Sabiha's Dilemma

AMRA PAJALIĆ

MELBOURNE, AUSTRALIA

https://www.pishukinpress.com/

First Published 2022

Pishukin Press

Cover design: Created using Canva elements

Previously published as *The Good Daughter* by Text Publishing

For content and trigger warnings please go to www.amrapajalic.com/themes

Pre-publication data is available from the National Library of Australia trove.nla.gov.au

Hardback edition ISBN 9781922871008

Praise

'... would be excellent for class study as it concerns matters of modern Australian multiculturalism, the question of belonging and issues of identity.' Fiction Focus

'... is a candid, insightful story and a realistic portrayal of a teenager in crisis.' Magpies

'A funny and challenging debut novel that has been described as the Bosnian answer to *Looking for Alibrandi*... a gritty and enjoyable novel, at times unflinching and dramatic.' Canberra Times

'... is the debut novel from new Melbourne author Amra Pajalić and it's one you won't want to miss! It's a funny and honest story about Sahiba, a teen girl growing up in Melbourne's western suburbs who's trying to deal with family traditions and her own desire to do what she wants. (5 stars).' Girlfriend Magazine

'Amra Pajalić writes with such honesty every young adult will empathise with her... While dealing with some ordinary "stuff" Pajalić's observations are sincere and often hilarious.' Bendigo Advertiser

'This multicultural story is frustrating, funny and sad with an ending that promises there is still much more to tell about Sabiha's life. I hope so. Loved it. Want more!' The Reading Stack

'Insightful... A spirited debut novel.' Herald Sun

'Written with a light and comic touch... Pajalić brings a fresh voice to

Australian Young Adult fiction through a funny, endearing, tough and ultimately resilient, first-person narrator.’ Viewpoint

‘Rewarding, poignant and occasionally chuckle-out-loud funny.’ Books Buzz

‘A raw and honest story about duty and the desire to run free. A strong new voice in Australian fiction.’ Melina Marchetta

‘It had me in stitches. Hilarious, poignant, gutsy and real.’ Randa Abdel-Fattah

‘Funny, sharp and insightful.’ Simmone Howell

A note on pronunciation:

Č č—Ch sound
Ć ć—a softer Ch sound
Đ đ—softer Dj sound
Š š—Sh sound
Ž ž—Dj sound

Chapter 1

When I stepped out of my bedroom ready to leave, Mum gasped. 'You can't go like that!' And pushed me back into the bedroom. We were going to a *zabava*, the Bosnian name for a party. *Zabava's* were organised twice a year, once as a community meet and greet, the second to celebrate *Ramadan*, the Muslim religious month of fasting. This would be my first attendance.

'Why not?' I demanded, my hands on my hips as I twirled. I wore a little black dress Mum bought for my fifteenth birthday. I'd grown in the year since and the dress moulded to my body. I wore the dress a few months before, when we attended a work barbecue for Dave, Mum's ex-boyfriend. Mum complimented me then.

'It's not suitable.' Mum rifled through my wardrobe.

Even though both my parents are from Bosnia, I didn't have anything to do with the community. When I was six-years-old Mum moved us to the inner-city. Now that I was sixteen we were back where we'd started—in St Albans.

Even though St Albans was established in 1887, at least that's what the plaque at St Albans train station said, you couldn't tell by walking through the bustling centre. The buildings are two-storey plain block structures with tin roofs. The shop fronts are a mix of European, who settled after the post World War II boom, and Vietnamese who came in the 1970s.

St Albans' only distinguishing feature was the streets formed into perfect rectangles, an absence of trees on nature strips and the fact that every second shop is a pharmacy catering to the ageing population.

There were always Yugos in St Albans and after the Balkan war in the early 1990s the population exploded with refugees from all sides settling there. It wasn't a coincidence that Mum and I moved away, while everyone else moved into St Albans.

I never thought of myself as Bosnian. I was born in Australia, all my friends were Australian, and if I thought about it all I would have called myself a true blue Aussie. All that changed three months ago.

'What's wrong with my dress?' I admired myself in the mirror.

'You're too, too...'

'Beautiful, hot, gorgeous, sexy.' I cocked my hip. The black dress brought out the highlights in my dark blonde hair. The V-line showed off my cleavage, while the mini skirt made my legs look longer.

My bedroom door was pushed open. *'Hajmo,'* my grandfather demanded that we leave. He caught a glimpse of me. *'Bože sačuvaj,'* he hissed, which meant 'God Save Us,' and turned his back so he couldn't see me.

'Bahra, nađi joj nešto drugo da obuće,' his torrent of Bosnian came in lightning-fast bursts. I understood that he wanted my Mum, Bahra, to find me something else to wear, what would people think if they saw how I was dressed, that I was a whore, and then I lost him.

'Did Dido call me a whore?'

'He said you look like a whore because of your make-up.'

My grandparents were supposed to come to Australia with my Aunt Zehra and her family after the Balkan War in 1995, but my grandmother's diabetes made her too ill to travel. When my grandmother passed away last year, my grandfather came to Australia and lived with my Aunt Zehra and Uncle Hakija.

Unfortunately for me that lasted a few months before Uncle Hakija and Dido couldn't stay under the same roof. Auntie Zehra manipulated Dido into leaving—apparently by telling him that Bahra needed to be with him after all these years. And then she served up a good dose of guilt to her sister about being the black sheep, and about all the embarrassment Mum caused by shacking up with an Aussie. So Mum caved in and she and I made the move back to the western suburbs. And Dido moved in with us. And my life became hell, because of him.

I checked my make-up in the mirror. My foundation was flawless, making my pale skin blemish free. The liquid eyeliner and eye-shadow brought out my green eyes. I was wearing the basic make-up any teenage girl would wear to an evening function.

'He's whacked, Mum.'

She glanced at my face quickly. 'You'll have to tone it down.'

'But I'm wearing regular make-up.'

'We need to make a good impression.' Mum sighed.

'You're saying we're not good enough.'

'No.' Mum put her hands on my shoulders. 'Tonight is a very important night. It's the first time we're attending a Bosnian function as a family and we're all anxious about looking our best.'

I had to admit tonight was Mum's night. During the refugee onslaught my Auntie Zehra's family had arrived from Bosnia and we'd managed to play happy families for a total of two years, before Mum and Auntie Zehra had a falling out. We hadn't had anything to do with each other during the ten years we lived in the inner-city, but tonight was The Reunion.

She hugged me, but I held myself stiff in her embrace.

'I look great.' I pulled away from her, forcing her to look at me. 'Don't I?'

Mum hesitated. 'Yes, you do—'

'What are we waiting for? Let's go.' I headed for the door.

'But this isn't an Australian function. This is a *zabava*. Everyone will be watching us, judging us, judging me.' Mum winced.

Mum and I weren't what you would call traditional Bosnians. More like exiles returning to the fold. Mum had made some bad decisions. At the age of eighteen, she married my father, who brought her to Australia. After my birth she had a nervous breakdown and went to hospital. My Dad left us because he didn't want a mental patient for a wife; so Mum embarked on what I called her 'Finding a Daddy' phase when she dated every Bosnian man in sight, supposedly to find a father for me. Some lasted a night, some a week, some a few months, but inevitably they all left us. She ended up getting a bad reputation and this was one of the reasons why we moved out of St Albans.

'Please Sam-Sabiha, be good for me.'

For years I'd called myself Sammie Omerović and so had Mum. It was the easier option because most Australians had to be taught to pronounce the 'h' in my name, and then there was the deciding incident.

I'd been looking forward to Grade 6 camp the whole year. We went to a farm in Victoria's countryside and I had fantasies of milking cows and riding horses, but what I hadn't envisioned was my camp leader and his wife. On the first day of camp Mr Howard asked all the students for their name. When it was my turn the conversation went something like this:

Mr Howard: 'That's an interesting name. Where are you from?'

Me: 'Thornbury.'

Mr Howard: 'No.' He laughed. 'Which country.'

Me: 'Australia.'

Mr Howard: 'Your name isn't Australian.'

Me: 'It's Bosnian.'

Mr Howard: 'Ah, so you're Bosnian.'

That should have been the end of the story, but then I met his wife.

Mrs Howard: 'Where is your name from?'

Me: 'I'm Bosnian.'

Mrs Howard: 'When did you come to Australia?'

Me: 'I was born here.'

Mrs Howard: 'So you're Australian.'

Me: 'Yes.'

While I had many conversations that went along these lines, what made this so different was that Kristy Newman, my Grade Six nemesis, witnessed both. She made the three-day camp a living hell by by calling me Sabiha-No-Country.

When I came home from camp I told Mum I wanted to change my name to something more Australian. By the time I began high school I had a clean slate and everyone knew me as Sammie Omerović. Now that we were embracing our ethnic roots I was Sabiha again...

'Bahra.' My grandfather was getting angrier with Mum.

'There's nothing suitable here.' Mum closed my wardrobe doors. 'Find something in my wardrobe.'

'Mum,' I whinged.

'Please Sabiha.' Mum gave me a harried look and went to answer Dido's demands.

I sighed heavily as I rifled through Mum's wardrobe. It used to be fun playing dress-ups in Mum's wardrobe when I was a child, but now it would be a disaster. Mum was a few inches taller than me and her figure was fuller. Anything I put on would hang like a sack.

As I pushed her clothes along a parcel fell at my feet. I bent and picked up a bundle of letters tied with a ribbon. I pulled a letter out, but it was written in Bosnian and I couldn't understand much. I glanced at the salutation and saw it was signed from 'Darko.' Another old boyfriend? But this name didn't ring any bells... I returned the letter to its envelope and tossed the bundle back to the bottom of the wardrobe. I'd make sure to come back and decipher them later.

'How did you go?' Mum asked as she rushed in.

'There's nothing here that will fit me.' I shut the wardrobe doors.

'Nice try.' Mum opened the doors.

'No way.' I cringed as Mum held out the dress to me. And that's how I ended up at the *zabava*, without a spec of make up and wearing the dorkiest outfit in the history of female fashion.

'Nice dress,' snickered my cousin Adnan as I sat in the chair next to him. I stiffened. His sister Merisa gave me a dismissive once-over. She was wearing a silver silk suit jacket and skirt that was fitted around her tall willowy body. She'd managed to toe the line between modesty and good taste without looking frumpy. Unfortunately I wasn't so lucky.

Adnan pinched a fold of fabric between his fingers. 'For your birthday I'll get you a subscription to *Vogue.*'

I went red. It was one of Mum's 'conservative' dresses. On her it was a knee-length fitted dress with a scooped neckline and almost skin-tight; but on my thinner frame the hem reached my calves and the scooped neckline was too low, so Mum had insisted I wear a top underneath. I looked like an op-shop reject.

'Read between the lines, buddy.' I lifted my hand, joining my thumb and little finger and keeping my other three fingers in a straight line. I caught my Aunt's eye across the table. Guiltily I put my hand down by my side.

'You look nice,' she called out.

I forced a smile. 'Thanks.' Adnan smothered a laugh. I elbowed him. Having a family was way overrated.

I examined what other people were wearing. If you say you're Muslim most people go to the stereotype of the turban-wearing, bearded Arab-man or the *hijab*-wearing subjugated Arab woman. They don't get that there are 1.5 billion people practicing Islam in 57 languages and that each ethnic group had a different way of expressing their religion. Since the Balkan War people know of Bosnia, but they don't know about

Bosnians. They don't understand why women aren't covered up and men aren't turbaned.

I hadn't known either, but since Dido moved in his pet project was to educate me about my 'roots.' He told me that Bosnians were ruled by the Turkish Ottoman Empire from fifteenth to the early twentieth century, that most Bosnians converted from the Bosnian Church to Islam. As a result we have a lot of Turkish words in our vocabulary and dress like Turks in Western fashion.

Most of the people at the *zabava* wore regular clothes. The men were in suits and the women wore loose clothing with no skin showing. There were a few older women who were covered up, but instead of the *hijab* they wore a headscarf. Single young men wore jeans and a shirt. Adnan said he'd tried to do the same, but Auntie Zehra ordered him to change into a suit.

Mum waved to someone. I turned and groaned. Safet and his sister Safeta were making their way over to our table. It was the Bosnian tradition to use one name in the family and add variations to it, the most popular being adding an 'a' to make names female.

'*Salaam Aleykum*,' Mum said, uttering the Arabic greeting, 'Peace be unto you.'

'*Aleykumu Salaam*,' Safet returned the greeting. Bosnians speak a Southern Slavic language, like most people in the Balkans, but they use a few Arabic words and greetings that they learnt, because all Muslims pray in Arabic. Mum introduced Safet as her special friend. In private she called him her boyfriend, even though they'd only been going out for a month. I was reserving judgement.

The men shook hands with Safet, my Uncle Hakija making a point of greeting him with *Zdravo*, 'Hello', to needle my grandfather. Uncle Hakija was still a fervent communist and a thorn in Dido's side. Dido explained that it was an insult to use non-Muslim greetings among Muslims. These were reserved for mixed company only.

I turned to find Safeta standing behind me, holding out her arms. I leaned in for the kiss on the cheeks, another custom. We were pretty relaxed about it. I used to have a Turkish friend and I'd never seen so much cheek-kissing in my life. They have the whole three-kiss thing down pat. We used to do the three-kiss thing too, but we dropped it because the Serbs have the same practice with their three-fingered crossing of the chest.

Usually I managed to avoid kissing, but Safeta was trying to impress and was over-compensating. She thought she had to win me over. She didn't know that Mum's boyfriends never lasted and that I'd stopped caring one way or another.

Safet and Safeta sat on the seats we'd been saving for them. Dido watched Safet with approval. Safet used to be a university professor before the war and was considered a catch, even though he worked as a taxi driver in Australia—that is, when he chose to work.

Soon after the preliminaries they moved onto their favourite game. Safet and Safeta were originally from Prijedor, while Mum's family came from Banja Luka, which was roughly an hour away.

'Do you know Ishmael Šahović and his wife Husna?' Safet asked, ash hanging off his cigarette. My Auntie and Uncle looked blank.

'He has a daughter Esma, and a son Faruk,' Safet's sister added. Auntie and Uncle shook their heads.

They could keep this up forever, trying to find a tenuous link, a friend of a friend of a second cousin whose mother was related by marriage to their grandfather five generations back.

When I called this the 'Connect the Bosnian Game', Mum told me off. She said that in Bosnia everyone knew his or her neighbours within a twenty-kilometre radius. Bosnia and Herzegovina was roughly half the size of Tasmania and had a population of 4.1 million, so even if you were dropped on the other side of the country by direction-challenged aliens, chances were you'd find people who knew someone you did.

Now that everyone was scattered to the four corners of the world this was the only way they had of learning about their former neighbours and creating a sense of community. They also trawled the telephone directories looking for possible relatives. When they found someone with the same surname they'd call to sniff out if there was a family connection.

Mum told me that Bosnians who arrived in Australia during the 1970s were desperate for kinship and that anyone with the same surname would become a cousin, whether they were a blood relative or not. Now that there was a larger population there was no need to settle like that.

As they talked I opened my bag and found my mobile. I typed in a message: 'Hope you're having a better time than me. Love Sammie.' I scrolled to Kathleen's name in my address book and pressed 'send'. Kathleen was my best friend. We were friends since primary school when Mum and I lived in Thornbury.

During the summer holidays we still saw each other regularly. She visited me once, but my grandfather was less than welcoming so mostly I travelled down her way and we met in the city or hit the op-shops and cafés around Brunswick Street, in Fitzroy.

In the week since I started Year 10 at my new school, St Albans High, we hadn't spoken much. I was used to seeing her every day, and then we'd call each other after school, or send an email or text message. I missed her. I returned my mobile to my handbag. When I tuned back into the conversation they were talking about the war, again. I was so sick of hearing about the war.

'I was on the front line,' Uncle Hakija said. 'That's where I got injured.' He touched his stomach. There was a collective sigh by the group. There weren't many men who could claim hero status. Most men fled with their families when the war broke out.

When he arrived in Australia Uncle Hakija had surgery to repair the damage to his gut. He attempted working for a few years, but his health was frail and he was in too much pain. Now he tended to the garden and ran errands, while Auntie Zehra and my cousin Merisa, who was 20 years old, worked as cleaners. In Bosnia, Hakija had been a veterinarian and Zehra was a nurse.

'I lost my wife and two daughters. My oldest would be Sabiha's age.' It was Safet's turn and he glanced at me. We all shook our heads on cue.

'My fiancé was a police officer in Prijedor. After Serbs seized the city he was arrested, with all the other officials and non-Serb leaders. I never heard from him. They were probably sent to Omarska,' Safeta said.

We all looked down, remembering the television images of emaciated men staring at the camera through steel fences. Omarska was the Serb-run concentration camp in which Bosnians were imprisoned, the Bosnian equivalent of Auschwitz. Even though I was sick of the constant talk about the war, when I remembered those images, I realised why they couldn't let it go.

I turned away and watched the Bosnian folk dancing on what passed as the dance floor. When Mum talked about attending the *zabava* I'd imagined a fancy ball, instead we were in a high school gym. There were folding tables and plastic chairs laid out in long rows from one end of the gym to the other with a walkway in the middle.

In the canteen attached to the gym the women were making food. Heavy clouds of cigarette smoke hung over the tables blending with the smell of sweat, onions and cooked meat. On the stage behind me a folk band were producing an ear-piercing tune. Some people would call it music, but I wasn't one of them.

While I watched the folk dancing it had seemed deceptively easy. Dance in a circle holding hands as if you're in a conga line and shuffle your feet in a quick two-step. But for some reason I lacked the necessary rhythm to transform the simple moves into a high-spirited jig.

When I tried dancing it looked like I was jumping on a pogo stick. Mum had natural rhythm. Her cheeks were flushed, a wide smile on her face as her feet kicked in unison with the other dancers.

As we walked back to our table a man stared at us. 'Isn't that Mustafa?' I asked Mum as we sat. Another ex-boyfriend—he'd lasted nearly a year and was one of the rare guys I'd liked. I smiled and lifted my hand to wave.

'Don't.' Mum slapped my hand down. 'He's with his wife.'

A little girl about eight years old sat on his lap. His wife noticed me staring. I looked away and met my Aunt's gaze.

Auntie Zehra cast Mum a scathing look. Mum blushed. Auntie looked like she was about to get stuck into her sister.

'I'm hungry,' I exclaimed loudly.

Uncle Hakija and Adnan stood to get *ćevapi* and soft drinks for us to eat. I loved *ćevapi*. The grilled skinless sausages made with minced beef or lamb, garlic and spices served on a Turkish roll with diced onion. While we were eating they resumed their conversation.

Uncle Hakija had a toothpick between his lips. 'The war happened because of who we are. It's backward the way everyone's identity is decided by his or her religious beliefs. We call Bosnian Catholics Croatians, or Orthodox Bosnians Serbs, even if their family has lived in Bosnia for centuries.'

Uncle Hakija's theory was that there were no problems when former Yugoslavia existed under the communist President Tito who led the Partisans to defeat the Nazis in World War II. It was only when Tito passed away in 1980 and communism was eroded that tensions started simmering as everyone sought independence.

Dido thumped the table. 'Those Orthodox Bosnians *are* Serbs. If they weren't why did they rise up in the *coup d' etat* even though they'd been living in Bosnia all their lives?'

'Just like you were a Muslim all your life.' Uncle Hakija made a dig at Dido's previous life as a communist. Dido was now a Born-Again-Muslim like most of the Bosnians since the war.

'I did what I had to do,' Dido defended. 'It was the only way to make a life.'

While those with religious beliefs weren't persecuted in Yugoslavia the way they were in other communist countries, they weren't promoted at work and given opportunities that communist party members received.

Safet clapped Dido on the shoulder. 'Come on friends, let's talk of happy things.'

Auntie Zehra covered Uncle Hakija's hand. 'We came to have a good time, not rehash old arguments.'

Dido and Uncle Hakija engaged in a staring contest. Safet and Safeta finished eating and left to speak to friends at another table.

Mum picked at her *ćevapi*. 'Do you want it?' she asked Uncle Hakija. He broke the stare, smiled and shook his head.

Auntie Zehra narrowed her eyes at them. 'You were always wasteful, Bahra.' Using a fork she transferred the *ćevapi* to her plate. 'You need to eat more.' She bit into a *ćevap* and chewed it with relish.

Mum scrunched her nose and watched Safet as he worked the room. 'I need to watch my figure.'

'If you put meat on your bones you'd be able to keep a man.' Auntie Zehra followed Mum's gaze.

'Not all men like big women,' Mum replied.

Uncle Hakija pinched the roll of fat bulging over Auntie Zehra's skirt. 'You should watch your figure too.'

She slapped his hand, hard. 'You should keep your eyes off other women's figures.'

Uncle Hakija rubbed his hand. 'I was joking.'

'He didn't mean anything by it,' Mum said.

'You're in your thirties yet you're as vain as a teenager,' Auntie Zehra attacked Mum.

Even though Auntie Zehra was forty-two years old to Mum's thirty-seven, she was right. Mum looked like she was twenty-something. She did push-ups and sit-ups every night to keep her figure trim, while Auntie Zehra's weight aged her face and the frumpy clothing she wore made her look like a senior citizen.

Auntie Zehra kept going, pointing at Mum. 'And you're dressed like a whore.' Mum's only fault was that she looked too good. Her knee-length dress fitted against her curves and her cleavage was just visible.

After over fifty years of living under communist Yugoslavia, there were only a few customs Bosnians practised in their everyday life that identified them as Muslim: the names they gave their children, drinking Turkish coffee, and the fact that male children were circumcised. Since the war they were groping for a new-found sense of identity after being pigeon-holed as Muslim; and while many of them didn't know how to be Muslim, they knew what didn't make the grade and what got gossiped about. Skimpy clothes, drugs and pairings with non-Muslims were at the top of the hit-list. Mum had already received two out of three strikes.

Mum picked up her glass and took a sip, her hand trembling. She wasn't good at confrontations.

'That's not—' I interrupted my Aunt. Adnan pinched me under the table. 'Ouch!' I exclaimed.

'Leave them to it,' he whispered.

'She's my mother,' I whispered back.

'She's her sister.'

I was about to speak, but he held up his fingers like he would pinch me again.

Uncle Hakija held Auntie Zehra's hand and looked at Mum. 'Bahra looks nice,' he pronounced.

Auntie Zehra's face was flushed and rivulets of sweat trickled from her temple. 'Keep your eyes to yourself.' She dug her nails into Uncle Hakija's hand.

'Zehra,' Dido snapped. 'This isn't the time.'

Mum and Auntie Zehra's bickering went back nearly twenty years ago when Uncle Hakija was courting Mum. Everyone expected that they would marry, but then my father came home from Australia to find a bride. Mum ended up marrying my Dad and moving to Australia, Auntie Zehra and Uncle Hakija married and stayed behind, and there's never been peace between the two sisters since.

In the quiet afterward, we heard a hushed whisper at the table behind us. 'That's the woman who's crazy.'

A woman at the table behind us scowled at Mum.

Chapter 2

Mum hunched in the seat beside me. Most of the Bosnians off the boat freaked out when they heard that Mum was bipolar. In communist Yugoslavia anyone who had a deformity or was afflicted were put in a home and separated from the rest of the population. Yet another reason why we avoided the Bosnian community.

'She may be crazy, but at least she's not dumb.' Auntie Zehra glowered at the woman. The woman turned away. 'Don't pay any attention to them,' Auntie Zehra told Mum. 'They're primitives,' she said, her voice loud enough to carry.

The woman stiffened, but she didn't look at us again. Mum smiled at Auntie Zehra, who nodded and kept eating her *ćevapi*. Mum fiddled with her dress, tugging the V-line to cover her cleavage.

'Merisa, give Bahra your jacket,' Auntie Zehra said.

Merisa sat on Mum's other side. She took off her jacket and handed it to Mum.

'You have to have to stop dressing like an Aussie.' Auntie Zehra reached across the table and squeezed Mum's hand.

'I know.' Mum smiled as she put the jacket on.

'See,' Adnan whispered in my ear. 'I told you.'

'Up yours,' I whispered back.

Adnan left the table and I breathed a sigh of relief. I leaned back in my chair and crossed my arms. It was still weird that these people had a claim on Mum. For so many years we'd been our own independent unit. Unlike most mothers and daughters we were friends, but now everything was changing. I was relegated to the sidelines. I checked my mobile—no reply from Kathleen.

Merisa stood. 'Where are you going?' Auntie Zehra asked.

'To the toilet,' Merisa replied.

'I'll come too,' I said, following her away from the table.

Inside the bathroom Merisa went to the mirror while I went to the toilet cubicle. As I washed my hands Merisa re-applied her make-up. I eyed her lipstick covetously. 'Can I have some?'

'I don't think this is your colour.' She used her finger to fix her lip line. I dried my hands using a paper towel directing a piercing stare at her in the mirror. Merisa sighed and handed me the tube. 'Don't break it.' She was such a tight-arse. I rubbed it on my lips. 'Not like that.' Merisa blotted my lips with a tissue. 'You don't want to be obvious or Dido will go crazy.'

Adnan waited for us in front of the toilet doors. He and Merisa walked away from the door leading into the gym.

'Where are you going?' I asked.

'To get some fresh air.' Merisa's tone was sharp. I knew I wasn't welcome, but I didn't care.

They hurried outside. I followed and heard snatches of conversation as we turned the corner. So this is where everyone under the age of twenty disappeared.

Merisa pulled out a pack of cigarettes from her handbag and popped one in her mouth. 'Anyone got a light?' she asked in Bosnian. A young man with a cigarette in his mouth flicked his lighter and put the flame to her cigarette. 'Thanks.' She exhaled smoke to the side.

He offered his hand. 'Mooki, short for Muharem.'

'Merisa.' She smiled as they shook hands.

Adnan moved to another group. I edged closer to Merisa and she introduced me. I said hello, not knowing whether to offer my hand or not. Most Bosnians seemed to be into the handshake thing, but it felt weird to me.

'Australian?' Mooki asked. Merisa nodded.

Another young man put his arm around Mooki's shoulders. 'What have we got here?'

Mooki introduced his brother Ferid.

I watched them like I was at a tennis match, my head bobbing from side to side as they talked. I knew Merisa was keen on Mooki by the way she tilted her head and laughed. I thought that Merisa was pretty when I first saw her, but once I knew her better her bitchiness erased my first impression.

Adnan appeared at my side. 'Got a light?' he asked Merisa. She passed it to him without looking away from Mooki. Adnan lit his cigarette and returned the lighter. 'Having a good time cuz?' Adnan put his arm around me and squeezed me against him.

'Let go,' I muttered, pulling away from him.

He laughed, pinching my cheek before sauntering off.

I turned and saw Dina watching me. Dina and I now went to the same school and even had classes together. Our grandfathers used to be neighbours in Bosnia and since my Dido moved to St Albans they'd reconnected. Her grandfather was Edin, my grandfather's chess-playing buddy and she was named after him. Her real name was Edina.

Last week, when I started at St Albans High, Mum talked to Dina's mum, Suada, and asked Dina to show me around. Grudgingly, she and her best friend Gemma let me hang with them if I happened to find them, but they didn't make it easy and were always moving.

Dina sidled up to me. 'Is Adnan your boyfriend?' she asked, her eyes following him as he rough-housed with his friends. Adnan went to our high school, but he was in Year 12.

'No,' I protested. 'He's my cousin.'

'Your cousin?' Dina said disbelievingly.

'Our mums are sisters.' Dina looked relieved and I realised that she liked him. There was no accounting for taste.

'Wow, you're Adnan's cousin,' she said it as if I was related to royalty.

You could call Adnan handsome. He was over six feet tall. He had bright blue eyes and brown hair, with a slight cleft in the chin. As his cousin I was immune to his charm since I was always the butt of his jokes.

'Why didn't you tell me you were related?' Dina said, pouting.

'What's the big deal?' I asked.

Dina shrugged and gave me a smug smile.

Adnan appeared at my side. 'Where is she?'

I looked around and saw that Merisa had disappeared.

'Mum's coming,' he grunted.

Auntie zeroed in on Adnan.

'Merisa's gone back to the gym,' Adnan said.

She walked on. I didn't have a good feeling. Her face was flushed and a vein was popping in her forehead, like when she and Uncle Hakija were arguing. Adnan and I followed. Even though I tried to give my feet the signal to turn back to the gym, I couldn't help myself. I wanted to see Merisa cop it.

Ten minutes later we found them. Merisa was leaning with her back against a building while Mooki had one hand above her head, his body nearly on top of hers. She turned her head away to exhale smoke and saw Auntie Zehra. Merisa stamped the cigarette under her foot. Mooki straightened and offered his hand to Auntie Zehra. After shaking hands, Auntie waited for us to start walking toward the gym before following in the rear.

'You should have been more careful,' Adnan said to Merisa.

'What's the big deal?' I asked. 'Merisa's an adult.'

When we were away from the crowd Auntie sped up and caught up to us. 'What were you doing with those boys?' Auntie demanded, her voice tense as she kept from shouting. She had Merisa's arm in an iron grip.

'Nothing, Mum.' Merisa was clearly in pain, but she didn't pull away.

I'd been looking forward to Merisa getting in trouble, but seeing the Auntie's scarcely suppressed rage, I wanted to get away.

'Zehra! Babo wants you to come inside,' Mum said as she approached. When Auntie ignored her, Mum tried to pull her away from Merisa. 'Now isn't the time.' Mum pushed herself between Merisa and Auntie, but as Merisa moved away Auntie went for Mum.

'Don't tell me how to discipline my child. How do you think I felt hearing about all the men you slept with?' Auntie Zehra's face was ugly as she leaned into Mum. 'Not even married men are safe from you.'

Mum put her hand on Auntie Zehra's arm. 'Zehra, there's nothing between Hakija—'

'I know there isn't.' Auntie Zehra threw her hand off. 'I'm keeping an eagle eye on you both because I know what you're capable of.'

Auntie looked around, realising we were in public. She stormed off. Merisa followed, rubbing her arm, Adnan in the rear.

I checked my mobile in order to avoid looking at Mum, and frowned at the blank screen. Usually Kathleen would have replied instantly. She carried her mobile everywhere. We would have spent the whole night sending each other messages. At least I would have had something more amusing to get me through this hellish night.

Back at our table Dido was talking to a man in a black robe. Even though Bosnians might wear Western clothes the *hodža*, the Muslim priest, wears a robe. Imagine an orthodox priest except the *hodža's* hat is white, minus the cross, of course.

'Here are my grandchildren,' Dido announced.

He introduced Adnan and Merisa. The *hodža* shook hands with Adnan, but Merisa didn't put her hand out. Women followed the Muslim custom of not touching a male who wasn't a blood relative, which was really weird because they shook hands and kissed everyone except the *hodža*.

'This is my Australian granddaughter.' Dido was being a such a suck-up.

'Sabiha,' I snapped. 'My name is Sabiha.'

Mum came to my side and put her hand on my back. I bit the insides of my cheeks.

'I'm reminding parents that *mejtef* is held at the Deer Park mosque on Saturday mornings,' the *hodža* said. 'So many children are woefully ignorant about their heritage and we need to correct this.'

I'd never been to *mejtef*, the Bosnian religious school. Mum had never followed any of that religious stuff, until now.

'Some *vlasi* know more about Islam than Bosnian children,' Dido spat out. *Vlah* was the worst insult a Muslim could give another Muslim. It denoted all non-believers.

'The parents are to blame. They accepted communism as their salvation and neglected their children's religious education,' the *hodža* said. 'Now they expect their children to become perfect Muslims overnight.'

Dido stared at the ground. Mum told me that during Dido's communist phase he'd once caught my grandmother teaching Mum and Auntie Zehra how to pray and beat them for embracing superstition.

'I will make sure my grandchildren attend,' Dido said, putting his arm around Adnan and me.

'I look forward to seeing you in *mejtef*.' The *Hodža* shook Adnan's hand and nodded at me before leaving.

When we reached the carpark Uncle Hakija and Dido began arguing. Hakija was furious that Dido said Adnan would attend *mejtef*. 'I will decide how my children are brought up!'

'I believed all the communist propaganda and look where it got me,' Dido implored. 'I will be judged for my sins on judgement day.'

'Superstition,' Uncle Hakija roared. 'There is no heaven or hell.'

Dido stared up at the sky. '*Allah* protect him.'

'There is no almighty God that protects and punishes humans. We are the controllers and destroyers of the Earth.'

'Blasphemy!' Dido yelled. 'You will bring down God's judgement.'

'Don't talk rubbish around my children,' Uncle Hakija warned.

'They're my grandchildren!' Dido yelled back.

'Stop it both of you.' Auntie Zehra got between them.

'Zehra, tell him that Adnan needs to go to *mejtef* and learn to be a good Muslim,' Dido urged.

'Zehra is my wife and she'll do as I say,' Uncle Hakija barked.

'Zehra,' Dido begged.

This was my aunt's fate. She was always used as a tug of war between my uncle and grandfather. Whichever way she decided there would be hell to pay. 'Hakija is my husband and he's the head of our family,' Auntie Zehra said.

Dido seemed to collapse as his bluster deflated. 'Then you're not my daughter any longer,' he said, walking away.

'*Babo*,' Auntie Zehra called.

'Leave him.' Uncle Hakija took her arm. 'He needs to calm down.'

'Another fun family reunion,' I grumbled as I followed Mum to our car.

Dido spent the rest of the weekend in a dark depression, muttering under his breath about ungrateful daughters. I hid out in my bedroom and avoided him.

***

On Monday at school when I walked out of History, Gemma and Dina were waiting for me. 'What's up?' I asked. It was the first time they'd ever sought me out.

'Nothing much.' Dina put her arm around my shoulders and turned me to walk towards the back of the school.

'Where are we going?' I asked.

'To the oval,' Dina said, a rare smile on her face.

'Yeah, to the oval,' Gemma repeated, laughing like a kookaburra.

'I'll meet you there.' I stopped walking. 'I have to buy lunch first.'

'No!' Dina exclaimed. 'You can have my lunch.' She held up her lunch box. 'I have *zeljanica*.'

My mouth watered. *Pita* was the Bosnian national meal and was made with pastry filling that was rolled into a cannelloni shape. Then the roll was formed into a spiral and baked. Cheese and spinach pita, which is what Dina was offering me, was my absolute favourite.

'I need something to drink too,' I said, testing Dina's resolve.

'Gemma will give you her juice.' Dina grabbed Gemma's backpack and pulled out her apple juice.

'Hey,' Gemma protested, snatching the juice back.

'Give it to her,' Dina said.

Gemma hesitated, before buckling under Dina's glower. 'Here.' Gemma threw the juice at me.

'Now can we go?' Dina demanded.

'Okay.' I shrugged and walked to the oval. I poked the straw through the juice box, hiding my grin as I sipped. They were so pathetic.

As we walked there was a dacking underway. Dacking and knackering were the two great traditions of my new school. Two boys grabbed an ankle each and knackered the victim's balls against one of the numerous poles holding up the walkways. The worst was when a third boy held the arms, so that the victim couldn't cup his balls to protect them.

Dacking was the reason that tracky pants were only ever worn to Phys Ed. Unfortunately for him the target hadn't received the memo. The bully went behind him and yanked his dacks and undies to his ankles. The guy in tracky dacks stood frozen, his cock and balls visible to the world, his pale face turning tomato red. When laughter broke out he awkwardly lurched down and pulled his pants up, at the same time trying to run, and nearly did a Jerry Lewis tumble.

'You should Pull the Dragon!' Gemma yelled as the target ran.

'What's Pulling the Dragon?' I asked.

'Dragon was the nickname of Dragan Blažić,' Dina said.

'He was so hot,' Gemma said dreamily.

'He graduated last year,' Dina continued. 'Someone dacked him and he stood with his pants around his ankles, letting the world see his equipment.'

'So what?' I demanded.

'He had the goods.' Gemma held out her hands a ruler length apart. 'And he always wore tracky dacks.'

'Yeah,' Dina agreed. 'He was never short of girlfriends.'

'But that guy there didn't have what it takes to Pull the Dragon.' Gemma giggled and held her index finger and thumb a centimetre apart.

'Let's sit here.' Dina pointed at a patch of grass beside the railing, on the other side of which Adnan was playing soccer with a bunch of guys.

'Yum,' I murmured as I swallowed the pita. 'Your Mum is a great cook,' I told Dina. Her stomach rumbled as I ate. Gemma ate her sandwich on the other side of me. She looked longingly at the juice.

Dina yelled out to Adnan when there was a break in play. A few minutes later he ran over and sat next to me. 'Yum, *pita*.' He snatched some from me.

'Cut it out!' I pushed his hand away and shoved the rest of the pita in my mouth.

'You're a pretty good soccer player,' Dina said.

'Thanks.'

'I always wanted to play.' She leaned toward Adnan so that she was halfway across my lap.

'It's not that hard,' Adnan scoffed. I made a gagging face only he could see. He laughed.

'What's funny?' Dina demanded.

Adnan pointed to one of his mates messing with the ball. When Dina peered at the boys, he wagged his finger at me. After a while Dina turned and talked to Gemma.

'You're such a love-me-do,' I said quietly.

'I can't help it if I'm stunningly handsome,' he preened, smoothing his hair with his hand.

'Vomit.' I put my fingers down my throat.

***

As word got around about my family connections I wasn't short of company. Whenever girls met me their first words were 'You're Adnan's cousin.' Every girl wanted to be my friend, any excuse to hang around near Adnan. When he came over to talk to me they'd drool while I rolled my eyes. By Friday I was sick of being the Adnan-Love-Boat-Link and hid in the library.

I was in the fiction shelves when I bumped into Brian who was in my General Maths class. We nodded at each other and I turned back to the shelf.

'So,' he said. 'You're Adnan's cousin.'

'What's it to you?' I retorted.

He blushed.

'I'm sorry,' I spluttered. 'Did you do your maths homework?'

'It's bloody hard and we're only doing General Maths,' Brian said.

'No matter how hard I try I don't get it,' I agreed. He was really cute. His eyes were dark chocolate brown and his brown hair was wavy.

'There you are.' Dina stood to my left. She gave Brian a once-over like he was old gum stuck to her shoe. 'Come outside.' She tugged on my arm.

I pulled away from her. 'Sorry, I'm busy.'

'See ya.' She flicked her hair and walked off, her anger following her like a smell.

'Another member of the Adnan fan club?' Brian asked.

I returned a book to the shelf. 'Yeah, I'm over it.'

'She's really good.' Brian reached around me and handed me the Tara Moss book I was looking at. He stood close and I breathed in his aftershave. Butterflies fluttered in my stomach. As I took the book it slipped between my fingers. He ducked and caught it at my knees. He straightened slowly, his face moving up my body as he did.

'Thanks.' I took the book from him. He was the first boy I met who read books and it made him so much cuter.

'Did you want help with your homework?' He looked straight at me, smiling. 'I've got my Maths book here.' He nodded toward his backpack.

My heart sped up and I blushed. 'Okay.' I followed him to the study area, checking out his butt on the way. As Brian showed me how he'd worked out the answers, his shoulder bumped into mine, and I fought to concentrate on what he was saying.

A boy dropped to his knees in front of our desk. 'Joshua King,' the boy said. 'I'm putting him on my hit list.' The boy pulled out his notebook and took Brian's pen.

I read the page upside down. *People to kill.* I blinked. Did I read that right?

'Why?' Brian asked.

'He tripped me in the hall,' the boy said.

Brian read out the next answer, but I widened my eyes and nodded at the strange boy with homicidal tendencies.

'Sabiha, this is my best friend Jesse.'

Jesse's blue eyes were curious. He didn't look like he was mentally deficient. 'We're in Phys Ed together,' he said.

'Right,' I said, remembering him.

When our teacher Mr Robinson left the gym to go to his office, all the boys in class decided to play dodgeball with Jesse as the target. As Jesse tried to protect himself from the basketballs bouncing off his body, everyone laughed. Jesse looked like he was going to cry. When Mr Robinson returned and saw the balls on the floor around Jesse he asked him what happened. When Jesse didn't say anything, Mr Robinson ordered him to put the balls away. The Phys Ed students laughed at his rising emotion and treated him like a wind-up-toy whose only purpose was their entertainment.

'That one's great.' Jesse took the Tara Moss book titled *Split* that Brian recommended.

'You've read it too?' My voice sounded overly surprised.

'I can read.' Jesse threw the book on the table.

He blushed and his eyes watered. What had I done? I'd just pissed off the guy who was probably voted most likely to go on a high school killing spree.

Chapter 3

I grabbed Jesse's hand before he could run off and add me to his kill list. 'I haven't met any boys who read,' I lied. Jesse's face cleared and my heartbeat returned to normal.

Since we moved to the western suburbs, whenever Mum dragged me to visit I'd been on the lookout for something to read to pass the time, but I hadn't seen any books in people's houses. It was so different from Thornbury where most houses had overflowing bookshelves and there were bookstores on almost every corner. The only bookstores in the west were the chain variety in shopping centres.

'I was just surprised to find someone who shared my passion,' I explained.

'Jesse's the book-lover,' Brian said. 'I just read what he tells me to.'

Just what the world needed. A book-loving psychopath.

Jesse glanced at his watch. 'I've got to stock up on my rations.'

Seeing my confusion Brian translated. 'He needs to get reading material for the weekend.'

'How long have you two known each other?' I asked after Jesse went to gather his books.

'Since primary school.' Brian put his Maths book away.

'Has he always wanted to kill people?'

'Jesse's not a weirdo or anything. He uses fantasy to deal with the bullying. He couldn't hurt anyone.'

'Good to know,' I said.

I was putting my books in my backpack when Jesse placed his books on the counter. 'This is a new title,' the librarian said as she scanned it. 'You have to write a recommendation since you're the first lender.'

Jealousy cut me. At my old school I was the librarian's favourite and got all the perks. I was allowed to borrow over my limit and got let off fines. It sucked being the new kid.

I was walking out of the school gates at the end of the day when Dina called me. 'Do you want a lift?' she pointed to her mum waiting in the car.

'No thanks.' I waved to her mum and walked on.

'I'll see you on Monday at the front?' she yelled.

I kept walking, a huge smile on my face. Instead of the oval, I planned on hanging around in the library with Brian again.

When I got home Mum's bedroom door was open. She knelt on her woven prayer mat with little pieces of paper spread around her. She'd only been praying for a few months; with five different prayers a day, she had a lot to learn, so she used the cheat method and read the prayers instead of reciting them.

She wore *dimije* (think Harem pants except three times as much fabric is used so they billow like a kite when you walk), a loose shirt and her head was covered with a scarf. Women were supposed to be modest while praying: they shouldn't show any flesh above the wrist or ankle, and only their face was uncovered.

I went to my bedroom and closed the door. I'd accessed my email at the school library and read an ambiguous message from Kathleen. When we lived with Dave I used his computer, but since we moved out I had to rely on the public library, or internet cafés, to type up all my work or to email.

I'd been sending Kathleen SMS messages every night since the *zabava*, but hadn't received a response. Whenever I called I received an out-of-service message, and her landline rang out. Her parents were cheap-skates and wouldn't get broadband, so most of the time the phone was busy because they were on the internet.

After agonising for another day, I'd finally sent her an email from school at recess. 'Haven't heard from you. Are we still on for tomorrow?' Her reply when I checked after school: 'Yes. Usual time, usual place.'

Was she ditching me? Had Shelley finally won? I hated Shelley. She was supposed to be our friend, but I still couldn't stand her. Back in year 7 Mum and Dave broke up for a few months. So Mum moved us out of Thornbury and I changed schools for six months. When Mum and Dave made up again and I returned to my old school, I found that Kathleen, my best friend had made a new best friend and we were supposed to be one big happy triangle. I'd been on Kathleen's back for years to ditch-the-bitch, but so far my entreaties had fallen on deaf ears. I always suspected that Shelley was out to steal Kathleen from me. What if she'd finally succeeded? I'd have to wait until tomorrow to ask Kathleen what was going on.

Mum poked her head into my room. 'What are you doing?'

'Ever heard of knocking?'

'Come with me,' Mum commanded.

She was standing behind the dining table 'Today we're making *pita*.' She handed me a pen and paper.

'What's this for?'

'To make notes.' She put on her apron.

'Will you test me?'

'Yes.'

'This is a waste of time. I don't need to cook.' I put the pen down.

'What will you do when you get married and have children?' Mum asked.

'Takeaway,' I snarled.

'Let's hope you make enough money to buy takeaway,' Mum said.

'Maybe I'll marry a chef.'

Mum let out a bark of laughter. 'As if a man who cooks all day for a living will come home and cook for you.'

'I know how to make *pita*.' I slouched in the chair. 'I've seen you do it enough times over the years.'

'Okay.' She put her hands on her hips. 'Tell me how you make the dough?'

I drew a blank. Of course I'd never paid attention. 'Flour and milk,' I said decisively.

Mum's eyebrows rose. 'Not quite.' She placed a bowl on the table. 'To make dough you need one tablespoon of salt, four cups of flour and two cups of warm water.' She waited for me to take down the recipe. I started writing. It wouldn't hurt to learn. I mean, I loved *pita*.

'Place the flour into a bowl.' Mum counted with her plastic measuring cup. 'Then add the salt and stir.' She held the jug of water with her right hand and poured it into the bowl while stirring with her left hand. 'Have a look.' She tipped the bowl. 'You knead until it forms into a ball of dough and leave it to rise for twenty minutes.'

I stood. 'I'll come back in half an hour.'

'Nice try.' She took a plate off the bench-top. 'This is dough I prepared earlier.'

I smiled at her television-chef imitation. Remembering myself, I formed my mouth into a straight line. There was no way I'd let her think I was enjoying this.

'As you can see, I kneaded this dough, then flattened it onto the plate and rubbed oil into the top.' Peeling off the Gladwrap, she placed the pancake dough on the dining table, in the middle of the white tablecloth.

She smoothed the dough using the Bosnian version of a rolling pin, a long stick the length of a broom handle, called an *oklagija*. The *oklagija* holds a special place in Bosnian life. Apart from being used for cooking, it's also used to measure kids and to beat kids. Whenever Mum told me stories about her childhood she'd inevitably end it with, 'And then Mum chased us with an *oklagija*.'

Thankfully she'd never shared that tradition with me. Mum's idea of discipline was talking to me until I buckled under the weight of her emotional blackmail.

Mum placed her fingers in the middle of the stick and rolled her hands onto it, while maintaining even pressure over the whole expanse of dough. After each roll she jerked the dough in another direction, flattening it evenly. 'Have a go.' She held out the stick.

I tried to manipulate the *oklagija*, but the wood pressed into my hands and made them itch. My lower back twinged as I bent over the table. My shoulders tensed and bunched up.

Mum stared at the misshapen dough. 'It's okay. I'll take over now.' She adjusted the dough with a few strokes of the *oklagija*; the muscles in her forearms taut as she manoeuvred the stick. She placed it in the middle of the table and folded the pastry over it. Lifting the *oklagija* in the air with one hand, she tugged the edges with the other, stretching the pastry into a see-through sheet.

'Can I have a go?'

She gave me the *oklagija*. My arm was nearly wrenched from its socket as I fought to hold it in the air. I tugged the dough, but instead of stretching it the way Mum did, I tore it.

'That's okay.' Mum took the *oklagija* and spread out the pastry sheet on the table. 'I'll cut that part off. Now we do the filling.' She removed another bowl from the fridge. 'I made the mixture for *zeljanica*.'

There were so many variations, you could pretty much think of an ingredient and there would be a *pita* based on it. *Zeljanica* was spinach *pita*, *krompiruša*—potato, *burek*—meat, *sirnica*—cheese, *tikvenica*—pumpkin, *maslanica*—layered with butter and cheese, *jabukovača*—apple, and there was also a *burek* variation with potato and minced meat.

'*Merhaba*,' Dido said as he came through the back door.

I was too busy scribbling to return his greeting and just moved my chair out of the way to let him pass.

'What's this?' Dido asked. 'Bosnian women don't write down recipes. They toss the ingredients together and make a meal.'

'I'm not Bosnian then.' I threw the notepad on the floor and left.

'Come back here,' Dido shouted. He reached for my arm, but Mum stopped him. 'Again! Where's her respect?' he ranted as I stomped down the hallway. 'A good beating would knock the stubbornness out of her. Give me the *oklagija*.'

A few minutes later Mum tapped on my bedroom door and pushed it open. I was lying on my side with my back to the door. 'Go away,' I muttered.

'Sweetie, he didn't mean to upset you.'

'Yes, he did. He loves putting me down.'

She sat on the bed. 'He doesn't. That's his sense of humour.'

'He's a pig.'

'Don't call your grandfather names,' Mum scolded without conviction.

I curled into a ball with my arms over my head.

'Sabiha, please come back to the kitchen.'

Sullenly I followed her back, but this time I didn't take any notes while she talked. After she finished making the *pita*, I hid in my bedroom until dinner. When I came out, Safet was already sitting at the kitchen table.

When dinner was over, I lay on a cushion in front of the TV. Dido was reading *Bosna Magazin*, the Australian Bosnian newspaper. I took the remote off the coffee table and switched the channel.

'Girl,' Dido growled behind me. 'I was watching that.'

'It's in Greek. You don't even understand what they're saying.'

He hogged the TV and watched nothing but news. He'd flip from channel to channel and watch every bulletin. Then he'd switch over to SBS and watch French, Arab, Russian, Ukrainian, and, of course, Greek news.

'I can understand that,' Dido insisted.

'No you can't.' I gripped the remote.

'I can understand Ukrainian and Russian and that's coming on next.' Even though the Russians and Ukrainians spoke in a different dialect, we used a lot of the same Slavic words.

'Mum!' I yelled.

'Bahra!' Dido yelled at the same time.

'Okay.' Mum put her hands out for us to stop. 'Sabiha can watch *Home and Away* while you and Safet play chess,' she said to Dido. 'After that Safet and I will leave and Dido will have the TV.' It was Friday night so Mum would stay at Safet's.

Safet lived with his sister who had a job packing shelves at Safeway and worked the night shift. Mum was in the habit of staying at Safet's until Safeta came back from work. Then Mum would sneak home around 6 a.m., while Dido and I were sleeping, and pretend she'd slept in her own bed. I'm sure Dido knew the truth, but he turned a blind eye.

'Can you give me money?' I asked Mum, knowing that she'd be dead to the world in the morning.

'What for?'

'I'm meeting with Kathleen in Brunswick Street for her birthday.' Six months older than me, Kathleen was turning seventeen.

'But tomorrow is *mejtef*,' Mum said.

'*Šta se dešava?*' Dido demanded to know what was going on and Mum dutifully explained. '*Nemože ona ići*,' Dido spat.

'Sabiha, maybe you shouldn't go,' Mum said.

'What?' I shouted. 'You've known about this for a month and now I can't go because of him!' I pointed at Dido.

'*Smiri se*,' Safet urged me to clam down.

'Shut up!' I yelled at him. 'This isn't any of your business.'

'Sabiha,' Mum gasped. 'Apologise immediately.'

My eyes burnt. I should have expected Mum to gang up with them like this. It was like she didn't have a mind of her own. 'No,' I said. There was a choking in my throat, but I sucked it up. I wouldn't cry in front of them.

'Go to your room.' Mum raised her arm and pointed.

'Thanks, I know where it is,' I said, charging past her.

I slammed my bedroom door and leaned against it, listening as all hell broke loose. Both Safet and Dido were going on about how I was out of control and needed to be disciplined. Mum wasn't saying much, apart from, 'Yes, I know.'

I threw myself onto the bed, muffling the sound of my crying in my pillow. After a few minutes I grabbed my journal from under the bed and began writing to vent my anger at Mum's treachery, the pen nearly pierced the paper.

My door burst open and Mum rushed in. 'Sabiha,' she yelled.

'Did you forget how to knock?' I demanded as I wiped my face and hid my journal under my pillow. I stayed on the far side of the bed, facing the wall.

I heard the door close. 'We need to talk about what just happened,' Mum said.

'Yes, we do,' I turned to look at her. 'You betrayed me.'

'No, I didn't.'

'Yes, you did. You knew I was seeing Kathleen this weekend and now you're demanding I go to *mejtef*. What gives?'

'It's important for you to go to *mejtef*.' She sat on the bed and was reaching to pat me.

'If it was so important, why are you only making me go now? I am sixteen years old!'

'You're right,' Mum said. 'It isn't important to me, but it is important to Dido. Think about him for a minute. He lost his wife a year ago. He spent the ten years before that living in desperate poverty in an alien part of Bosnia because he'd lost his home in the war.'

My resolve was crumpling.

'The only reason my parents had food was because we were sending them money. He's in a new country where he doesn't know the language and has no community.' Mum held my hand. 'He needs this. He needs a sense of belonging. We need to make an effort for him.'

'What about me?' I threw off her hand. 'What about what I need?'

'What if you saw Kathleen tomorrow and the week after you went to *mejtef*?'

'I'm seeing Kathleen tomorrow no matter what,' I said.

'Yes, but will you have enough money?' She held up a fifty dollar note.

I wavered for a moment. I really did not want to go to *mejtef*. I could think of thousands of other things that would be much more pleasant. Having my eyes gouged, my body torn apart by wolves. But I needed that money.

I'd used all my money for Kathleen's birthday present. Usually it wasn't a big deal if I didn't have enough cash. Kathleen would lend me the money and I'd pay her back when I wheedled it out of Mum. But things were so weird since I moved to St Albans. Kathleen and I just weren't as close.

'Take it or leave it, Sabiha,' Mum said.

'Okay.' I took the money. 'I'll do it.'

'Now you apologise to Safet—' Mum led me to the door.

'Whoa!' I broke her hold. 'Who said I would apologise?'

'You were rude to Safet—' Mum started.

'He was rude to me,' I interrupted. 'He had no right to interfere—'

'He's my boyfriend and one day he might be a part of this family—' Mum interrupted.

'Or he might be your ex-boyfriend in a few weeks if your track record holds true,' I interrupted.

Mum snatched the money out of my hand and went to walk out.

'Okay, okay.' I stopped her. 'But it's not fair—'

'I don't care what you think.' Mum gripped my arm hard. 'He could be my chance for happiness, my chance to put everything right and to make Babo proud of me. You will not ruin this for me, Sabiha.'

There was desperation in her eyes. While I knew that it was important for her to get respect in the community, I didn't realise she was willing to sacrifice so much, including me.

'Please,' Mum added. 'For me...' She held out the money. I took it and followed her.

'Je si li joj pokazala Boga njenog?' Dido demanded to know if Mum put me in my place. The Bosnian version of 'Did you send her to meet her maker?'

'Sabiha has something to say.' Mum put her hand on my shoulder.

'Sorry,' I said to Safet, then turned around and left, my hand over my pocket where the money was. I heard Dido yelling, then Mum placating him by announcing that I'd be going to *mejtef* next week.

'Next week is a long way away,' I said under my breath. I spent the night in my room writing a short story about an evil mother who abandoned her child to an orphanage in order to marry a millionaire.

***

Kathleen sat at a table outside *Retro*, our favourite café on Brunswick Street. 'It's been ages.' I hugged her. 'I missed you.'

'Me too.' She hugged me back.

'It's so good to be out of the suburbs.' I sat down and picked up the menu.

'Hey Sammie!' Shelley sat opposite me.

I frowned at Kathleen. What happened to lunch on our own? Kathleen shrugged.

'Geez, I haven't seen you since you moved,' Shelley said.

'I know.' It wasn't an accident. The highlight of my move to St Albans was that I didn't have to see Shelley any more.

Kathleen placed her bag on the table and rummaged inside. 'Where's my lip gloss?' she muttered.

'Have you made any friends at your new school?' Shelley asked.

'I've got all the friends I need right here,' I replied.

'My cousins Sharon and Karen live in St Albans. I can hook you up?'

'Thanks, but no thanks,' I said. As if.

Kathleen found her lip gloss and ran it over her lips. As she placed her bag on the ground she shook the table and her coffee spilt on the saucer. 'Shit!' she exclaimed.

'I'll get you some serviettes,' Shelley said.

'What the hell is she doing here?' I hissed at Kathleen after Shelley left.

'She wanted to see you.'

'What for?' I demanded.

'You are her friend too.' Shelley returned and mopped up Kathleen's coffee. 'Thanks Shell,' Kathleen said. Shelley always made me look bad in front of Kathleen by being Miss Perfect. 'I have to go and wash this off.' Kathleen pointed to the stain on her skirt.

After she left Shelley searched through her handbag. 'I've got something for you.' She pulled out an envelope and put it on the table. 'It's a birthday invitation—'

'I've got plans.' I cut her off. Where did she get off playing like we were best buds, when we both knew we hated each other's guts.

Shelley opened her mouth, about to argue, but then thought better of it. 'Don't say I didn't invite you,' she said with a tight smile. She returned the envelope back to her handbag and pulled out an iPod. She put the earphones in her ear. 'Mum bought it for me. It was $250.'

I didn't look at it. Shelley was a show-off. When Shelley's parents divorced they split custody of their daughters. So her sister went to live with her mum and Shelley lived with her dad. Shelley's mum bought her whatever she wanted because she felt guilty that Shelley didn't live with her. Shelley wanted me to admire her iPod but, if I asked to listen to it, she'd make up an excuse not to let me touch it.

'I'm listening to Pink,' Shelley said.

'How original,' I replied. Pink was Kathleen's favourite singer. Shelley was always doing that. Whatever Kathleen liked, so did Shelley.

She pressed stop on her iPod and peered at my bare thighs. 'Is that another op-shop bargain?'

'No.' I tugged at my denim mini down and yanked my tank top up. Both were op-shop bargains that I changed into at Flinders Street train station.

It was March and it was chilly. Mum was hassling me about wearing 'appropriate' clothes, which meant looking like a dork, so I left the house in one outfit and changed into another. Although it was technically too cold for this outfit, I had to make a stand against Mum, even if she didn't know it.

'At least I dressed up.' I gave Shelley the once-over.

Her barrel torso and skinny legs were covered in a Nike top and pants. 'I got this for half price at DFO.' Shelley smoothed down her top. 'It was down from $120 to sixty.'

Every time we went out she wore her Nike crap and went on about how much it cost. She claimed her look was sporty, except instead of muscles she had a spare tyre around her waist. My theory was that she was trying, unsuccessfully, to hide her lard. I didn't know what Kathleen saw in her.

Kathleen returned. 'All clear.' She took a sip of the remains of her coffee.

'Oh no!' Shelley lifted a bag from the ground. 'Some coffee got on your birthday present.'

'I better open it now.' Kathleen took the bag and pulled out a beautifully wrapped box with a card attached. She read it. 'Oh,' she gushed. 'That's beautiful.' She reached over and kissed Shelley on the cheek.

What was the big deal? As Kathleen unwrapped the box I read the card. *Dear Kathleen, You've been a tower of strength during all my dramas. I don't know what I would have done without your supportive shoulder and words of comfort. I hope you have a great 17th birthday. Love forever, your best friend Shelley.*

I wanted to crumple the card. How dare she?

Kathleen pulled out a Nike top and a Pink DVD of her Aussie concert tour a few months back.

'Thanks. You're the best.' She hugged Shelley.

'Now we match,' Shelley said.

'I'm putting it on right now.' Kathleen stood beside Shelley. 'How do we look?' she asked me.

'Great,' I lied. They were like a Weight Watchers before-and-after photo.

'I thought you'd like it.' Shelley touched the DVD. 'Since you didn't get a chance to see her in concert.'

Kathleen avoided my gaze as she thanked Shelley.

'Why don't you give Kathleen her present now?' Shelley gave me a fake smile.

'I've already given her my present.'

'What did you get her?' Shelley asked.

'Tickets.'

'Movie tickets,' Kathleen interrupted. 'We went to see *Twilight* over summer.'

Shelley smiled. She thought she'd won the competition and got Kathleen the better present. Kathleen made me promise I wouldn't tell Shelley about her *real* birthday present. It was an easy promise to keep when I didn't see Shelley, but now that her sneering face was taunting me I fought the urge to tell.

'I heard it was a great movie. I hope you threw in lunch, Sammie,' Shelley said.

I fisted my hands. She pissed me off. I couldn't let her get away with this. But if I argued back Kathleen would be angry with me. She was always telling me to be the better person and not let Shelley's insecurity rile me.

'You just told me that you bought your Nike top at DFO for sixty bucks.'

'Sammie,' Kathleen gasped, while Shelley blushed.

'At least my present was more than fifteen bucks,' Shelley said.

'So was mine. I bought her Pink—'

'Sammie, don't—' Kathleen cut me off.

'—concert tickets,' I finished.

'But your parents wouldn't let you go,' Shelley quizzed Kathleen.

Kathleen's parents were devout Christians and they saw Pink as the devil's tool. They didn't allow her listen to her music and if they found out that Kathleen went to a Pink concert, they'd ground her for all eternity.

'She slept at my place.' I beamed at Shelley. Despite my other issues with Mum she was the coolest parent of the group. Whenever we did something that Kathleen's parents didn't approve of, she slept over at my place.

'I didn't know.' Kathleen put her hand on Shelley's. 'It was a surprise birthday present.'

'That's okay...' Shelley took a deep breath, pretending she was holding back tears. 'The only thing that matters is that you had a great birthday. Excuse me.' As she stood to leave there were tears glistening on her cheeks. Shit, maybe she really *was* crying?

'Why did you have to be such a bitch?' Kathleen hissed at me after Shelley had gone to the bathroom.

'She started it,' I muttered. 'She was making fun of my birthday present.'

'You know she didn't mean anything by it,' Kathleen said. 'She does that to make herself feel better about not living with her Mum.'

'I'm sick of it,' I said. It was always about poor Shelley. There was always a drama going on that demanded Kathleen's attention. I had problems too, but you didn't hear me going on about them twenty-four seven.

'I'm sick of *this.*' Kathleen got up and followed Shelley.

My stomach dropped. I knew that I gave Kathleen the shits by arguing with Shelley all the time, but I'd never seen her so pissed off. 'I'll come with you.' I stood.

'Really?' Kathleen said, that one word imbued with suspicion as we faced off.

'I'm sorry. I shouldn't have let her get to me.'

'It's Shelley you need to apologise to,' Kathleen said, as she marched past the staring waiters. I was nodding and looking at the ground as I trailed behind her.

We found Shelley in the toilets dabbing her face with a wet paper towel. 'Are you okay?' Kathleen asked, putting her arm around her.

'I'm fine,' Shelley gasped. 'Things at home are getting to me.' She jammed her asthma puffer into her open mouth.

I restrained myself from dry retching. Kathleen hugged her. I wanted to scream in frustration. She always bought Shelley's stories hook, line and sinker. I mean grow up. Shit happens. Deal with it and shut up.

'Listen Shelley,—' I had to swallow as the apology choked in my throat. 'I'm sorry about before,' I finally managed.

'Thanks.' Shelley turned back to Kathleen. 'It's getting worse at home.'

I wanted to strangle the cow. I apologised and all she had to say was thanks. What about her freaking apology to me? She was mean to me first. Kathleen glanced at me. I arranged my face to show appropriate concern.

'What's going on at home?' I asked. Now Kathleen couldn't say I wasn't being friendly to the skank.

'Dad says he wants me to go and live with my Mum,' Shelley said.

'Let's talk about it.' Kathleen ushered Shelley to the door. I needed to go to the toilet, but if I didn't go with them Kathleen would have another reason to be pissed off. 'Are you sure he really means that,' Kathleen asked when we were back at the table.

Shelley wiped her face. 'Since Alana's been there, he's been saying it more and more.'

Her father's girlfriend had moved in a few months before and things were bumpy ever since. Shelley's dad was spending a lot of time with his girlfriend's daughter and Shelley felt left out.

'Maybe he's under stress from the changes,' Kathleen said.

'I don't know,' Shelley said. 'But I can't go back to Mum's.'

Every second weekend Shelley and her sister stayed over at one of their parents together. 'Why not?' I asked.

'When I stayed at Mum's last weekend her boyfriend walked in on me having a shower and tried to touch my boobs,' Shelley said.

'Tell your Dad,' I said.

'I can't.' Shelley twisted a tissue between her hands. 'Then he wouldn't let me visit Mum again.'

'Everything will be OK.' Kathleen hugged Shelley as she sobbed. 'You *have* to tell your dad about what happened.' Shelley shook her head. 'What about your sister?' Kathleen asked. 'He could try it on her too.'

'He won't,' Shelley insisted. 'She's only ten.'

'She'll be a teenager soon and then what will happen?' Kathleen said.

Shelley's mouth fell open like she was catching flies. 'You're right,' she said. 'I have to talk to Dad. I'll do it tonight.'

'Good.' Kathleen hugged her again.

'Thanks Kathleen,' Shelley said. 'You're my best friend.'

There it was again. She was having a dig at me. I glanced at Kathleen, but as usual she was oblivious. Why did she always notice when I had a go at Shelley, but never when it was the other way around?

'Anyway, I'd better get going,' Shelley stood. 'I only dropped by to say hello to Sammie.'

'Thanks.' I felt off-centre. If I'd known she was only staying for coffee I wouldn't have let her get to me.

'I'm glad to hear things are going well at your new school,' Shelley said.

Kathleen looked at Shelley all dewy-eyed. I couldn't believe she was buying into this. Shelley hated me as much as I hated her.

'I hope things get better at home,' I finally got out, almost choking on my own hypocrisy.

'Thanks,' Shelley said. 'I'm sure it will be fine.'

After Shelley left, Kathleen lifted her coffee and sipped, keeping her eyes straight ahead.

'What's going on?' I asked.

Kathleen shrugged.

'Did you get my SMS last Saturday?' I asked.

She shook her head. 'My brother tossed my phone into the toilet.' Kathleen's younger brother and sister were always destroying her stuff. I should have known there was a reason like that for her not to reply.

'I'm sorry I told Shelley,' I said. 'But she started it.'

'You promised,' Kathleen said flatly.

I bit my lip. She was really pissed off. When Kathleen was hysterical and loud, she blew off steam and was over it. It was when she was calm and cold that you had to worry. This was her grudge-keeping mode.

'I'm sorry, Kathleen,' I said. Sucking up might soothe her.

'You're always sorry, Sammie.'

'Shelley didn't apologise to me,' I said.

'What for? You were the bitch.'

'So was she. While you were away wiping your skirt she put me down big time.'

Kathleen shook her head. I could tell she didn't believe me. As usual she cast Shelley in the role of the victim and I was the villain.

'Anyway it's better that she knows sooner rather than later. Aren't you getting her hopes up?'

Kathleen gazed at me questioningly.

"*Love forever, your best friend Shelley*,' I read out from her birthday card. 'You're *my* best friend, not hers.'

'No, I'm not.'

My eyes smarted. It was true. Kathleen wanted to dump me.

Chapter 4

'I mean I'm not just *your* best friend,' Kathleen jumped in when she saw my face. 'I'm Shelley's best friend too.'

'But you can't be,' I blurted.

'Why not?'

'You can only have one best friend. That's why they're the best.'

'Grow up, Sammie,' Kathleen said.

'But we promised each other.'

We made the vow at the end of Year 6. Kathleen was supposed to go to a private Catholic school, while I was enrolled in a public school. We feared we would be split up forever and promised each other we'd be best friends for life, no matter what. Then her Dad's concreting business ran into trouble and her parents couldn't afford the private school fees so we ended up at the same high school.

'We're not in primary school anymore. We can have more than one friend,' Kathleen said.

'So you can break promises, but I can't.'

Kathleen sighed, but didn't say anything. I tried making conversation, but she kept replying in monosyllables.

'Do you want to go to an op-shop?' I asked finally.

'I better go check how Shelley's doing.' Kathleen stood.

'But we were supposed to spend the day together.' I winced at how whiny my voice sounded.

'I'm not in the mood today.' Kathleen packed her things in her handbag. 'We'll get together another time.'

'I probably won't have the chance again. Mum expects me to go to Bosnian school on Saturdays.' I wanted her to stay with me. I desperately needed to talk to her about the changes in *my* life.

'Since when has your Mum made you do anything?' Kathleen asked.

I knew she didn't believe me. She knew Mum as the cool Mum who let me do whatever I wanted. She didn't know the Born-Again-Muslim-Mum.

'See you later.' Kathleen gave me a brisk hug and kiss, the kind you give to an acquaintance that you feel obligated to touch.

'See ya,' I said, my voice husky. A tear crept down my cheek, but Kathleen didn't look at me as she said goodbye. As she walked off I wanted to shout for her to stop, to talk to me, to be my best friend again, but I wasn't sure she'd listen. I'd pushed her too far and I didn't know if she'd ever come back to me.

Instead of going home, I went window-shopping by myself. I dawdled at the usual shops Kathleen and I liked, but it wasn't the same. Usually Kathleen and I critiqued each other's fashion choices and tried on awful outfits to get a rise out of each other. The day would fly by so fast I wouldn't notice the time.

A woman walked past, her bright-red hair glinting in the sun. It was Frankie, Mum's best friend. I ran after her. As she glanced at a shop window, however, I saw from her profile that it wasn't Frankie. But it gave me the idea to go see her. I always liked talking to Frankie. I could get to her house in ten minutes by tram. She lived two streets from us when Mum and I lived in Thornbury with Dave. I rang her on my mobile, but her phone was busy.

Frankie also lived around the corner from Kathleen. I hesitated as the tram pulled up. If Kathleen saw me, she'd think I was stalking her. Maybe it wasn't a good idea to visit Frankie? But I really needed to talk to someone. Stuff it. I got on the tram.

Walking up Clarendon Street I was struck again at the differences between St Albans and Thornbury. In Thornbury the houses were narrow and jammed next to each other, the majority semi-detached. There were hardly any front or backyards. A lot of houses had chairs on the front porch where people sat and chatted to passers-by. The streets were narrow and full of cars because there wasn't any off-street parking.

In St Albans the houses were on huge blocks. There was distance between neighbours. The streets were bare, the cars parked in driveways and garages. You only saw your neighbours if they walked past your house or worked in their yard. All the social activities took place in the backyard, away from neighbours' eyes.

I was nervous as I knocked on the door. I hadn't seen Frankie since we moved. She and Mum saw each other at least once a week and talked on the phone often, but I didn't know when Mum had last spoken to her.

'There you are—' Frankie opened the door with a smile. Seeing me on her doorstop she stopped mid-sentence and her face creased in consternation. I was clearly not who she was expecting. 'Is your Mum with you?' She scanned the street.

'No, it's just me.'

'Oh.' Frankie held the door.

'I'm sorry.' I was an idiot. 'I should have called first, but I was in the neighbourhood.'

'Don't be silly.' She reached for me. 'You're always welcome, Sammie.' She gave me a big hug. 'Sit down. I have to make a phone call.'

I walked to the living room at the back of the house. Frankie was a perpetual student who worked part-time at a pub. She'd been renting this house for five years and all the furniture was second-hand.

Frankie and Mum met in a doctor's surgery when I was little, and their friendship had grown over the years. She'd been like an aunt to me and, before Mum met Dave, I used to stay with Frankie when Mum was in hospital. Even though my real aunt, Zehra, offered to take me in, I preferred Frankie's because it meant I stayed at the same school. Plus she was cool to live with.

She went to the bedroom with the phone and closed the door, but the windows to the living room and bedroom were open and I heard her. 'You'll have to come by later. Sammie's here.... I don't know, I'll call you when she's gone.'

I shifted on the sofa uncomfortably. I'd stuffed up her plans. 'I can't stay long,' I said when she emerged from the bedroom.

'Stay as long as you like,' Frankie said. 'I've got nothing on.' Frankie went to the kitchen and made us coffee. She passed me a cup before sitting on the sofa opposite. 'What's new?'

I told her about the past few months. As I talked my limbs loosened. I hadn't realised how stressed I was.

'Of course it's difficult getting along with your grandfather,' Frankie said, after I complained about Dido. 'Just because you share the same DNA doesn't mean you will instantly like each other. You have to develop a relationship.'

'I wish you'd tell Mum,' I said. 'She expects me to be the perfect granddaughter and accept everything about him, when he wants to change everything about me.'

'She has a lot of guilt about not being there for him over the years,' Frankie said. 'She's over-compensating. Give her time and she'll calm down.'

When Frankie glanced at the clock I saw I'd been gas-bagging for over an hour. 'I better get going.' As she led me down the hall, I knew I'd overstayed my welcome. 'I'll tell Mum to give you a call,' I said.

'It's okay,' Frankie said. 'I know she's busy.' She kissed me on the cheek. 'See you soon, Sammie.' She closed the flyscreen behind me. Before I reached the footpath I heard her on the phone.

Despite her being distracted, it was still a relief to have talked to Frankie. She had made me realise that I shouldn't feel guilty about not liking my grandfather. We were strangers and suddenly we were living under the same roof and were supposed to act like best mates.

I caught the tram from Thornbury to Flinders Street Station and then a St Albans train. Once we'd left the inner city at Footscray station, the view out the train window got bleaker. Grey industrial buildings rose across the landscape, signposts of the future in factories that awaited the youth of the western suburbs.

Last week, I read an article in the local paper, the *St Albans News*, about how fewer than half of high school graduates would go on to tertiary education, and most of those were vocational apprenticeships and training courses. The majority would get a trade or go on unemployment benefits. It was different from my old school where most students didn't contemplate anything other than studying at university.

The woman sitting opposite me thought I was looking at her. 'Going home from work, dearie?' she asked.

'No, I met up with a friend.'

'I'm going home after a day out away from the neighbours,' she said.

I nodded. I hated it when strangers talked to me on public transport. Usually I'd either be reading or listening to music, but today I didn't feel like it reading and I'd left my headphones at home.

'Bloody Greeks are chasing me out of my house so they can move in more of their family.'

I eyed the train door, wondering if I had the guts to make a run for the next carriage.

'They're cursing me.' She looked around to see if anyone was watching us. 'They put an evil white feather on my front lawn. Bloody wogs,' she muttered under her breath.

'This is my stop.' I bolted for the door. We'd pulled into Sunshine station, three stops before mine, so I ran two train carriages down and re-entered the train.

As I found a seat, I couldn't get the conversation out of my head. That woman would never have confided in Kathleen. Kathleen's dusky skin and dark eyes and hair from her Italian heritage marked her as non-Anglo. With my blonde hair and green eyes, people thought I was Anglo. I called myself Sammie and never thought about my parents being Bosnian, but now it was different. I felt like I was out of a club I thought I was a shoo-in for.

When I got home there were boxes strewn across the living room floor. Mum was amongst the packaging. 'What's going on?' I asked.

Mum slashed open another box. 'I went shopping.' She pulled out a gold-coloured metal telephone stand with glass shelves. 'What do you think?'

'Nice.' I squinted as the light bounced off the gold.

'I got a matching coffee table and lamp tables.' Mum arranged the telephone table.

She moved our old coffee table halfway into the kitchen. We only bought it a few months ago when we moved out of Dave's house.

'What's wrong with our old furniture?' She was usually such a tight-arse and only bought me clothes once a year. I only got two pairs of shoes: one for summer, one for winter.

'Nothing.' Mum wiped her forehead. 'I thought it was time for a change.'

'Where's our old TV cabinet?' It had been replaced with a monstrosity that took up the whole wall.

'Dido thought it was tatty so we put it on the lawn and someone took it away.'

I wanted to swear. I loved that TV cupboard. I was the one who found it at a garage sale. It was made of dark wood and was ready for the tip. But

Dave sanded it back and repaired the shelves and Mum and I painted it. It was our creation and one of my great memories of our past life.

Mum was changing the house to look more like other Bosnian homes. All Bosnians had the same decor: the L-shaped sofa, the glass-covered coffee table with the knitted tablecloth underneath, a wall unit for the TV, and a matching shelving unit that had glass doors, where you kept drinking glasses and *fildžani*, the Bosnian version of special china you rarely use.

When we lived with Dave we collected our furniture from op-shops and garage sales. It was funky and grungy. Now there were knitted doilies on surfaces and Mum had already filled the big new TV cabinet with glasses and knick-knacks.

'I'll be giving those bits and pieces to Safet.' Mum pointed to the old coffee and lamp table.

I should have known her sudden loosening of the purse strings had something to do with Safet. She didn't fart these days without his permission.

'There's something for you in the kitchen,' Mum said.

'You bought me a TV!' I shouted when I saw it on the kitchen counter.

'Technically it's for Dido.' Mum stood behind me. 'He and Edin can play chess and watch TV here, and leave the living room for you.'

'Why can't I have my own TV?' I asked.

'Because I can't afford a television in each room. If you don't want it, I can return it,' Mum said.

'No, no,' I said hurriedly. 'It's great.'

Dido came in and his face darkened when he saw the new furniture and TV. 'Where did you get the money from, Bahra.'

'Credit card.' Mum squeezed the box she was holding.

'You can't afford a credit card!' Dido shouted. 'Give it to me.' He held out his hand.

Mum snapped open her purse and handed him the card.

He rushed to the kitchen and banged drawers until he found the scissors. 'I paid off the mortgage by selling my house in Bosnia and now you want to make us homeless!' He cut the credit card and threw it in the bin. 'No more spending,' he growled.

Mum nodded, her head bowed.

'I saw Frankie,' I said, after Dido had marched out.

'How is she?' Mum asked absent-mindedly, her focus on the stubborn packing tape around the box in her hands.

'She said she hasn't heard from you in a while.'

'Mmm,' Mum murmured, ripping open the final box. The phone rang.

It was Safet. I went to my bedroom and lay on the bed. Why didn't Mum and Frankie care about not talking to each other? As far as I knew, they hadn't had a big falling out; they just seemed to have stopped calling each other. It was as if the distance between the suburbs created an invisible shield cutting them off from each other.

Was that happening with Kathleen and me? What if our friendship was only based on seeing each other at school and now that we didn't, it was over?

On Sunday I pretended I had heaps of homework and spent the day reading books, hoping each time the phone rang that it was Kathleen. But she didn't call.

***

The next week at school I hung around with Brian and Jesse at lunchtime. On Thursday we were sitting on the benches in front of school when Dina and Gemma came over.

'Hi.' I eyed them curiously. We hadn't been bosom buddies in the past week. In fact I was doing my best to avoid them.

Dina scrutinised Brian's face and ignored me. 'You're wearing foundation,' she burst out shrilly voice.

'It's Clearasil,' Brian said without skipping a beat.

We examined his face. His cheeks and chin were covered in large purple pimples that were muted under a layer of orange cream.

'Looks like foundation to me,' Gemma said.

'Why aren't you on the oval?' I stared them down. Since I'd been hanging around with Brian and Jesse, Dina had backed off from stalking Adnan.

Dina smiled. 'Do you want to join us?'

'Sure,' Brian jumped in before I had a chance to say no.

As we walked to the oval Jesse and Brian fell in behind us, while Gemma and Dina took position on each side of me. 'You shouldn't be hanging around with Brian,' Dina said.

'You don't want his reputation to rub off on you,' Gemma piped up.

'What reputation?' They avoided my gaze. What did they know about Brian? Dina checked to see that Brian and Jesse were far enough behind not to hear her. I sidled closer to her, nervous about what she had to say.

Chapter 5

'He's gay,' Gemma whispered.

'Yeah,' Dina whispered. 'Your family will be upset if you hang around him.'

'No, he's not,' I growled.

'How do you know?' Gemma demanded.

'I know.' I blushed remembering the way he walked close to me. His constant little touches when we were together. I didn't think I was hot, but I knew when someone was flirting with me. Backstabbing cows. I stopped in my tracks. 'If you care about your reputations it's best if Jesse, Brian and I don't go to the oval.' I raised my voice so Brian and Jesse heard me.

Dina grabbed my arm and gave Brian and Jesse a fake smile. 'I don't care.'

'Yeah, I don't care,' Gemma said, less certainly.

'Good.' I smiled at them. We reached Adnan's group and I sat between Jesse and Brian, forcing Dina to sit next to Brian. Jesse opened *The Shining* and began reading.

'That's the best Stephen King novel, isn't it?' I smiled at Jesse but he just nodded back and kept reading.

Brian watched the soccer players intently and a wave of unease overcame me at the hungry look in his eyes. Maybe Dina was right? Had I misread his signals?

'Why did you want to come to the oval?' I asked him.

'Change of scenery.' Brian's face became serious.

Dina caught my eye, 'I told you so,' written on her face. I wanted to poke my tongue out at her; instead I flicked my hair over my shoulder.

I waved at Adnan. He came over during a break, loping across the grass, his naked torso glistening with sweat. I forced myself not to glance at Brian. I was scared of what I'd see.

'Hey, cuz.' Adnan reached out and slapped my hand in a high-five.

I introduced Jesse and Brian. Jesse nodded at Adnan and went back to reading. Brian offered his hand. 'That was a nice header, mate.'

'Thanks.' Adnan threw himself onto the grass in front of me.

'You been playing long?' Brian asked.

'Since I was this tall.' Adnan put his hand below his upturned knee.

'Do you follow European league?' Brian asked.

'Whatever I can see on SBS.' Adnan shrugged. He untied the top from around his waist and used it to wipe the sweat off his face.

'My Dad installed a satellite dish so we watch all the games.'

'Sweet.' Adnan put down his top.

'Hi Adnan.' Dina's eyes were glued to his chest.

'Hey,' Adnan replied without looking at her. 'You play?' he asked Brian.

'Yeah.'

'Let's see what you've got?' Adnan stood.

Brian leaped up. He was dressed like he was going to a formal: pleated pants and a short-sleeved shirt. He took off his shirt and folded it, leaving on his T-shirt. 'Get ready to be dazzled,' Brian said. Adnan laughed and slapped him on the back.

'Gees, he'll ruin his make-up,' Dina said. She and Gemma sniggered.

They began playing and Adnan's mates blocked Brian, but he didn't back off. I elbowed Jesse and nodded toward the oval. He glanced up before returning to his book.

Brian hounded the players until he isolated a chubby kid and stole the ball from him. The players pulled together into defensive positions and tried to block him. He feinted around them and kicked the ball to Adnan who scored a goal.

The guys took him seriously after that and the game returned to the normal easygoing camaraderie. When the lunch bell rang they shook hands with Brian and slapped him on the back. Dina and Gemma were gobsmacked.

Adnan and Brian ran over to us. 'You really can play,' Adnan said as he picked up his backpack.

'Thanks.' Brian put his shirt on.

'Same time tomorrow?' Adnan put his hand out for a high-five.

'You're on.' Brian slapped his hand.

'See ya cuz,' Adnan called as he ran off.

I fell into step with Brian on the way to class. The teacher gave us a Maths problem to do in teams and Brian and I paired up. 'I didn't know you played soccer?'

He frowned as he worked the calculator. 'I haven't played since primary school.'

'Why not?'

Brian shrugged.

I grabbed his arm and squeezed. 'How come?'

'Once guys decide you're a gay they don't want to touch you in case they catch it,' he hissed. It was like he'd read my mind. 'I'm sorry for taking it out on you,' Brian said. 'It just gets me worked up.'

I put my hand on his shoulder. 'They're stupid people spreading stupid rumours.' I knew it. Of course he wasn't gay. The teacher called out and we turned to the front. For the rest of the lesson we copied from the board.

The bell rang. 'Meet you at the front,' Brian said as he headed to the door.

I nodded and packed my backpack. The three of us were going to Sunshine library together after school. Sunshine Library or Scumshine, as it was called by those who lived there and had reason to know, was three times bigger than the St Albans library. Thankfully it also had unlimited borrowing so I'd have books to read for a while, as long as I kept renewing them so I didn't cop a fine.

Jesse was by himself. 'Where's Brian?' I peered around him.

'He's coming. I can't make it tonight,' Jesse said.

'Oh, that's too bad.' Happiness crept into my voice. I would be alone with Brian. Jesse looked cut. 'I mean, we'll miss you,' I jumped in, interjecting sincerity in my voice.

'Don't worry, Sabiha, I know what you mean.' Jesse picked up his backpack and turned to leave.

We both saw Brian approaching.

'You okay?' Brian asked.

'Mum's not feeling well,' Jesse said. He handed Brian a list with Stephen King and Dean R. Koontz titles scrawled on it. 'Can you get me some books?'

'What's up with him?' Brian asked after Jesse left.

I plastered a clueless look on my face. 'What's wrong with his Mum?' I asked, even though I didn't really care. I was happy to have Brian all to myself. This was my chance to find out if he liked me.

Brian shrugged. 'We'd better get going.'

We caught the train from St Albans to Sunshine. Usually I went to the library on my own. Kathleen wasn't much of a reader, so I was rapt to find a companion.

On the train, Brian's face became serious. 'You know when Dina said I was wearing foundation?'

I waved my hand like I was pushing away a bad smell. 'She's a turd.'

'I *am* wearing foundation.'

I examined Brian's face. He'd applied the make-up expertly, blending it into his neck so there was no tell-tale jaw line to give it away. I didn't know what to say. I wasn't jumping to conclusions again. 'Do you wear foundation all the time?' I asked softly, aware of the other passengers around us.

'Only when I break out.' Brian touched his left cheek where there were nasty pimples.

'Foundation just makes it worse, you know.' I knew from experience. 'It doesn't allow your skin to breathe and makes the pimples stay for longer. You should wear a tinted moisturiser.'

'Really? Thanks,' Brian said uncertainly.

'You're welcome.' I felt like I'd dodged a bullet.

At the library we pointed out our favourite novels. I borrowed JD Salinger's *Catcher in the Rye* on his recommendation. He agreed to read Stephenie Meyer's *Twilight*, even though he needed some convincing. Gothic vampire romances were a new thing for him.

While he discovered Bella and Edward, I checked my emails. Kathleen had sent me a meme of cute furry critters and a line saying she was sorry for being crabby on Saturday. I took comfort in the fact that she hadn't forgotten me.

As we walked back to the station I winced and shifted my backpack straps. I'd left my schoolbooks in my locker so I'd have more room, but as usual I'd gotten over-excited and borrowed fifteen books. Now I had to suffer.

Brian took off his backpack. 'Let's swap.'

'Are you serious?' I couldn't believe my luck. He'd only borrowed five books. 'Thanks,' I said, catching up to him.

Brian smiled. 'My weight-lifting is paying off.'

I peered at his biceps and then at his chest, and saw the firm outline of muscle. 'You weight-lift?'

He nodded. 'At least an hour after school. Do you think I'm a freak?'

'Because you weight-lift?' I squeaked.

'Because I wear make-up.' He slanted his eyes. 'Sometimes I wear eye-liner and mascara too.' He started gabbling. 'There are heaps of guys who wear make-up.' Brian didn't look at me, but he did slow his pace. 'The Killers, Good Charlotte, The Chemical Brothers…'

I strained to remember other rock bands. 'Yeah, it shows you're interesting. It's not gay, it's fashionable.'

Brian smiled. 'You're a good friend.'

When the train drew up at St Albans station, Brian helped me put on my backpack, leaving his hands to rest on my shoulders. We were the same height. His eyelashes were thick and spiky, his eyes a soft, velvet brown.

'I had a great time.' He leaned in.

He was going to kiss me. My eyes closed as his face went out of focus. His lips brushed against my cheek. My eyes flew open and I blushed. I hoped he didn't see me close my eyes. 'I had a great time too.' My voice was husky.

'See you tomorrow,' Brian said.

I took a few steps and glanced over my shoulder. He was watching me. I turned back and resisted looking behind me again. I'd never met a boy like him. He was sweet and gentle, but still did boy things like weights and soccer. The boys I knew before hadn't prepared me for someone like Brian.

As I remembered the flutter in my stomach when he kissed my cheek, his lips soft and gentle, I broke into a shit-eating grin. It was wonderful, nothing like the jaw-wrenching, slobbery mashing of the lips that Joshua, my only other boyfriend, inflicted on me.

***

Two girls were standing on the corner of my street. 'I think that's her,' one of them said.

When I met their gaze they looked blank. They followed me down the street. Hearing their footsteps in time with mine made my heart speed up. At my house, they kept walking without looking back. I breathed a sigh of relief. I was imagining it.

My stomach rumbled. I dropped my backpack in the hallway and went to the kitchen to make a sandwich. I reached into the breadbox. 'There's no bread!' I yelled.

'Here.' Mum took out a ten-dollar note from her purse. 'Go and buy it.'

'Why didn't *you* buy it?' It drove me mad when there was no bread. It wasn't like she didn't know what time I was coming home from school, or that I'd be hungry. 'What were you doing all day?'

'I was busy,' Mum said. 'If you want it, you get it.' She put the note on the table.

I grabbed the money and slammed the back door. 'Busy, my arse,' I muttered under my breath. 'Busy sleeping in until noon.' Mum claimed that her medication made her lethargic, that she needed to sleep like a hibernating bear. My version was that she was lazy.

'Sabiha!' Mum yelled. I stopped in my tracks and kicked the stair. She heard me. 'Buy milk too.' Mum stepped out holding a five-dollar bill.

'I don't drink milk!' I yelled. 'If you want it, you get it.'

Walking back, I held the sliced Vienna loaf under my left arm. I split the top of the plastic bag and pinched off bits of bread and ate them. The girls from the corner of my street were following me again. I sped up and heard footsteps pounding behind me. Something smacked into me and I dropped the bread. Fists pummelled me and the half-chewed bite of bread fell out of my mouth. Arms pulled me up.

One of the girls held me while the other one slapped me in the face, once, twice, before she punched me in the stomach. I went down, my knee landing on the bread and grinding it into the concrete. They high-fived each other and ran away, their feet echoing down the street.

The bread I'd chewed was by my foot. My stomach heaved and I dry retched, moaning with the violent jerks. My ribs ached. I wiped the spittle off my mouth and picked up the squashed bread. I looked up as the girls ran into the next street.

'Girl,' Dido called when I walked through the front door. 'Come here.' I heard the clacking of wood on wood. He was playing chess with his buddy Edin. When he played chess he acted like I was his waitress.

I went into my bedroom and sat on the bed, cradling the bread in my arms. I heard my grandfather speaking and then footsteps. My bedroom door opened.

'Sabiha, didn't you hear your grandfather?' Mum asked. Her face crumpled in concern. 'What happened, baby girl?'

'Some girls hit me,' I gasped between sobs.

'Who?'

'I don't know them. I think they live in Cottle Street.' Mum hugged me and I cried, the plastic bag with the bread rustling as we squashed it between us.

There were tears in Mum's eyes. 'Where did they hit you?'

My ribs were throbbing. I lifted my T-shirt, but there wasn't a mark on my skin.

Dido appeared in the doorway. 'What happened?'

'She was beaten up.'

'Get her out there to smash their skulls,' Dido urged.

I sobbed, hiding my face behind my hands. Waves of embarrassment washed over me every time I remembered the way the girls hit me like I was a scarecrow. I didn't put up one decent punch.

'Leave us, Babo.' Mum closed the door in Dido's face. When I finished crying she wiped my face with a tissue and gave me another one to blow my nose. 'Let's go.'

I followed her into the hallway. 'Where?'

'To the police.' Mum put on her shoes.

'No, no. We can't.' I knew what happened to dobbers. The girls would just bash me even more.

'We're not letting them get away with this.'

At the police station Mum spoke to the policewoman at the counter while I played with my sleeve. 'Are you sure you want to press charges?' the policewoman asked. 'If the girls live near you it means your daughter will be an easy target for retaliation.'

'But they beat her up,' Mum exclaimed. 'Practically in front of our house in broad daylight.'

'I understand that.' The woman shuffled paperwork. 'Sometimes reporting it makes these things worse.'

'Come on, Mum.' I pulled her arm. 'Let's go.'

'But, but, this can't happen,' Mum insisted, putting her hands on the counter. 'You're supposed to help.'

'You can fill in the incident report form' The policewoman picked up her pen and waited.

Mum let me pull her away from the counter and back into the carpark.

'Why should the police waste their time?' Dido said when Mum told him. 'The girl needs to defend herself.' He stared at the chessboard as he plotted his next move. Edin watched Dido, his chubby face creased in a smile.

'It's okay if your granddaughter gets beaten in front of her own house?' Mum demanded. 'Next time they can come into the house and beat her up.'

Dido held a pawn, his hand hovering above the board as he decided where to place it. Edin tensed in anticipation, waiting for Dido's move.

Mum threw up her hands. 'Why stop there?' she yelled. 'Maybe we can help them rob us by throwing our things onto the street?'

'Do you know them?' Dido asked, finally looking up, a cigarette clenched between his teeth.

'No.'

'They live in Cottle Street.' Mum pointed toward the milkbar. I cursed my big mouth. 'Bobbie from next door will know them.' Mum headed for the front door. Bobbie was a little old Greek lady who lived in the same house since she came to Australia fifty years ago. She knew everyone.

Dido and Edin kept playing chess. *'Šah Mat,'* Edin exclaimed joyfully as he declared checkmate. 'Three out of three?' Edin asked as he pushed the figurines off the board. They always played three games of chess to determine the winner.

'We'd better wait for Bahra.' Dido collected the pieces and returned them to the box.

I gulped. This was serious. Dido was saying no to a game of chess when he was on a losing streak. I prayed that Bobbie's nosiness would fail her and she wouldn't know the girls. I wanted to pretend the attack never happened.

Mum returned a few minutes later. 'Bobbie knows them. She says the girls are sisters and that they live at 30 Cottle Street.'

"*Hajmo*,' Dido muttered as he walked out the front door, Edin following his footsteps.

I let them stride ahead of me, hoping that I could return home when they weren't looking. I think Mum read my mind because she slowed. 'Don't be scared,' she said as she took my arm. 'Nothing can happen to you while we're with you.'

I thought I'd had crappy days since Dido moved in with us, but today was going down in the history books as the worst day ever.

Dido and Edin moved up the footpath. Dido pounded on the front door. A man and woman answered. The two girls hid in the darkness of the hallway behind them. I hadn't noticed before, but they were dressed alike, as if they were twins, even though they obviously were not.

Mum pulled me forward. 'Your girls attacked my daughter.' Mum lifted up my T-shirt, but I yanked it down.

'I'm sure it wasn't our girls,' the Twins' mother said.

'Is that them?' Mum asked in Bosnian. I wanted to lie, but I couldn't show Mum up. I nodded jerkily. Mum turned back to the parents. 'Your daughters attacked her in front of our house.'

'What is she saying?' Dido demanded.

'They're calling Sabiha a liar,' Mum said in Bosnian.

Dido smiled and stepped closer to the girls' father. He was a head shorter and had to look up. 'You're calling my granddaughter a liar?' he asked in Bosnian. Mum translated.

'We're not calling anyone a liar. We're saying a mistake has been made.' The Twins' father lifted his hands in supplication.

Mum shook her head. 'He's being a smartarse.'

'He thinks we're liars,' Dido spoke to Edin in Bosnian. Even though Dido was like a small boy compared to the Twins' father's hulking body, his bluster made him puff up like a rooster. 'Can you believe that in this country children can be attacked in front of their house? Then the parents of the criminals can lie to your face?' Dido's voice escalated into a booming shout.

The Twins' parents glanced at each other nervously.

'That's enough,' Mum said. 'Let's go.'

Dido ignored her. His face was red and the vein on his neck bulged. 'And the police tell you to piss off when you report a crime. If you raised your kids properly there wouldn't be crime.'

Mum tried to pull Dido away, but he wouldn't budge. While Dido shouted Edin bellowed every English profanity he knew. 'Fuck, piss, shit, prick, dirty dog, arsehole.'

'You'd better leave!' the Twins' father shouted.

'We have to go.' Mum tugged on Dido's sleeve. He jerked away from her, his tirade unrelenting.

'We'll call the police!' the father shouted back.

'Yes, call so they can arrest your criminal daughters,' Dido shouted, recognising the word police.

'Let's go,' Mum commanded, inserting herself in front of Dido.

'Tell them they better keep a watch on their daughters because if I have to come here again I'll give them the beating they've been asking for,' Dido said.

'And I'll be beside him.' Edin raised his fist in the air.

Mum walked off without translating. 'Tell them,' Dido demanded.

'Keep your girls away from my daughter or we'll be back.' Mum finally wrenched Dido away and pushed him towards the street.

Following Dido as he strode ahead, Edin hitched his pants over his potbelly, his gait roly-poly as he shifted his girth with each step. 'We showed them,' he said to my grandfather.

Chapter 6

'That was so embarrassing,' I hissed to Mum as we walked home.

'At least they won't be bothering you again.'

'That's how a real Bosnian deals with bullies,' Dido said.

'So I'm not a real Bosnian because I don't shout at people like a maniac,' I spat, and marched ahead of them.

'What the hell's her problem?' Dido asked.

'Nothing,' Mum answered tiredly.

'Three out of three?' Edin asked, eager to continue their chess tournament.

'You're on,' Dido said.

***

The next morning I waited out the front of school. Brian and Jesse crossed the street and waved. Brian kissed me on the cheek. 'You're early today.'

Jesse hung back. We hadn't gotten the hang of the touchy-feely thing.

'How's your Mum?' I asked him.

'Good.' He stared at his feet.

I frowned at Brian, but he just shrugged.

'Why are you early?' Brian asked as we walked to our bench.

'I can be on time.' I climbed with them to sit on the table with our feet on the bench in our usual formation. Jesse, Brian and then me.

Brian took off his backpack and threw it on the stool. 'Not that I've seen.'

'I did my Maths homework. You can copy my notes.'

'Who are you?' He peered into my face. 'What you done with the real Sabiha Omerović?' He lifted my hair and looked into my ear.

I laughed despite myself. 'Do you want to see?'

'You betcha.' Brian tickled my waist. 'Cause I don't believe you did it.'

I unzipped my backpack and searched for my notebook. 'It's here.'

'Sure, sure.' Brian patted my head.

I jerked away. 'It is.' I tipped everything onto the table and checked each notebook. 'I left it in the library.'

'Are you sure the dog didn't eat it?' Jesse asked.

'Smartarse,' I muttered.

'Let's go and a look.' Brian gestured for me to lead the way.

'Miss Swan!' I called out as I ran to the counter.

'Looking for this?' She held out my notebook.

I smiled and hugged it to my chest. 'Thanks heaps.' I turned to give Brian and Jesse a triumphant look.

'It was a pleasure having your company this morning, Sabiha,' Miss Swan said.

'I wonder why a girl who can't be on time to class would be early to school?' Brian asked when they caught up with me. 'Are you blushing?' He peered at my cheek.

My left cheek was red from the Twins' slaps and I'd put blush on my right cheek.

'Perhaps she has a new crush she's stalking?' Brian nudged Jesse suggestively.

'No, I wanted to avoid the crowds,' I said sarcastically.

Brian and Jesse guffawed. Brian cupped his ear. 'We have a late-breaking announcement. Sabiha Omerović, a sixteen-year-old schoolgirl from St Albans, Victoria, this morning woke at the crack of dawn and scurried to school to avoid the monstrous crowds at peak hour.'

I was starting to get that empty, sick feeling in my gut.

'Congestion peaked at 8.30 a.m., but thankfully no one was crushed to death. Keep tuned and we'll have more updates later.' Brian shifted his eyes from side to side as if he was reading a teleprompter. 'And now we go to Jesse James, our on-location correspondent who has a live interview with our fearful schoolgirl.' Brian turned to Jesse.

'When did you develop this fear of crowds?' Jesse thrust an imaginary microphone in my face.

'Piss off!' I pushed his hand away and ran to class.

During Drama I joined another group for improvisation and ignored Brian. At recess I hid in the library and read Sylvia Plath's *Bell Jar*. It wasn't until fourth period in History that we were together again. Instead of sitting in my usual spot in the back row with Jesse and Brian, I sat in the middle row. During class Gordana passed a note onto my lap.

What's up your arse?-B

I turned and stared at Brian. He stared back.

Nothing-S. I scrawled and passed the note back. Ten minutes later it returned.

What's with the mood swings?-B

What's your problem?-S I passed the note back.

You were a bitch to Jesse-B

I glanced over at Jesse. He was slumped in his seat. When class finished we met at the door. Lunch was subdued. Jesse avoided me and didn't join in the conversation.

'You two have English together now, don't you?' Brian said to me when the bell rang. 'I'm off to Science.' He headed down the corridor.

Jesse stood next to me like a lump of wood. 'Let's get going,' I said, my voice fake cheerful.

When it got hot I took off my jumper in class, Jesse's eyes were on my elbows. I followed his gaze to the bruises where one of the Twins held me.

'What happened?' he asked.

'I fell.' I put my jumper back on, turning to see if anyone else had noticed.

'Is that the reason you came to school early?' Jesse pushed.

I didn't respond, pretending I was engrossed in copying the teacher's notes. I felt his stare on me throughout class, but I ignored him. During sixth period a knot gathered in my stomach as I watched the clock hands move toward going home time. My big plan was to run home. I'd put all my heavy textbooks in my locker. I thought about hanging around after school, but I was more likely to bump into the Twins later in the evening.

Jesse and Brian waited for me at the school gates. 'Let me see,' Brian demanded as soon as I was in earshot.

'What?' I played dumb.

Brian grabbed my top and lifted. I slapped his hand away and wrenched my top down. 'Arsehole.' I looked nervously at the students walking past.

'Let me see,' Brian insisted.

'Fine.' I stomped behind the bushes. When I was satisfied we were hidden from everyone, I lifted my top.

Brian whistled between his teeth as he gently touched my skin. 'Those are beauties.'

'Who was it?' Jesse asked.

I pulled my top down and stood awkwardly between them, trying to figure out how to fob them off.

'Was it your Mum?' Jesse asked softly into the silence.

'As if,' I laughed.

'Who was it?' Jesse persisted.

'Some girls.' I waved my hand dismissively.

'That's why you came to school early?' Brian asked.

I nodded, on the verge of tears. Brian put his arm around me. 'I'm such a loser,' I said into his shoulder.

'My bully was Tommy Jones in Fifth Grade,' he said.

'Mine was Joe O'Shea in Year Seven,' Jesse said.

I laughed. 'We're all losers.' I found a tissue in my pocket.

'Stay away from them,' Brian said.

'No shit Shirl.' I screwed up the tissue in my hand.

'Who are they?' Jesse asked.

'Bitches who live in the next street from my house.' I blew my nose.

'You're stuffed,' Brian said.

'I know.' I chucked the tissue at a bin and missed.

'We'll walk you home tonight,' Jesse said.

'Really?' I asked Brian.

Brian nodded. 'We'll catch the bus back.'

I hugged him. 'Thank you,' I whispered into Brian's ear. I opened my eyes and gave Jesse a gummy smile. 'You're the best.' Jesse smiled back.

'Which way do we go?' Brian asked.

'Straight down Main Road West.' I pointed.

The train tracks divided Main Road into East and West. Most of the kids at my new school, including Brian and Jesse, lived on the east side of St Albans. Walking from school to the train tracks was easy. When we crossed over to the West side the nerves kicked in. We were now officially in the danger zone.

Brian put his arm around my waist. 'We're here with you.'

I tried smiling, but my face was frozen. Now that Brian and Jesse were my escorts I realised I'd been conned. What would they do if the Twins came after me? And even worse, what if they tried to do something and got attacked? I'd lose the only friends I had.

I stopped. 'You can turn back now.' As I spoke it seemed as if the sun disappeared and sinister shadows stretched across the footpath.

Brian put his hand on my shoulder. 'We don't mind.'

I clasped Brian's hand. 'You've gone so far out of your way.'

'What if they're waiting for you near your house?' Jesse asked.

My palms were sweaty. 'I don't want you caught up in this bullshit.'

Jesse searched my face. His cheeks reddened. 'I'm not scared of stupid girls.'

'I know you're not.' My voice was flat, revealing my doubt.

Brian smiled. 'We've been bullied by worse.' He turned me to face Main Road West.

I was unconvinced, but tried to hide it. He took my hand in his and walked with me. Jesse hung back. He was still upset. When we got to my corner I waved across the street. 'There's the bus stop.'

Brian nodded and surveyed my street. 'We'll walk you to your house.'

I let out a sigh of relief and squeezed his hand. When we were two houses away I stopped. 'You can go back now 'cause I don't want my Mum to know.'

Brian kissed me on the cheek. 'I'll see you at school.'

Jesse stood a few metres away.

'Thanks guys,' I said. Jesse turned and walked off. Brian smiled ruefully and followed him.

I watched Jesse's back and felt angry. Why did he have to be so sensitive? I couldn't say anything without him taking it the wrong way. I tried to chill, remembering he'd walked me home, completely out of his way, to protect me. That pissed me off more. He was such a pushover.

When they were halfway down my street, I scuttled up my driveway. Even though the street was deserted, it was as if the Twins were hiding behind a tree and laughing at me.

I was reading in my bedroom when the phone rang, Mum answered. A few minutes later she burst into my room. 'Suada just called!' Suada was Dina's Mum.

'You got a phone call.' I did a fake cheer.

Mum squinted at me. It was her version of a dirty look, but she just looked like the sun was in her eyes. 'She was driving past and saw you kissing a boy.' She was always driving through our street, dropping off or picking up Edin, her father.

'I wasn't kissing a boy,' I said. Suada and her husband were Born-Again-Muslims too. A year ago they'd found Dina's brother with marijuana in his room and kicked him out. I could just imagine how she was spinning this story.

'Were you with a boy in front of our house?'

'Yes,' I said. 'But—'

'You're too young to have a boyfriend.' Mum paced.

'He's not my boyfriend,' I raised my voice.

She stopped abruptly. 'Is he Muslim?'

'I can have a Muslim boyfriend?' Maybe I'd found the loophole in her reasoning? I almost saw the hamster turning on the wheel in her brain as she thought.

'No,' Mum said uncertainly. 'You have plenty of time for boys.' Mum swept my hair behind my ear. 'Who was this boy you were kissing?'

I jerked away. 'He was someone from school.' I threw my book on the bed. 'And we weren't kissing.'

Mum sneered with disbelief.

'You believe that short-sighted cow over me?'

'Don't call Suada a cow.'

'But you agree she's short-sighted?'

'I didn't say that.'

'You didn't dispute it, so I assume you agree.'

Mum had the hamster-on-the-wheel look again. 'I don't want you walking with any more boys.' She opened the door.

'I'm at a co-ed school,' I yelled as she closed the door.

I almost felt sorry for Mum. She didn't have it in her to match my comebacks. Sometimes I felt like I was torturing a helpless puppy. And other times, like today, I felt like a million bucks.

***

The next morning I was in the library at 8.00 a.m., typing a story, when Brian sat next to me. I'd left later than yesterday so I didn't freeze my tits off waiting for the library to open.

'You're early.' I pushed my things off the table to make room for him.

'So are you.'

'Where's Jesse?' I asked.

'He's at home.'

'Is he still angry at me?'

'No, he's busy,' he said.

'Doing what?' I demanded.

Brian shrugged. 'What are you up to?'

I didn't answer straight away. Jesse was such a sulk. I opened my mouth to whinge to Brian, but thought better of it. 'English homework,' I said instead. 'Let's go outside?'

While we were waiting for Jesse, Adnan arrived. 'You playing today?' he asked Brian.

'Yeah,' Brian said. 'Been watching the cup?'

As they talked about soccer my eyes glazed over. Who cared? One group of idiots fought to get the ball from another pack of idiots and, if they managed to score a goal, one pack of idiots cheered while another pack of idiots booed. Big deal.

Jesse walked up the street. He waved when he saw me looking at him. I didn't wave back. 'Did you have any problems this morning?' he asked.

I shook my head. There was grease on his jeans, but I didn't tell him.

'Do you want us to walk you home tonight?' he asked.

Adnan broke off his conversation with Brian and interrupted us. 'Why would they walk you?' he asked.

'She got attacked on the way home yesterday,' Brian said.

'So?' Adnan said as if it was my fault.

'Up yours.'

'She was hurt,' Brian said.

Adnan was angry. I didn't smile, but I wanted to. He caught me at my locker between class breaks. 'Why didn't you come to me?'

'What are you talking about?'

'When you were bashed.'

'Why?' I put my Maths textbook in my backpack.

'Next time, come to me for protection,' he hissed.

'Get real,' I said. 'You've never cared about protecting me.'

He gripped my arm hard. 'You embarrassed me today,' he muttered. 'I shouldn't have to to find out what happened from Brian.'

I wrenched my arm away. 'You embarrassed yourself jerk-off.' I pushed him away and walked off.

At lunchtime we went to the oval, but I adopted Jesse's trick and read Melina Marchetta's *Looking for Alibrandi*. Adnan tried to talk to me, tapping me on the leg to get my attention. I moved away. At the end of school, as I walked towards the front gates, three figures stood immobile.

'Do you want us to walk you home tonight?' Brian asked.

Adnan held my arm and squeezed. 'I'm visiting my grandfather.'

'I can walk by myself.' I was getting sick of being special-needs.

'I'm going that way,' Adnan said.

'You haven't seen Dido since the *zabava*,' I shot back. Dido and Aunt Zehra were going through another stand-off after the family reunion night.

Adnan put on a pained expression. 'We don't know how long he'll be around.'

'Puh—lease,' I muttered under my breath so only he could hear.

'We'll see you tomorrow.' Brian slapped Adnan's hand and kissed me on the cheek.

'See ya.' I waved. Jesse lifted his hand and waved clumsily as he left. What a dork. 'Quite a performance,' I said.

Adnan smiled. 'I have a gift.'

'The gift of being a bullshit artist.'

He laughed. That was the thing about Adnan: he was impervious to insults. Adnan gestured at Safeway. 'Let's go inside.'

'What for?' I followed him in through the electronic doors, grumpy that he thought I was his lackey.

'Research.' In the cereal aisle he took out a notebook and listed various items. After ten minutes or so, when I was about to scream with frustration, he closed his notebook.

'What was that about?'

'It's how I'm making my fortune,' he said mysteriously.

'You're going to be a homemaker.'

'I've got a much better plan,' he retorted.

'And?'

'Not telling.'

'Wanker,' I muttered under my breath. He smiled slyly.

We walked the rest of the way home in silence.

'Little one, make us coffee,' Dido barked as we entered the living room. He was playing chess with Edin, his right hand poised above the chessboard.

'Is that how you greet your only grandson?' Adnan smiled beside me.

Dido hugged him. 'Ado,' he caressed his head, his eyes were glassy as if he was about to cry. 'Did Zehra come?' He looked at the doorway for my aunt.

Adnan shook his head.

My grandfather hugged him. 'You're Dido's brave one.'

Disgusted at Adnan's performance, I went to the kitchen to make a sandwich. 'Can I have one?' he called out.

I took my plate and sat at the table. I waved at the bread and condiments on the kitchen counter. 'Help yourself.'

Adnan made a pitiful face. 'After I walked all this way to protect you. You should show me some respect.'

'You—I—' I was so pissed off I couldn't speak. His only motivation was his macho pride. I slapped my sandwich on the plate and passed it to him. 'Your Mum will go off at you for coming here.' Auntie Zehra's temper was legendary.

'Probably.'

'Aren't you scared?' I asked.

'I've got a plan.'

'And?'

'Watch and learn.' He leaned back and picked his teeth with a toothpick.

'Sabiha, coffee!' Dido shouted from the living room.

I opened my mouth to shout back that he could make it himself, but Adnan put his hand on my arm. 'I'll help,' he said.

I squinted. 'What are you up to?' He *never* helped around the house.

He did his usual inscrutable smirk. He carried the tray out to the old men. 'I'll pour.' He sat on the ottoman and poured coffee in the three *fildžani*. Dido raised his eyebrows in surprise, before he smiled. I left them to their mutual appreciation club.

I was in my bedroom writing about my day, well actually about signs that Brian liked me, when Adnan walked in. 'Were you raised in a tent?' He wasn't big on respecting other people's privacy. I put the diary in my desk drawer.

He sat on the bed. 'I'll teach you self-defence.'

I frowned. 'What for?'

'So you don't do your punching-bag imitation for every bully.'

I stuck my middle finger up.

'Come on. It'll help.' He tugged my arm.

Reluctantly I followed him into the backyard. 'This is stupid,' I moaned.

'The first thing to learn is to deal with movement.' He shadow-boxed at my head. I flinched. 'You need to stop closing your eyes.' He imitated me, screwing up his face.

'You look like a toothless hag.'

'Come on. Let's get serious.' He punched again.

I flinched.

He stopped and put his hands on his hips. 'What's the worst that can happen?'

I gave him a dirty look.

'Okay, one more time.'

He aimed for my face, giving me time to see him coming. I clenched my muscles, determined to stand my ground. As the fist approached my face, I squeezed my eyes shut and hunched like a turtle hiding in its shell.

He put his hand on my shoulder. 'I'm doing this for you.'

With my eyes on his face I didn't see his fist pull back. It wasn't until my guts pushed into my spine that I knew he'd punched me. I dropped to my knees, holding onto Adnan's arm as I heaved for breath.

Chapter 7

'Embrace the pain,' he urged, his eyes glittering with joy.

Bile rose in my throat and I gagged. Adnan pulled away and I fell on the ground. After a few minutes my breath came back, but my stomach throbbed. I sat up.

Adnan crouched beside me. 'That wasn't so bad.'

'Arsehole.' I aimed a punch at his stomach.

'Not bad.' He caught my fist in mid-air and pulled my thumb out of my fist. 'Try again.'

I lifted my foot and hit him in the stomach.

He fell on his arse with a grunt.

I scrambled to my feet and walked off.

'We've just started,' he called.

The fly screen burst open and Dido stood in the doorway. 'What's going on here?'

'Adnan punched me.'

'I'm teaching her how to fight,' Adnan said.

'Good,' Dido said. 'She will stop being a cry-baby.' He went back into the house.

Adnan grabbed the fly screen before it closed. 'Any time you want more fight lessons, let me know.' He closed the door in my face.

When I went back into the living room Adnan was watching TV. Dido was scowling, but didn't shout at him to turn if off. 'Turn off the TV,' I said. 'It's ruining Dido's concentration.'

'Is it okay if I have it on softly?' Adnan lowered the volume with the remote control. Dido grunted without looking up from the chessboard.

I sat on the floor next to Adnan. I was in a bad mood. Cheesy game-show music played. The camera panned to a cheering audience. 'George Georgiou. Come on down,' the voiceover proclaimed. A man ran down the aisle waving his arms. Another three people were called down. They jumped as if they were in a mosh-pit, smacking kisses on each other's faces and hugging like they were at a wedding. 'You are our first contestants on *The Price is Right*. And now your host, Larry Emdur,' the voiceover proclaimed, while the host made tacky small-talk with the contestants,

I leaned closer to Adnan. 'This is your big plan?' I laughed.

'Quiet,' Dido shouted.

Adnan grinned.

I shifted and 'accidentally' hit him with my elbow.

He nudged me back and shushed.

The camera focused onto a stereo and the contestants were asked to estimate the price. After they each locked in a price the host slid a card out of an envelope and read the correct price. The contestant who estimated the closest, without going above, had the chance to play for another, much more expensive prize and ultimately the opportunity to play for the showcase. At each stage of the game Adnan guessed the price of the prizes and was uncannily correct. By now Dido and Edin were watching too, cheering with glee when someone won.

Adnan handed Dido the remote when the show finished. 'That's the only TV show for ethnics,' he said in Bosnian. 'Every other show is whitewashed with Anglo-Australia. Look at *Home and Away, Neighbours, McLeod's Daughters*.'

'What about other game shows?' I asked.

'On *Temptation* you have to be a rocket scientist on stupid local trivia.'

'What about *Wheel of Fortune*? All you have to do is spin the wheel.'

Adnan was scornful. 'And then you have to guess the phrase.'

'The phrase is pretty obvious.'

'For someone born in an English-speaking country. All these shows are made for people born here. This,' he pointed to the TV where the credits on *The Price is Right* were rolling. 'This is the only show for us ethnics. It's the one thing we're good at. Prices and bargaining.'

What Adnan said made me feel odd, like I was seeing my country for the first time. I was in no man's land. To the Aussies I was Bosnian, to the Bosnians I was Aussie. In the inner-city I'd been Sammie Omerović, second-generation Aussie. Now I had all this Bosnian baggage to drag around and I didn't know how to carry it.

Edin left. Dido and Adnan sat across from each other on the sofa while I sat on the floor, pretending to watch TV.

'Does your mum know you're here?' Dido asked.

I glanced over my shoulder; Adnan was shaking his head.

'Will you tell her?'

'You know Mum,' Adnan said. Dido coughed his usual smoker's cough that sounded like he was about to lose a lung. 'You're sick.' Adnan held Dido's hand.

'I'm fine.' Dido cleared his throat and spat his phlegm into a tissue.

Adnan became thoughtful. 'If you were sick Mum would be here like a shot.'

Dido lay on the sofa, adjusting the cushion under his head. 'Can you hand me my blanket?' Adnan reached for the blanket and covered Dido from head to toe, tucking him in like a child.

'Where are his pills?' Adnan asked. I pointed to the pillbox on the TV cabinet. Dido opened one eye and watched as Adnan put his pills on the coffee table. Dido smiled and within a few breaths he was snoring.

Adnan smiled as he picked up the phone. 'Mum?' his voice quivered. 'Dido's not feeling well.'

Auntie Zehra arrived within ten minutes. She must have driven with squealing tyres and burnouts. She cried when she saw Dido lying on the sofa.

Adnan touched her arm. 'He had a bad turn.'

Dido opened his eyes and held out his hand. 'Zehra.'

She dropped to her knees beside the sofa. 'Babo, how are you?'

Dido kissed her hand. 'I'm glad I saw you again before I died.'

'He's not that sick,' I told her.

'He needs to sleep,' Adnan jumped in, glaring at me.

Dido patted her hand. 'Come and visit me tomorrow.'

Auntie Zehra was torn. Adnan helped her up. 'Come on, Mum.'

She nodded and kissed Dido on the cheek. I walked them to the door. 'Where's your mother?' she asked.

'She's at Safet's.' I'd hardly seen her the past week, which wouldn't have been that bad, except that I copped being Dido's servant.

'She should be at home taking care of the two of you,' Auntie said.

'She'll be home soon,' I replied, scowling.

She shook her head. 'I'll be back tomorrow.' She kissed me on the cheek.

***

On Saturday morning, my mood worsened as I remembered what was awaiting me.

'Sabiha, get up!' Mum burst into my room and flung open the curtains.

'I think I'm sick.' I crumpled into the foetal position and clutched my stomach.

'No way.' Mum ripped the doona cover off me.

'Ohhhh,' I groaned, hiding my head under the pillow.

'I'll have breakfast ready by the time you've showered,' Mum said as she walked out, leaving my bedroom door open.

I pushed the pillow off my head and looked at the empty doorway. Who was this woman and what had she done with my real mother? She'd never woken me up and made me breakfast before I went to school, but today she was Mrs Homemaker because it was my debut as a Born-Again-Muslim at *mejtef*.

It took me a while to get dressed because I had to dig out my daggy clothes—the ankle-length loose skirt I had at the back of the wardrobe.

I gasped as I walked into the kitchen. 'Strawberry pancakes!' They were my favourite: spread with strawberry jam, sprinkled with crushed walnuts and pecans, filled with strawberries, and then rolled into a burrito shape. I took a bite. So far the *mejtef* experience wasn't so bad.

'Sabiha, it's important you make a good impression,' Mum lectured while I ate. 'The *hodža* is making an exception for you.'

Mejtef was organised like school: children progressed through different levels with their age group. Despite not having been to *mejtef* I had been placed in my grade level, with the expectation that Dina would help me keep up.

I nodded absently, the tart taste of strawberries hitting my tongue and taking me to a happy place.

***

'Do you want me to come with you?' Mum asked me as she pulled up in the mosque car park.

'I'll be OK.' I reached for the doorhandle, puffing myself up with false bravado. She drove off and I turned to the mosque.

It was a square white building with the familiar dome roof and minaret that was traditionally used to broadcast the call to prayer. I'd only been to the mosque once before with Mum and everything had been a blur.

I entered the front glass doors into a hallway with shoe shelves against each wall, where prayer-goers left their shoes before entering the prayer room that was covered with a colourful red carpet. Muslims prayed on the ground so there were no pews or seats in the prayer room.

There was a kitchen where an informal café operated selling Turkish coffee, *pita* and *ćevapi*. I walked past rooms fitted with taps and sinks for the prayer-goers to take their ablutions before performing their prayers, and then I entered the classroom where *mejtef* was taking place.

I slid into the empty seat beside Dina. 'So how does this work?' I asked anxiously. I hoped it wouldn't be like school where they made the new students stand and talk about themselves while everyone stared as if they were a zoo animal.

'The *hodža* talks, we listen.' Dina continued scribbling in her notebook.

I fought the instinct to elbow her in the ribs. She was such a prissy bitch. Students milled around, chatting to each other. A few threw curious glances my way. For once Dina's self-involvement worked to my advantage and she didn't perform any introductions.

The *hodža* walked in wearing his traditional black robe. Everyone sat. 'We have a new student, Sabiha,' he said in Bosnian, nodding at me.

My fists clenched as I waited for him to call on me.

'Last week we were talking about the correct conduct for a Muslim man and woman and we're continuing this discussion. In the *Kuran* it states modesty is a priority for both men and women. Men are to cover their torsos and to be covered from waist to knees. Women are to be covered from their neck to wrist, and waist to ankle. When they pray women also cover their hair.'

'Great, we're being sent back to the dark ages,' I muttered.

'The general perception by non-Muslim society is that the requirement for modesty in Islam is a way of subjugating women. But we know that if women are covered, they are judged by their intellect and not purely on their physical appearance.'

I stared down at the notepad I'd brought and drew hearts while the *hodža* continued talking about what it meant to be a good Muslim. This was the first time I'd heard about both men and women having to practice modesty. People only talked about how Muslim women were treated unfairly by having to cover up, but nobody mentioned that men were supposed to be doing the same.

I recalled the way some men looked at me when I wore skimpy clothes. If I didn't wear revealing clothes, would they pay attention to me properly? Mum tried to convince me that you could be both modest *and* fashionable. I wasn't buying it? Why should I have to compromise myself for other people? Most of the time I dressed to feel good for myself, not for anyone else. And what was the big deal about modesty? Shouldn't women be respected, regardless of how they looked? I wished I had the guts to ask the *hodža* that question, instead I tuned out while the lecture continued.

After talking for fifteen minutes, the *hodža* taught us a new prayer. He recited a few words in Arabic and then the students repeated them. We had to enunciate the Arabic words properly. After saying the prayer in Arabic the *hodža* recited the translation in Bosnian.

'Your homework for next week is to learn this prayer and be able to recite it when I call on you.'

I stopped myself from swearing. I had enough real homework without this.

'Sabiha, see me before you leave,' the *hodža* said while students headed for the doors.

Shit, he'd heard my smartarse comment about the dark ages.

'This will also be your homework too for next week.' He handed me a sheet of paper with the heading Five Pillars of Islam. 'Because you haven't had the chance to learn the basics you have to work harder to catch up.'

'So I have to learn both these things?' I held up the other handout he gave us with the new prayer.

He nodded and handed me a book. 'And this is what we use for the junior *mejtef* classes. You should read it, too.'

'When am I supposed to do my school work?' I demanded. 'I mean, that's a lot of stuff to learn.' I stopped when I realised how harsh my voice sounded.

'Just learn the Five Pillars,' he said. 'It's more important you know the basics.'

'Thank you,' I said meekly.

'But you will have to start learning at the same pace as the other students,' he said.

I nodded without answering. What a crock. First I was forced to participate in this whole makeover experiment and now I was being persecuted by having to be Miss Islam overnight. I so had to find a way to get out of this.

***

On Monday morning Brian rode to school. 'Here you go.' He wheeled the bike over to me.

'What do you mean?'

'As much as Jesse and I would love to walk you home every night, it's not going to happen. *Voilà*'.' He waved at the bike and smiled at me. 'With this you'll be an independent woman again.'

'But I can't pay you.' I rubbed the handlebars in wonder. With this means of escape I would never be at the Twins' mercy again.

'It was hanging around Jesse's house.'

I snatched my hands off it. 'It's Jesse's bike?'

'I think it was his sister's.' He pointed at the V-shaped bike body. Jesse joined us. Brian grabbed Jesse into a bear hug. 'Where were you?'

Jesse punched him on the arm. 'We were supposed to swap riding the bike to school.'

Brian gave him a cheeky smile. 'I like the fast life.'

Jesse turned to me. 'Do you like it?' he asked with a shy smile.

'I love it.' I stopped short. Taking a present from Brian was okay, but being beholden to Jesse, I didn't know if I could do that. I wasn't even sure if he liked me. I mean, he was always avoiding me. It seemed like a weird game. My hands sweated as I tried to find the words to tell him I couldn't take it. He'd either spit the dummy or cry. 'I—, I don't—.' I glanced at Brian, pleading.

Brian took pity on me. 'She doesn't know if she can take it for free.'

'And I have no money to pay for it,' I added.

'How about a trade?' Jesse asked.

'Okay.' What would Jesse want from me?

'Bring in your CDs so I can load them onto my computer.'

'That can't be the trade for a bike.'

'That's your fee for borrowing it for a year.'

'Really?'

Jesse shrugged. 'It was rusting in the backyard since my sister bought a car.'

'Thanks.' Before he could react I kissed him on the cheek.

He blushed. 'It was nothing.' He put his hand through his hair. 'I'd better get going.'

'Where are you off to?' Brian asked.

'Gotta do something,' Jesse mumbled.

'He was fixing it before and after school yesterday,' Brian said.

I felt guilty: I'd made it obvious I wanted to be alone with Brian, so Jesse was avoiding spending time with us.

'I'm not looking forward to tonight,' Brian moaned as we walked to the bike-shed.

'What have you got on?' I bent and locked my new bike with the padlock Jesse had attached.

'Are you high?'

'No.' My hands were covered in grease.

'You really don't remember?'

I found an old hanky in my backpack and wiped my hands. 'Keep it up and I'll turn you into a grease-monkey.' I jumped toward him with my dirty hands outstretched.

He held his arms up in surrender. 'It's parent—teacher night.'

'Oh,' I groaned.

'How speaketh you of such matters as if they meaneth nothing?' He dropped dramatically to one knee, his hand to his forehead and pretend-swirled an invisible cape around himself. 'How now, why speaketh thee as if thy school affairs are not life and death?' I walked off and he ran after me. 'My parents will hear about my lack of "progress".' He made air quotations. 'And I'll be stuffed.'

'My Mum never comes.' I forced a smile at the sight of Brian's face. 'She's never on my back about homework.'

'You're lucky,' he said.

'What can I say?' I laughed. 'I'm blessed.'

We split up in front of the gym. My words replayed themselves in my head. *'I'm blessed. I'm blessed.'*It sounded like a slow-motion effect on television. I didn't feel lucky. I felt like no one cared.

Mum hadn't come to my parent—teacher interviews since Grade 6 when all my teachers praised me. Since then all she looked through my end of semester reports to see if I was in trouble. Her motto was: if you're not doing badly, why should care?

Whereas other overseas-born-parents went on about the sacrifices they made so their kids could finish school, Mum was so mellow about the whole thing, she wouldn't even notice if I didn't go to school.

All day everyone bitched and moaned about parent—teacher night. We were supposed to organise interview times in fifteen minute slots. Adnan and Brian skipped their usual soccer game, and since Dina and Gemma had congregated to watch them, we all had lunch on the oval instead.

'I only get them to meet my favourite teachers and ignore the rest,' Dina said at lunchtime. Her parents were typical: they expected her to do well, but didn't know enough about the school system to take a real interest.

'My Mum gets a copy of my timetable at the beginning of the semester and checks off that she's met with everyone,' Brian said. 'I think I'm failing Geography.'

'I think I'm failing Maths, History and Phys ed,' Gemma interrupted.

'How do you fail Phys ed?' I asked.

'I dunno,' Gemma said.

'What about you?' I asked Jesse.

'My sister's coming tonight,' Jesse said.

'What about your mum and dad?' Gemma asked.

'My Dad's dead and Mum isn't feeling well.'

Adnan shook his head dismissively.

Gemma caught him. 'You have nothing to worry about Einstein,' she said. Adnan had featured in the school newspaper as the high-achiever in his year level.

'Capitalism breeds pride in mediocrity,' Adnan spat out.

All eyes rested on me. There was only one thing to say. 'What's up your arse?' I burst out.

He stared at us like we were scum. 'You have every opportunity to be what you want, to achieve anything you want and all you do is brag about how to avoid hard work.' He stood. 'In Yugoslavia anyone would be ashamed to fail a class let alone repeat a year; yet here it's cool.'

Everyone bowed their heads at the force of his scorn. 'Who the fuck died and made you king?' I asked. He pivoted on his heel and left. 'Arsehole,' I called after him.

'It's not his fault,' Dina said.

'Just because you like him doesn't mean you have to make excuses for him,' I said.

'It can't be easy. His Mum and sister are the breadwinners in the family since his dad can't work,' Dina insisted heatedly. 'His whole family depends on him to achieve something with his life.'

'He's still an arsehole.' I sort of agreed with Dina that it must be difficult for him, being the great hope of his family. They all gave up their dreams and pinned their wasted ambition on Adnan. Still that was no excuse for him to bust everyone's balls. We finished lunch in silence.

Brian invited Adnan and me to his house after school until the interviews began. Jesse and I got my bike while Adnan and Brian waited at the front. 'Give me the key,' Jesse said.

I handed it to him and he unlocked the padlock which I'd stupidly locked near the bike-chain. 'Sorry,' I said. His hands were covered with grease.

'It's OK.' He pulled out tissues and wiped his hands.

'You've got to be the only guy in the world who carries tissues.'

'It's to give to the girls that I make cry.'

I laughed despite myself.

Brian and Adnan walked ahead, leaving Jesse and me to follow. 'Here.' Jesse took the bike from me and wheeled it beside him with one hand.

'I can do that.'

'But I can do it better.' Jesse smiled. 'I'm reading a great book at the moment.' He reached into his backpack with the other hand. The front cover was black with a line of red hearts to the title that read, *The Messenger*. 'It's an amazing book. Everyone's raving about it. I've read other books by Markus Zusak, but this is the best.'

I turned it over and read the blurb about a guy whose normal life is turned upside down when he receives mysterious missions. 'It sounds great.' I handed it back to him. 'I'll have to chase it up at the library.'

'Keep it,' Jesse said. 'I've already read it.'

'Thanks.' I put it in my backpack.

Some boys from our Phys ed class walked past. 'Hey Jesse, you want to play dodgeball?' They all laughed.

Jesse blushed. I avoided looking at him. We walked along in awkward silence. 'Why don't you tell them off?' I asked, angry at him, and angry at them.

'Why?' Jesse said. 'So they can have a go at me again? Anyway, they'll get their own.'

'When you kill them?' I remembered his hit list.

'I've already killed them,' Jesse said with a sly smile.

Shit, why did I always get involved with the crazies?

'Here, look—' He reached into his backpack again and handed me a magazine, *Voiceworks*.

'I don't get it,' I said.

He took it back from me and turned to the title page. I read the item above his index finger. '*Massacre* by Jesse James.' I flipped to page twenty-two and read the first line. 'You wrote a short story?'

Jesse nodded shyly. 'Yeah, and I found this magazine that only publishes writers under twenty-five.'

I stopped walking and read while Jesse hopped on the bike and wheeled round and round.

The short story was a string of vignettes, scenes from the perspective of a high school student. In the first vignette he stood in a pool of blood with dead students around him, then the story shifted through different points of view and moments in time to show how he came to that moment. It was a quick read. There was a lump in my throat when I got to the end. 'Wow,' I said. 'It's amazing.'

'Thanks.' Jesse put the magazine back in his bag.

'Why didn't you tell anyone?' I asked.

He shrugged, looking away.

'If people knew about this they'd leave you alone. You're so talented.'

He smiled.

'Have you had other things published?'

Jesse nodded.

'Where?' I hit him in the arm. 'I can't believe you didn't tell me.'

'I've entered a few short story competitions in the teenage category,' Jesse said. 'The council runs an annual competition and I won last year. There's also the library competition.'

'How many have you won?'

'I got first and second prize in two competitions.'

'I didn't know you were a writer,' I exclaimed. I thought I knew Jesse. I'd written him off as a loser, but all this time he was doing these amazing things. 'Can I read your other stories?'

Jesse nodded.

'Cool,' I said. We walked on. 'I write a bit too. I've only submitted them to Miss Partridge, though!' I laughed quickly. 'But I've sometimes thought about doing more.'

'You can,' Jesse said. 'My sister got me a membership from Writers' Victoria. They send out a newsletter every month with a listing of short story competitions and places to submit. You can read my back issues.'

'Thanks,' I said. He was being so nice. Shamefully, I remembered every nasty thought I'd had about him.

'If you want,' Jesse cleared his throat. 'I can read your stories and tell you what I think.'

'Okay,' I said. 'Really?'

'And maybe you can read my stories before I submit them too. We can be critique partners.'

'You want *my* feedback?' I asked. 'But you're a much better writer. You've been published and everything.'

'My sister used to proofread for me, but now she's busy with uni.'

'I'd love to!' I said. This day that had begun so crappy, was becoming awesome.

'Come on!' Brian yelled back to us.

'Which is your house?' I asked Jesse.

He nodded at the houses on the left.

'Jesse!' A young woman called from in front of the house across the street.

Jesse handed me the bike. 'I'll bring that stuff we talked about to school.' He hesitated.

The girl saw my bike. She had Jesse's blue eyes and curly, blonde hair, but she was tall and lithe while Jesse was not much taller than me.

'You must be Sabiha,' she said as she approached. I nodded. 'I'm Sarah, Jesse's sister.' She rested her arm on Jesse's shoulder. 'He's told us about you.'

Jesse's cheeks reddened. 'Let's go, Sarah.' He steered her toward the house. 'We have to leave soon.'

'Would you like to come in?' She turned back to me.

Just then I heard my name and saw Brian and Adnan, waiting for me at the end of the street.

'She has to go,' Jesse said.

'Another time.' Sarah made it sound like a date.

'See you tomorrow, Jesse,' I said.

I ran to catch up to Brian and Adnan, wondering what Jesse told his sister about me, and why. Brian unlocked the door. Adnan and I automatically bent to remove our shoes. Brian grabbed Adnan's elbow and pulled him up. 'Keep them on.'

It felt weird wearing shoes in the house.

'Want a drink?' Brian asked. We sat on the stools at the kitchen counter. 'I'm having a sandwich.' He got a bottle of Coke from the fridge and poured us a glass, then pulled out a loaf of bread from the pantry. 'Any takers?'

We nodded. I cut thick slabs of tasty cheese and put it on my buttered bread.

'There's tuna and tomato, too,' Brian said.

'I want to taste the cheese.' I bit into the sandwich. It tasted like heaven. Mum only bought cheap cheese that looked like cream cheese smeared on a plastic wrapper.

'How come you're circumcised?' Adnan asked Brian.

I nearly choked on my sandwich.

Chapter 8

'How the hell would you know that?' I demanded when I got my breath back.

'I saw his cock at the urinal,' Adnan said.

'Well, what sort of a question is that?' I returned my sandwich to the plate.

'It's a guy question.' Adnan was irritated now.

'Is it?' I asked Brian.

'Yes,' he said. 'I'm circumcised because I'm Catholic.'

Adnan frowned. 'But Catholics don't circumcise.'

'The Irish Catholics I know do. What about you?'

'All Muslims circumcise.' Adnan took a sip of Coke. 'Is it popular in Australia?'

'All my brothers and Dad are,' Brian said. He topped up our glasses.

'What's it with you and circumcision?' I asked. There was only so much talking about dicks that I wanted to do.

He gestured in frustration. 'Back in Yugo-Land only Bosnian-Muslims circumcised their boys and we were treated as backward by the Serbs, Croats and the Commies.'

I pushed my sandwich away. 'I can't eat anymore.'

'It's much more popular in America than in Australia,' Brian said.

'Bullshit!' Adnan exclaimed.

'Who cares?' I shouted, desperate to change the topic. This was the one time in my life I wished I knew something about soccer or footy or whatever boys talked about.

'You should,' Adnan said. 'I can't believe Auntie Bahra has neglected your sex education. I'll show you. Where's your computer?' he asked Brian.

'Don't have one,' Brian said.

'Shit.'

'My brother has a magazine,' Brian offered.

'Go get it.'

Brian came back and flung the magazine on the counter in front of Adnan. The pages flopped open, showing a man and woman in a flagrant sexual position. I turned away, my cheeks burning.

Adnan flipped the pages. 'Look here.' He thrust the magazine at me.

'I don't want to.'

'You need to see what an uncircumcised cock looks like.'

I couldn't resist. The man wore jeans and a shirt. The shirt was unbuttoned all the way showing his hairy, muscled chest; and his cock hung out of his unbuttoned jeans. The uncircumcised cock looked like it was covered in a sausage skin and the tip became untied.

'Here's the circumcised one.' Adnan pointed.

In front of a guy dressed as a mechanic was a woman on her knees, her hand holding a helmet-headed cock as she aimed it for her mouth.

'I don't get it.' I peered at the page. 'How does that...' I pointed at the uncircumcised cock. 'Become that?'

'You pull the foreskin taut over the head.' Adnan held his hands out over an imaginary cock. 'And then snip.' He made a scissors gesture with his fingers. 'The skin retracts and it's tied under the head.' He did a tying motion around his imaginary cock. 'And there you are, all done.'

'So it looks different,' I said. 'What's the big deal?'

He clutched his head like he was in pain. 'Didn't your mum teach you anything?'

'You should write a book.' I rolled my eyes.

He paused. 'That's not a bad idea.' That was the trouble with sarcasm. People could put their own spin on it. 'The problem with this,' Adnan tapped the uncircumcised cock. 'Is that the foreskin needs to be lifted and washed inside to keep it clean. When the guy has sex he has to roll back the foreskin to reveal the glands?'

I shrugged. 'I still don't get it.'

'Try having sex with this.' He flipped between the pages. 'And then try with this and you'll see which is the superior product.'

I arched my eyebrow. 'You seem to be speaking from personal experience.'

He stuck his middle finger in the air.

'How come Muslims get circumcised?' Brian asked.

'It's part of our religion,' Adnan said. 'One of the pillars of Islam.'

'No it's not,' I snapped. 'The five pillars are: the profession of faith in *Allah*, the five daily prayers, paying of alms, fasting during *Ramadan* and the pilgrimage to *Mecca*, which is compulsory once in a lifetime for those that can do it.' I recited them effortlessly.

My plan had been to forget the *hodža's* homework from *mejtef*, but then Dina had told me I'd be expected to recite the Five Pillars in front of class. There was nothing like the fear of public humiliation to provide incentive.

'Do you do all those things?' Brian asked.

'No way,' Adnan said emphatically.

'We never used to, but now Mum is trying to catch up for the years when she didn't do anything.' Her current gripe was about not eating ham because she'd found out I ate a Hawaiian pizza at school, when for years ham and bacon was a regular shopping list item. 'The reason we circumcise is for the same reason that we don't eat pork—'

'Because it's in the *Kur'an*,' Adnan interrupted.

'No, it's not,' I snapped again. 'It's in the *Hadith* which means it's a tradition that was practised by Muhamed and then became a tradition for all Muslims.'

'Who actually is Muhamed?' Brian asked.

'Muhamed is the last prophet.' It was sort of fun showing off my new knowledge. 'First there was Moses, then Jesus, then the prophet Muhamed who received messages from God that were collected into the *Kuran*.' I'd been skimming pages from the junior *mejtef* book.

Adnan waved his hand. 'I'm a communist and don't believe in all that superstitious crap. Anyway, that's not the real reason we circumcise.'

'Really, Brainiac,' I taunted.

'Yes, really. Circumcision began because people living in the desert found it necessary to maintain hygiene. Just imagine sand, heat and foreskin.' He shuddered.

'So now you're the fountain of knowledge, are you?' I demanded, shoving my face in his.

'At least I'm not brainwashed by religion.' Adnan and I glared at each other.

'Did I tell you about my party?' Brian interrupted.

'Party?' I demanded.

'My folks are visiting my Mum's family in the country in a few weeks and my brother and I are throwing a party.'

'Cool.'

'I want a costume party, but my brother reckons people won't go for it. I'm thinking comic book characters.'

'That's a great idea.' I glanced at Adnan, but he was flicking through the magazine again.

'Hey, Sabiha, let me get that poster for you.' Brian had an extra Justin Timberlake poster.

I followed Brian down the hall. His bedroom was so neat. Just as well he'd never see my bedroom and realise what a slob I was.

'Hey Adnan, come here!' he called.

'In a minute!' Adnan was still engrossed in the men's magazine.

Brian streamed music from his mobile and sat on the bed, plumping the pillow under his head. 'Tonight is going to be hard.' He rubbed his hands over his face.

'You're doing okay at school.'

He smiled at me sadly. 'That's the problem. I'm doing okay.' I sat on the bed next to him. 'My Dad only allowed me to stay at school as long as I got good marks.'

'He doesn't want you to go to school?' I was shocked.

'He's a brickie,' Brian said. 'My two older brothers are a plumber and an electrician. They all expect me to be a tradie like them and start an apprenticeship now.'

I put my hand on his. 'What do you want?'

Brian shrugged. 'Dunno. What about your mum?' He turned to look at me and I felt his breath on my face.

'Mum doesn't care what I do. She doesn't really have expectations I have to live up to.'

'It sounds like you've got it as bad as I do,' he said.

'Mmm,' I murmured.

There were flecks of yellow in his eyes. My lips tingled with the expectation of a kiss. Our heads nudged closer.

'Shit, I'm late!' Adnan burst into the bedroom.

Brian and I sprang apart as if we'd caught fire. Adnan's eyes narrowed. He glanced at his watch. We clambered to our feet and followed him out.

'See you at school,' he called. The slam of the front door reverberated.

'I'll help you with the dishes.' I picked up the discarded plate from the counter and took it to the sink.

'We've got a dishwasher.' He opened the door and put the plates in as I handed them to him, our fingers touching.

The awkwardness eased and we were once again two mates hanging out together. We both stiffened when we heard the sound of car doors closing. 'My folks are home,' Brian said.

'Shit, I should leave.' I squeaked with panic.

'Relax.' Brian squeezed my arm.

The back door opened. Brian was the spitting image of his mum: he had her colouring and delicate facial features. Brian's father was a big man, almost as tall as he was wide. His blue singlet stretched across his basketball tummy. His arms were lobster-coloured from being outdoors all day. Brian introduced me, his hand on my back. His mum said hello, while his father stared at me in silence.

'I'd better get going,' I said.

I always felt uncomfortable around friends' parents. I was used to calling people by their first name, and not acting as if adults were superior. Some parents hated that. At least Kathleen's parents did. Kathleen pulled me aside and asked me not to call them by their first name, but rather Mr and Mrs Gianni. The whole time we'd been friends I'd avoided addressing them.

Brian's mum turned around. 'We can give you a lift to the school. When are your interviews?'

'At six-thirty, but it's okay. I've got my bike here.' I waved towards the front of the house.

'It's too late for a young girl to be riding at this time of night. Frank.' Brian's mum turned to his father.

'Brian, put the bike in the car,' his dad said.

When they'd gone, Brian looked at me quizzically.

'I don't want your parents to think I'm a loser because my mum isn't attending parent—teacher interviews.'

'They wouldn't think that. Seriously. My dad thinks I'm a loser for going to school, remember,' he whispered.

Brian's father drove to school like a programmed android. Eventually his mother tried to fill the silence, but petered out after two sentences about the weather.

At school Brian took my bike out of the station wagon. 'See you Tuesday.'

'Aren't you coming to school on Monday?'

'I swear, Sabiha.' Brian was exasperated. 'Monday is a public holiday.'

'Oh…' I remembered how I'd been surprised at Mr Kumar's deadline for our Science assignment on Tuesday, but since I hadn't planned on completing it, I hadn't paid much attention. I sat on my bike.

'Aren't you coming inside?' Brian's mum asked.

'My folks will meet me here.' I nodded vaguely at the car park. I was about to push off when I heard my name. I turned and saw Auntie Zehra, with Merisa and Adnan.

'Where are you going?' Auntie Zehra asked.

'Home.'

'Isn't your mum coming?' she demanded.

I shook my head.

'Does she know where you are?'

I shook my head again.

Auntie Zehra clucked in annoyance. She grabbed my arm and I clambered off the bike. 'Merisa, you go with Sabiha to meet her teachers.'

'It's okay.' I tried to stop, but she kept tugging me along as I waved goodbye to Brian and his parents.

'If your mother won't take an interest in your schooling then I'll have to.' Auntie Zehra squinted at my bike and then at the dark around. 'You were going to ride in the dark?'

I nodded.

'You don't have any reflectors on it.' She pointed at the bike and shook her head.

'It's only supposed to get me from school to home and back,' I muttered.

'Adnan, fix her bike tomorrow.'

I started to protest, but Adnan glared at me. At the library they waited while I locked my bike to a pole. 'But I didn't make any appointments,' I complained as we walked in.

'Merisa, you explain it to them,' Auntie Zehra said briskly, then she and Adnan disappeared into the crowd.

Merisa hung her handbag across her shoulder so it criss-crossed her body. She took out a notebook and pen. Why did she have to be so bloody organised? It took a while to see all my teachers because we had to wait until they finished with their official appointments. Auntie Zehra and Adnan joined us at the end.

Auntie looked smug and I knew that Adnan had received glowing reports, the turd. It made it even worse when all my teachers had said something along the lines of 'Sabiha has potential, but doesn't apply herself,' which translated as: 'She might be smart, but we don't know.' I expected Auntie to rip into me.

She shook her head in disappointment. 'No wonder you're not doing well.' She rubbed my back. 'Auntie Zehra will take care of you.'

This did not sound good. I untied my bike. 'See you later.'

Auntie Zehra grabbed my arm again. 'We're taking you home.' She hitched her handbag higher as we walked arm in arm. 'Your mum and I are due for a little chat.'

Wonderful. Another family night of torture.

When Auntie Zehra walked into the house she and Mum squared off like two roosters in a cockfight. Auntie Zehra glanced at Dido. 'You have more colour in your cheeks.'

'You know how it is at my age.' Dido put on his pitiful old man routine. 'Every day is a gift from God.'

Auntie Zehra nodded and sat. Mum watched her warily. Merisa, Adnan and I shuffled into the kitchen and I stealthily opened the back door. I knew the signs and this would be a situation when you needed a quick exit. Adnan nodded in approval and we huddled next to the back door, eavesdropping on the conversation in the living room.

'I was at parent—teacher interviews at Adnan's school,' Auntie Zehra said. 'I didn't see you there.'

'I don't need to go. Sabiha does well at school.'

'Merisa!' Auntie Zehra yelled. 'Bring me your notebook.' Merisa took the notebook in, then returned to the kitchen. Auntie Zehra read out my teacher's reports.

It sounded much worse now. My Science teacher hated me because he caught me reading in class. My Literature teacher said I had the ability to deconstruct texts, but I showed apathy. At my old school I'd breezed through Literature with As, but I didn't like my new teacher and found it hard to focus in class.

The only positive report was English where the teacher said I showed promise with my writing, but I needed to address tasks in a disciplined manner. I always picked the creative option and wrote a short story, but we only do that three out of six assignments and I'd used up my quota.

'It's a new school. She needs time to settle,' Mum said.

'Perhaps if you spent more time being a mother, and less time with your boyfriend, your daughter would be doing better at school.'

'Zehra,' Dido said, but it was too late.

I agreed with her, but when she said it I wanted to rip her head off. Defences sprang to my lips. 'She does the best she can.' People were always talking about Mum's parenting. As if being bipolar made her mentally deficient.

I headed for the living room, but Adnan and Merisa dragged me out the back door and into the backyard. 'I have to help her.' I tried to pull away from them. After the night at the *zabava* I'd promised myself I wouldn't stand by again while my aunt attacked Mum.

'Dido will help her,' Adnan said.

'The only thing he does is put people down.'

'They want to help, not hurt her,' Merisa said.

I was unconvinced. All anyone wanted to do was dump on Mum. 'I need to hear.' I crept closer to the door.

They were talking normally and it looked like the crisis passed. Dido and Auntie Zehra were telling Mum that she had to take me in hand and discipline me. I winced. It wasn't looking good for me, but at least Mum was OK.

Adnan and Merisa went into the living room while I made myself a sandwich. I didn't get to eat my sandwich at Brian's after Adnan's dick conversation. I ate quickly and walked through the living room.

Mum wasn't letting visitors interfere with her Friday night routine. 'If I'd known you were coming I wouldn't have made plans to go to Safet's.'

'Going to do your homework?' Adnan shit-stirred as I walked down the hall.

'Where's my lamp?' I called from my room

Mum was putting on her shoes in the hall. 'I gave it to Nura.'

I didn't know Nura, but I knew that she'd arrived in Australia a few months ago. Over the past few months Mum had given our possessions to anyone who expressed an interest. 'But it's my lamp,' I whinged. This wasn't the first time she'd pillaged my bedroom.

"*Allah* will provide.' She picked up her handbag and left the house.

I hid my favourite clothes and make-up and was heading back to the living room when I heard Auntie Zehra.

'Babo, you have to find out Safet's intentions.'

'He's looking for a wife.' Dido's voice was gruff. 'It's normal, he lost his wife and children in the war.'

'I have no doubt about that, but have you thought about why he's settled on Bahra?'

'She can still be a good wife to him. She can cook, she can clean.' Dido was nodding to himself as he spoke.

'Yes, she can, but can she have another child? She's barely been a mother to Sabiha and it's a miracle she turned out so well. Bahra can't deal with having a baby.'

Dido didn't say anything.

'We're her family,' Auntie Zehra said. 'If we don't look out for her no one else will.' She waited.

I heard the clinking of china, but still Dido didn't say anything.

'If you don't talk to him then I will.'

'All right, I'll talk to him!' Dido shouted.

'Ask him about how will he support her,' she urged. 'He's supposed to be a taxi driver yet he barely does a shift a week.'

'He has a war injury,' Dido protested.

'Injury? He's supposed to have a sore back yet I saw him at Cash and Carry in Laverton with a car part that weighed more than he does.'

'He was a Professor in Yugoslavia.' Dido talked about Safet like he was a messiah and, according to Bosnian community, he was. Anyone who was a doctor or a professor was like a celebrity and Dido would get a lot of cred if one of his daughters married a professor.

'And now he's too good to get a job that will dirty his hands,' Auntie Zehra sniffed. 'Why should he when his sister Safeta works to support him? He's latched onto Bahra because she owns her house and gets a pension. If he marries her he won't ever have to work again.'

'Zehra, stop it.' Dido sounded tired. 'He treats Bahra well.'

Auntie Zehra was silent. 'He doesn't look like a man who's capable of taking care of anyone, but himself,' she said in a rush. She couldn't help herself.

'If she's with him she won't be screwing around,' Dido exploded.

I wanted to yell at him.

'Bahra deserves better than being a meal ticket,' Auntie Zehra said.

'Do you see anyone else lining up to be with her?' Dido demanded. 'I know you're right, Zehra, but if she marries him she'll be with a Muslim. She would have stability and respect.'

I went to my bedroom. I hated what Dido said and I hated him for saying it, but I wanted that thing so badly I could almost taste it. Respect. If Mum married Safet, people would stop treating her like she was a joke. We'd finally be normal and Bosnians would no longer regard us as an exotic soap opera. Maybe with Safet our luck could change. I made a vow: I would stop being a bitch to Safet. If he wanted to be with Mum, then I wouldn't stand in his way.

I needed to change my headspace. I grabbed my journal and began writing an article for the local newspaper competition—it had to be on a community issue, so I plundered my *mejtef* experience and scribbled about what the mosque meant to the Bosnian community. The prize was publication.

Auntie Zehra called me. She, Merisa and Adnan were putting on their shoes. Auntie kissed me on the cheek. 'Adnan will come tomorrow to fix your bike.'

'I'm going to *mejtef* in the morning.' Why couldn't I have a parent who was a communist?

'I'll come in the afternoon,' Adnan said. 'You can make me lunch as a reward.' He waggled his eyebrows.

'Help yourself,' I muttered.

I went to the kitchen for a glass of water and saw Mum's pill-box on top of the fridge. Her medication was in a weekly pill box because she had to take her tablets throughout the day. I reached for it. The Friday night compartment was full. Shit. No. It was happening again.

Chapter 9

I ran for the phone and flipped through our address book looking for Safet's number. 'You forgot your meds,' I blurted when Safet put Mum on.

'I've got the Lithium with me,' Mum said blankly. 'I'll be fine with them and I'll take the others when I come home.'

She hung up and I felt like I'd missed an oncoming train. These white tablets were the mortar that held Mum's sanity together. If she stopped taking them it was all over.

'What's the matter?' Dido asked.

'I thought Mum didn't take her pills.'

'Did she?'

'Yes,' I said.

'She's an adult, she can take care of herself.' He butted out his cigarette.

I returned the pill-box back on top of the fridge. It was easy for him to be relaxed. He didn't know what happened when she got sick. The way she broke into a thousand pieces and it took months for her to recover into something resembling the person she was. But thankfully I didn't have to worry about that now because she was still taking her medication.

When I came home from *mejtef* the next day Adnan was in the backyard. My bike was upside down and he was attaching reflectors. 'Where is everyone?' I asked.

'I haven't seen your Mum,' Adnan replied. She mustn't have come home from Safet's yet. 'And Dido was meeting someone for coffee in St Albans.'

Adnan's phone was blasting a Bosnian rock song I'd never heard before. 'Who's singing this?' I asked.

'Bijelo Dugme.'

'White Button,' I laughed. 'That's a funny name for a group.'

'It's no funnier than *Duboko Ljubičasto, Željezna Djevica, Kotrljajuće Kamenje.'*

Deep Purple, Iron Maiden, Rolling Stones.

'OK. Point taken.'

The song was a mixture of a folk song, a rock ballad and a classical symphony. I liked it, but could only understand one word in ten.

'What's it called?' I asked.

'Pediculis Pubis,' Adnan answered, tipping the bike upright.

'What does that mean?'

'You have to understand the context.'

'You don't know how to translate it to English.'

Adnan laughed.

'What?' I shouted. I was sick of being the butt of his private jokes.

'All done.' Adnan kicked the stand. 'I'll translate the song...if you make me a sandwich for lunch.'

'Fine.' I slammed the screen door behind me. He always seemed to get his way. Adnan opened the door and walked past me. He returned to the backyard with a pen and paper. While I prepared us roast beef sandwiches I heard the song rewinding and fast forwarding.

'It's ready,' I shouted, and sat to eat.

He came in and slid the notepad toward me.

I pointed at the paper. 'These aren't even Bosnian words.'

'It's Sarajevo jail slang. Inmates learnt to speak really fast in a simple code,' he pronounced proudly.

'They're singing about crabs?'

Adnan laughed.

'It's about a sexually transmitted disease,' I screeched.

Adnan laughed louder. 'Come on, it's still a great song.'

'To you maybe,' I said.

'I'll send you the playlist to listen to.' He passed me his empty plate. 'That was a beautiful sandwich, Sabiha.'

'Thank you.' Why did I fall into the trap of serving him?

He patted his belly. 'I'm still peckish.'

'Do you want another one?' He had me over a barrel, what with the bike and then explaining the song. If only he didn't turn everything into a bargaining match.

'Thanks.' He smiled, his big blue eyes twinkling. He ate the second sandwich in four bites. 'That was absolutely yummy. You know what I want to eat now.' He paused, looking at the ceiling. 'I'd love a caramel dipped in dark chocolate.

I frowned. That sounded so familiar.

'It would make my tummy tingly,' Adnan continued.

I gasped. 'You bastard!' It sounded familiar because I wrote in my diary that Brian's eyes were like caramels dipped in dark chocolate, and how being around him made my tummy tingly. 'You read my diary.'

'Of course not.' He smiled smugly.

I hit him. I got in a few slaps across his head and shoulders before he grabbed my hands. 'Let go you prick!' I shouted. 'I'll kill you!' I struggled, managing to slide my hands out of his grip and belt him across the head.

Mum chose this moment to arrive home.

'What's going on?' Mum pulled me away from Adnan.

'That prick read my diary.'

'Did you do that Adnan?' Mum asked.

'No.' Adnan put on a hurt face. 'I'd never do that.'

'He's lying.' I reached past Mum to hit him.

'Sabiha, you can't attack a guest in our house.' Mum grabbed hold of my shoulders.

'How can you believe him over me?'

'I'd better get going.' Adnan stood.

'Thank Adnan.' Mum looked at me expectantly.

'I'm not thanking him.'

'Sabiha,' Mum gasped.

'It's okay,' Adnan said, as he closed the front door.

'Sabiha, I'm disappointed in you. You should behave better than this.'

'He should know better than to go through someone's personal belongings.'

'Stop lying,' Mum said wearily.

I calmed down as her words cut through me. 'When have I lied?'

'You lied about kissing a boy in front of our house.'

'How many times do I have to say it, he kissed me on the cheek.'

'Suada saw you,' Mum said. 'People are talking.'

'So what?' I said.

'They shouldn't be talking about us,' Mum said. 'I'm doing everything right, but all they remember is what we do wrong.'

'Who cares?'

'I do. Sabiha, be good for me,' Mum urged.

'I am.' I was on the verge of tears. 'I'm doing everything you want—'

'That's not true,' Mum cut me off. 'Safet says—'

'This is all about him isn't it?' I demanded. 'All you care about is impressing him.'

'That's not all I care about—'

'Yes it is. Since you met him you act as if I don't exist.'

'Please, Sabiha,' Mum sighed. The phone rang. 'Don't exaggerate,' she said over her shoulder as she went to answer it.

I waited for a moment, but she settled on the sofa, like I wasn't there. I went to my bedroom and slammed the door. I served Dido like his own personal waitress, I played the good daughter whenever we were in company, I even went to *mejtef* and gave up my Saturday morning, *and* I worried about my mother's wellbeing. And what did I get in return?

The second drawer of my desk was open. Adnan hadn't returned my diary to its right place. At least he hadn't found Mum's old love letters from Darko that I had hidden under my bed. But I would have to find a new hiding place. I cringed as I re-read my entries. I'd written about Brian on nearly every page. I crumpled onto the bed in embarrassment. Adnan would never let me live this down. Grabbing a pen I began a new entry, all about Mum. I'd filled six pages when there was a knock on the door.

'Sabiha?' Mum opened the door and stuck her head in. 'Can you please help serve our guests?'

'Are you for real?' Did she think I forgot about our fight in an hour?

'Please,' Mum pleaded. 'I need your help.'

I wanted to tell her to get stuffed, but her look of desperation got to me. 'All right,' I said. 'But you owe me.'

She walked ahead of me to the living room. 'This is my daughter Sabiha.' She made the introductions in Bosnian. Safet was on the sofa and Dido on the armchair. 'This is Arnesa and her husband Nermin, and Arnesa's mother Enisa.'

'*Merhaba*,' I said.

'Sabiha, do you remember me?' Arnesa pulled me down for a smacking kiss on the cheeks, her moustache brushing my face. 'I used to care for you when you were little.' She put her hand at waist height.

I telegraphed an SOS with my eyes to Mum.

'Arnesa used to live in our street before we moved to Thornbury,' Mum explained.

'You used to love to eat my *hurmašice.*' Arnesa squeezed my hands. 'Do you remember?' She kissed my hands as if I was a baby again.

I stared at her like a deer in headlights. There was no graceful way to get out of this one and I should know, I'd been caught so many times. They always begged me to remember them. But I had no memory of them. Once a woman asked me if I remembered her rocking me to sleep when I was six months old. I'd learnt to look at them with a faint smile and wait until they got involved in the conversation and forget about me.

'Ona je isti otac,' Nermin said.

My ears pricked. Arnesa's husband had just said that I looked exactly like my father. Did that mean he knew him?

'Yes, she does.' Mum put her hand on my shoulder and pulled me to her side. 'Arnesa and Nermin were our neighbours when I was married to your father,' Mum explained.

'Where is Esad?' Nermin asked.

'He lives in Hobart,' Mum answered.

My father had re-married soon after divorcing my mother. I knew he had more kids. I guess they were my siblings, but since I'd never met them and wasn't likely to, I never thought about it much.

I used to pester Mum with questions about my Dad or pore over the photo album containing the few photos of their wedding and marriage. But whenever I probed Mum she took on that wounded look and changed the subject. In the end I'd stopped asking, figuring that if he didn't want me in his life, then I didn't want anything to do with him either.

'Come here Sabiha.' Mum tugged me to the kitchen. 'Prepare the *fildžani,*' she ordered.

I reached for the demitasse coffee cups in the glass cabinet, as she got the *džezva*, the Bosnian coffee pot, and spooned coffee into it. 'I don't want to go to *mejtef* any more,' I told her as I helped.

'Tough.' Mum placed the saucepan of boiled milk on the stove to warm.

I caught sight of the thick cream floating on top and turned away. 'But you said that you owed me.'

'No.' Mum put the kettle to boil. 'You said I owed you.' Mum counted the *fildžani*. 'Okay, you know what to do now. When the water boils pour it into the *džezva*, place the *džezva* on the stove until the coffee starts frothing and then add three teaspoons of sugar. Then bring the coffee out,' Mum instructed.

'I'm not your maid,' I said defiantly.

Mum stepped closer and grabbed my arm. 'You are my daughter and you will do what I tell you while you're under my roof,' she whispered. 'I'll leave you to it.' She let go of my arm and left.

I heard her crowing to the guests that I would serve coffee and my hurt flickered into anger. The only reason she needed my help was to show off. She didn't care about me or what I wanted.

I didn't understand how we'd come to this. Mum and I used to talk to each other like girlfriends. Yet now she was turning into a dictator. The kettle boiled, I poured the water into the *džezva,* put the *džezva* on the stovetop, then stirred the coffee and waited for it to froth.

My hand stilled. I was doing what she wanted. I was performing like a circus monkey trained to do a new trick. I lifted the *džezva* over the sink and started tipping out the coffee. No, it was too simple. I lifted the *džezva* upright. She'd only make another pot.

Looking around the kitchen for a tool of revenge my eyes settled on the sugar canister. Right next it was the salt in an identical canister. The only difference was the name on the lid. Perfect. I spooned three tablespoons of salt into the *džezva* and put it on the tray.

Mum would be judged as a mother by how well I perform domestic tasks, especially the making of coffee. Coffee to a Bosnian is like Guinness to an Irishman. Refugees who'd been in Bosnia during the war spoke about grinding rice instead of coffee beans while under siege. It's more than a social custom, it's a source of national pride and identity.

I carried the tray to the living room. I'd thought we were friends, but if Mum wanted to play the role of the traditional mother, that left me with the role of the rebellious daughter. I clunked the tray on the glass-top coffee table.

Arnesa's mum, Enisa, counted the *fildžani*, her lips moving and her head bobbing. 'Won't she be drinking coffee?' she asked.

'She's sixteen.' Mum poured the first *fildžan*, stirred it by gently tipping the cup, then poured the coffee back into coffee pot.

'I was married when I was her age,' Enisa said.

I gave Mum a warning look. She handed me a *fildžan* on a saucer. 'Pass this to Dido and get yourself a *fildžan*.'

I returned with a *fildžan*, handed it to Mum, then sat on the floor beside her. Now it was a just matter of who'd take the first sip.

'She's a real beauty,' Enisa said, her *fildžan* approaching her mouth. 'She won't have any trouble finding a husband.'

She was talking about me as if I was a heifer on the market. I opened my mouth, but Mum grabbed my hand and squeezed a warning. 'She's got a few years yet.'

I moved my hand away and smiled as Arnesa's mum tipped the *fildžan* toward her mouth. *Drink, you old bat. Drink.*

'Pičku materinu,' Dido swore loudly. Everyone froze. He'd used the traditional Bosnian profanity that translated as, "Your mother's vagina." 'There's salt in the coffee.'

Mum took a sip of her *fildžan*, her face puckering in disgust. 'My apologies.' She collected all the *fildžani*. 'I'll make another coffee.' She walked into the kitchen calling my name. 'What did you do?' she demanded, loudly, so they could all hear what a disciplinarian she was.

'I put sugar in it.' I lifted the salt canister.

'That's salt.' Mum tapped the lid furiously. 'This is sugar.' She pointed to the other canister.

'Well?' I asked loudly—I could play this game too. 'They both look the same.'

Mum grimaced.

I stormed out of the kitchen and slammed my bedroom door behind me. I threw myself on the bed, muffling my laughter in the pillow. It was perfect. I pictured Mum's face when she realised there was nothing she could do. On the surface it was a simple mistake anyone could have made.

After the guests left Mum came by to apologise. I played the hard-done by daughter and tried to get out of *mejtef* again. She 'promised' she'd think about it. I knew she was just saying that to get me off her case.

***

On Monday morning I woke late and smiled when I remembered it was a public holiday: I could eat my cereal while watching TV. I crawled out of bed and opened the sliding door to the living room. My bleary eyes and sluggish brain took a moment to process what I was seeing.

The sofa cushions were on the floor and Mum and Safet were sprawled over them, their naked bodies entwined, their faces slack-jawed with surprise as they stared at me. Mum was on top and they were both red-faced and sweaty.

Chapter 10

'Ohhh,' a scream emerged from my throat, like I'd walked into a horror set and seen a dead body. 'Fuck, fuck,' I whispered as I stumbled to my bedroom, my stomach heaving.

Mum burst into my room. 'Why aren't you at school?' she shouted, breathless.

I looked and saw she'd put on a nightgown, but it was almost transparent and she was still naked underneath. 'Eooww,' I groaned and turned away from her. 'Because it's a public holiday.'

'Listen.' She lowered her voice. 'There's no need to tell Dido about this.'

'Where is Dido?' I asked.

'He went to meet Edin at the mosque café.'

'So you thought it was your chance for public sex?' I grabbed my pillow and held it to my stomach, still reeling from what I'd seen.

'It's my house.'

'I live here too.'

'You're right,' Mum said. 'Listen, Sabiha, Dido would be embarrassed—'

Safet stuck his head in the doorway. 'Why isn't she at school?' he demanded.

'Get him out of here!' I shouted, hiding my face in the pillow. The image of his black curly chest hair matted against his sweaty, naked torso appeared before my eyes and it made me feel ill.

Mum went into the hallway, leaving my bedroom door open so I could hear what they were saying. 'You have to go,' she said.

'But I haven't finished.' I heard smacking noises like they were kissing and my lips curled in disgust. 'Send her to school so we can finish,' he said.

'I can't,' Mum said. 'It's a public holiday.'

He groaned. 'Bahra, why didn't you tell me?'

'I'm sorry,' Mum said. 'All the days blur together. I'll come to your house as soon as I finish talking to Sabiha.'

'I'll be waiting,' Safet said. I heard footsteps and the front door slammed.

'Sabiha,' Mum said softly. 'Can I come in?' I didn't answer. The bed dipped as she sat on it. 'I didn't know today was a holiday.'

I turned to look at her. 'Why would you?'

She flinched. 'I know that you're angry with me.' She lifted her arm. I glared at her in case she thought about touching me. She sighed and folded her hands onto her lap. 'But there's no point telling Dido.' She started crying. 'I try so hard,' she whimpered. 'I've embarrassed Dido so much over the years. I can't disappoint him again.'

Why did she always manage to make me feel sorry for her? She was the one who did the wrong thing, but I was the one who felt guilty. I knew I couldn't tell Dido. Imagining that conversation made my head swim.

'I won't tell,' I muttered between clenched teeth.

Mum wiped her face with her hands and smiled.

'But,' I said, before she got her hopes up. 'I have a request—' I let my sentence hang in mid-air.

'You're blackmailing me again?'

I refused to feel guilty. She pushed me to this. If she'd been reasonable we wouldn't have entered this war of attrition, but now I had no choice.

'What do you want?' she asked.

'No more *mejtef*.'

'Dido would never allow it.' She stood and paced between my bed and the door.

'Dido doesn't need to know everything.'

'I can't let you drop out of *mejtef*—'

'Fine, it's your funeral,' I snapped, ready to storm out.

'But I can tell the *hodža* that you're sick next Saturday.'

I thought about it for a moment. I could just continue being sick. After all it wasn't in Mum's best interest to bust me in a lie. All I had to do was pretend to go to *mejtef* and she'd be forced to cover for me. 'Deal.' I put my hand out.

Mum shook my hand. 'You're impossible.'

I hugged her, momentarily full of love and joy. 'You're the best, Mum.'

She hugged me back. 'You know I love you and if I'd known you were home I never would have—'

'Okay, okay...' I pulled away from her, the nausea returning. 'I'll also need money to keep me out of the house on Saturday.'

'You have no shame,' she scolded, before leaving my bedroom.

I needed breakfast. I lay back on the bed. I'd give Mum a few minutes to clean up the living room before I went to eat.

***

The following Saturday I woke 'to get ready for *mejtef*.' I wore my denim skirt with tights underneath and a scooped neckline knit top. I put on a jacket and carried my lipstick and eyeliner with me, just in case Dido was around. With one last look in the mirror, I was ready for a day of fun. I entered Mum's bedroom and kicked her bed. 'Pay up!'

'What—' she wriggled like a giant trapped caterpillar.

'Come on.' I kicked the bed again.

The week had flown by. The only tricky part was keeping my mouth shut about our plans for Saturday. I couldn't chance anyone at school finding out, especially not Adnan or Dina, so I'd sworn Jesse and Brian to secrecy.

Mum opened her eyes. 'What do you want?'

I threw her handbag onto the bed. 'For "*mejtef*." My fingers made air quotations. She had her hamster-on-the-wheel look. This wasn't good. 'Fine.' I headed to the door. 'If you don't want to keep your side of the bargain—'

'Here.' Mum thrust a twenty-dollar note at me. I kept my hand held out. She slapped another ten-dollar note on my palm.

'Ta.' I kissed her on the cheek.

***

'Hi guys.' I was cheerful as I walked up to Brian and Jesse who were waiting at the bus stop. We were catching the bus from St Albans to Highpoint Shopping Centre.

Brian kissed me on the cheek and yawned. 'It's the break of dawn,' he squinted.

'It's nine a.m.' I kissed Jesse on the cheek. He didn't kiss me back, but at least he didn't flinch either. We were slowly relaxing with each other. After our talk on parent—teacher night we'd been sending each other our writing via email. But somehow it was still easier communicating by writing than face to face.

'Is it too early for you?' We had to keep to my timetable to I could fake I went to *mejtef*.

'No.' Jesse smiled. 'But then I wasn't the one who stayed up half the night watching a Justin Timberlake special.'

'Brian!' I whacked him on the shoulder. 'I thought we were going to watch it together.'

He shrugged. 'It's Justin.' As if that explained everything, and unfortunately it did.

The bus arrived and we climbed on. 'I hope you're up to re-watching it with me,' I said as I bought a ticket.

'Of course,' he said. 'It's Justin.'

I rolled my eyes. 'That better not be your only sentence today.'

He smiled and followed me down the aisle. We sat at the back of the bus, I got the window seat with Brian next to me and Jesse at the end. I wanted to go to the city, but Brian and Jesse vetoed that suggestion. They'd been outraged I hadn't had the proper indoctrination to the western suburbs culture, apparently, Highpoint was where it all happened. When the bus stopped we headed into the complex. Most of the shops were still opening and the walkways were empty and silent.

'I told you it was barely dawn,' Brian gloated.

'There's Justin.' I pointed at a shop window.

'Where?' Brian stared around him wildly.

Jesse laughed silently beside me.

'Very funny.' Brian walked off. He stuck his middle finger in the air and kept walking. We stumbled after him, weaving drunkenly as laughter overcame us. When we caught up he was in a café ordering a cappuccino. I added a hot chocolate to the order and Jesse got a juice. Brian sat moodily as we waited. When the cappuccino arrived he looked at it like a lost love.

I took a sip of my hot chocolate. 'Your hair looks great today.'

'Thanks,' he said grudgingly. 'I've got to go to the loo.'

When he was gone Jesse made sucking noises. 'Shut up,' I said.

'Before I forget.' Jesse opened his satchel. 'I read the piece you wrote about the Bosnian mosque.'

'You did?' I crossed my legs. 'Because there was no rush.' I'd sent him my article a few days ago, expecting him to send me his comments via email. I composed my face into an expression of interest, even though I was cringing inside.

'There were some great paragraphs.' He pointed to a few lines where he'd put red ticks. 'I've also made suggestions.' While Jesse was talking about my story Brian returned to the table and sipped his cappuccino.

'Thanks, Jesse.' I squeezed his hand. 'That's really helpful.'

Jesse smiled. 'I hope the newspaper likes it too.'

Warmth filled me. Jesse was the first person I'd entrusted my writing to: he'd clearly read every word and, while he was speaking to me about it, he made me feel like the most important person in the world. I wanted to hug him. We'd been gazing into each other's eyes. I glanced at Brian. He winked. I blushed as embarrassment hit me. Brian thought I liked Jesse.

'Here's my story.' Jesse handed me a sheaf of papers.

'I'll read it and get back to you.' I put both stories in my handbag.

By the time we finished our drinks the shopping centre was jumping. We inspected clothes we couldn't afford. Jesse and I ducked into a bookshop and Brian dragged us out. Brian became hypnotised at the music store, and Jesse and I frog-marched him out, each holding onto an arm while he tried to make a break for it and return. We watched the latest Batman movie which was awesome. It was at the food court that we began to disagree.

'Maccas.' Brian glanced at the golden arches.

'I'll pass.' I hated McDonald's. Sometimes it was like I was the only person in the world who did. Brian and Jesse's faces fell. 'I'll do the rounds and find you,' I told them.

On the other side of the food court was a couple chewing each other's lips off. The girl was familiar. She pushed her hair off her face and I recognised Dina. My reaction was to hide, but *mejtef* was finished so I was in the clear, and anyway Dina saw me.

'Hi Dina.'

'Hi.' She avoided my eyes.

I waited for her to say something. She blocked my view of the guy. As the silence stretched out uncomfortably I got angry. 'You must be the boyfriend.' I moved around her and held out my hand. Up close he didn't look like a high school kid.

'Tony,' he offered, shaking my hand.

'How long have you been together?'

'Six months,' he said.

'Dina never mentioned—' I started to say.

'Okay, let's go.' She grabbed my arm and strong-armed me away from Tony. 'We're going to the Ladies, hon,' she called back to him as she pushed me into the women's toilets.

'What's your problem?' I demanded.

Dina shushed me and checked under the toilet cubicles. 'Okay.' She gave me the all-clear.

'Paranoid, aren't we?'

'You don't know what it's like having to hide like a criminal,' she said.

'What's the big deal?'

We had so much in common: our parents were both Bosnian-Muslim, our granddads were best mates, we were the same age and we saw each other six days a week between school and at *mejtef*, yet it was like we were from different planets. This was finally my chance to bust her open and see what was inside.

'Because my parents have found religion,' she said bitterly. 'And now I'm supposed to be the perfect Muso girl.'

'Well, I get some of the same treatment, you know. But you don't seem to have it too bad.' I nudged my head toward the food court. I still couldn't believe it. At school she pretended to be a regular girl who had crushes, and yet she was in a relationship.

'My parents don't know about Tony.' She blew her hair off her face. 'No one knows except you.'

'Not even Gemma?' I asked.

She shook her head.

'You've been friends since forever. How can she not know?'

'If my parents find out about Tony they will kick me out of the house like they did my brother,' she exclaimed in frustration.

'Why take the chance?' She was putting herself in a world of trouble for a boy. How could she be so dumb?

'I have to!' Dina shouted. She grabbed hold of the vanity and watched me in the mirror. 'I love him.' She burst into tears.

I broke her gaze, uncomfortable at her raw emotion. Dina was usually bloodless and cold, but now I realised that she kept her emotions submerged because she was living a double life.

She turned and squeezed my hand so hard I thought she'd fuse my fingers together. 'You have to promise me you won't tell anyone about Tony,' she begged. 'Not even Brian and Jesse,' she added as if she'd read my mind.

'I promise.'

She searched my face to see if I was telling the truth. She finally let go of my hand. 'Thanks.' She turned and opened the toilet door. 'I hope you're someone I can trust, Sabiha.'

I flinched as the door shut behind her. Her last words were like a barb in my gut. I'd already betrayed Kathleen's trust, blurting our secret to Shelley about going to the concert. I inspected myself in the mirror. Was I someone who could be trusted?

Dina and Tony were gone by the time I got out of the toilets. When I found Jesse and Brian, they'd nearly finished their lunch.

'What took you so long?' Brian asked.

'It took me ages to decide.' They smiled as they glimpsed my tray. After talking to Dina I'd been so rattled I'd ended up at Red Rooster.

'You got the lesser of the two evils, did you?' Brian grinned as he lined his McDonalds next to my tray.

'Are you okay?' Jesse frowned at me.

'I'm fine.'

'You picked well.' Brian stole a fry.

I spent the rest of the afternoon preoccupied with Dina's secret. How could her parents banish their only son?

When I got home, Mum was making dinner. It was one of the rare evenings we'd have a meal together like a real family. Safeta and Safet were out visiting so Mum stayed home.

'How come Dina's parents kicked out her brother?' I asked her.

'He disobeyed them,' Mum said. 'He used drugs.'

'What? He made one mistake.'

'He wasn't a Muslim,' Dido piped up. Anyone who didn't conform to the Muslim credo, even in the slightest way, was branded a non-Muslim heretic by Dido.

'Do they think God will reward them for throwing away their son?' I asked Dido.

'Yes.' He hit the table with the palm of his hand. The plates shook and goulash spattered the tablecloth. 'Abraham was willing to kill his son to prove his faith to *Allah* and that's what Dina's parents did.'

'That's disgusting,' I spluttered. 'What sort of a God would do that?'

'*Allah* wanted to know that Abraham believed,' Mum explained 'So he hid from his eyes that he was killing a lamb, instead of his son.'

'Would you throw me away if I had a *vlah* boyfriend?' I asked.

'Sabiha.' Mum put her hand on mine. 'Of course—'

'If you married a *vlah* you would be no granddaughter of mine,' Dido hissed.

'It's not as if you care that I'm your granddaughter now, so it's no big loss. What would *you* do?' I turned to Mum.

'I'd disinherit you,' Mum said.

'You hypocrite!' I pushed myself away from the table and the chair clattered to the floor. 'You won't have a daughter for much longer.' When I got to my bedroom I wanted to scream.

Mum barged in. 'We're only doing what's best for you. Think about what would happen to you if you married someone who wasn't Muslim?'

'You married a Muslim and look how that turned out.'

'I know you think we're old-fashioned—'

'You had *vlah* boyfriends,' I interrupted her.

'Yes, but I never married any of them.'

'What about your first boyfriend?'

'How do you know about Darko?' Mum stopped dead.

'Mmm... you raved about him once when you were sick,' I lied.

I'd tried to read Mum's letters from Darko and had managed to translate a few words. They wanted to marry, but their parents were against the marriage because Darko was Serbian and Mum Bosnian. Pretty much the same as your Romeo and Juliet scenario.

'But Sabiha, if I had married him, how would my life be right now? Our people were killed because they are Muslim.' Mum was speaking like she was possessed. 'My family lost their homes and started again in a country that is alien in language and culture. And what would have happened to my children? To be half and half with their loyalties torn. To belong to neither and be hated by all.'

'What about me?' I shouted. 'Both my parents are Bosnian, but to him I'm the Australian granddaughter who still has to fulfil his expectations.' I pointed to the living room where Dido was waiting for the rest of his dinner. 'To the Bosnians I'm Australian, and to the Australians I'm Bosnian.'

'Imagine how much worse your struggle would be if both your parents weren't Bosnian.'

'I'm Australian.' I spat out. 'I can marry anyone.'

'Can you really?' Mum asked. 'Why do you think I left Dave?'

Dave was the only one of Mum's boyfriends that I'd liked. He was the closest thing I'd ever had to a father.

'I thought he left you.' I trailed off as Mum shook her head.

'I left him.'

'He was nice.'

'He was a *vlah*.'

'That's bullshit.' This was the first time we talked about Dave and I wouldn't let her bag him. He was the only decent man I knew. After they broke up he sent me a Christmas card, but I never replied because I thought he'd dumped Mum like all her other men had.

'I'm not saying he didn't love us both,' she added. 'But all the things he loved in the beginning he wanted to change in the end. He didn't like our food, didn't like me talking Bosnian or having any Bosnian friends, and when Dido came to Australia, Dave didn't understand that I had to care of my father.'

Everything changed when my grandmother passed away. Mum had a crisis when her mother died: she was wracked with guilt for not visiting her parents after she moved to Australia, despite her mother's entreaties.

After Dido came to Australia and lived with my Auntie Zehra, Mum wanted to hang around her family more. The one time we visited with Dave had been a disaster because he couldn't speak Bosnian and nobody spoke English with him.

'Mum, Dave wasn't the problem. Dido is the only one who cars about where people come from.'

'You get asked where you come from all the time when your name isn't Australian,' Mum said. 'So it's better to stick to your own community.'

'That's just because people are curious.' I defended it, even though I hated the question. When I was asked it made me feel like I didn't have the right to call myself Australian.

'And how do they react when you tell them you're Muslim?' Mum demanded.

I remembered all the ways that I avoided the Muslim tag. As soon as people heard the M word their gaze sharpened, and then the questions would start: why was I not covered up, what was *Allah*, and where was Bosnia?

'You don't admit it to me.' Mum headed for the door. 'But at least be honest with yourself.'

Mum was paranoid. Like Frankie said she was overcompensating for her guilty conscience and was being a Try-Hard-Bosnian. But I was Australian and that crap didn't apply to me.

Maybe Mum was right and some people treated us differently for being Muslim, but not everyone was like that. The movie ticket stub I'd saved from my trip to Highpoint was on my mirror. Brian and Jesse were Australian, but they didn't give a shit. They cared about was me, Sabiha Omerović, without all the Bosnian baggage.

There was a knock on the door. Mum poked her head in my bedroom door and handed me the cordless phone. 'It's Dina.'

'Thanks.' I took the phone, avoiding Mum's questioning look. 'Hey Dina, how are you?'

'Did you tell anyone?' she demanded.

Chapter 11

‘Hold on…’ I covered the mouthpiece. ‘Is there anything I can help you with?’ I asked Mum. She left. I checked that the door was properly closed. ‘Okay, I can talk now,’ I told Dina. ‘No, I didn’t tell anyone.’

‘All right, all right,’ Dina said. ‘Don’t get snappy.’

There was a silence as we both tried to think of something else to say. ‘How did you organise seeing Tony?’ I asked.

‘I told my parents I was stopping at the library, but I still had to be home by two. Some of us aren’t like you.’ Her voice was sharp.

‘I can’t go anywhere,’ I protested.

’You didn’t have to go to *mejtef* this morning.′

‘Don’t tell anyone, but I kind of lied.’

‘So you’re in the same boat,’ Dina’s voice was too happy for my liking.

‘Kind of… Yes, I’m in the same boat,’ I admitted. It was difficult acknowledging that the freedom I used to have, that my friends envied, was being restricted now.

‘Maybe we can help each other.’

‘I’m listening.’

‘I’m guessing your mum is cracking down just like my parents. No going out. No friends who aren’t Muslim and definitely no boys.’ Dina steamed ahead while I nodded to myself. ‘What if we became best friends?’

How the hell was I getting out of this?

‘Of course we wouldn’t really be friends at all,’ Dina said.

‘Of course,’ I repeated. Did she think she was too good for me?

‘If we let our parents think we’re friends and we call each other every night, then we could call whoever we wanted.’

Dina was a genius, but I wasn't telling her. 'That's a great idea,' I said instead, keeping the excitement from my voice. 'We can even organise weekend outings and hook up with mates.'

'And we can have fake sleepovers.'

That wouldn't do me any good. There was no one I wanted to sleep over with. Then Brian and our near kiss popped into my head. My lips tingled.

'But that's down the track,' Dina said briskly. 'We should set a time to call each other. How is seven o'clock onwards?'

'Works for me.'

'We have to keep to the same timetable with our boy—, I mean with our friends, otherwise we'll get caught. So we have to be off the phone by eight.'

'Uh, sure.' I thought I was good at working the system, but Dina amped it to a whole other level. I was her apprentice and she was my master.

***

On Monday Gemma and Dina waited at the school gates as I rode up. 'Cool bike.' Dina hugged and kissed me like we were long-lost sisters.

'I have to put it in the bike-shed,' I said.

'We'll come.' Dina put her hand through mine and walked with me. Gemma followed, watching us suspiciously.

'You're making us look suss,' I muttered to Dina in Bosnian.

Dina saw Gemma following and let go of my arm. 'What are you doing slow-arse?' She thrust her arm around Gemma's and tugged her until we were walking in a line.

I let out a sigh. I felt like I'd sold my soul to the devil. While pretending to be friends with Dina was convenient, I did not want a touchy-feely relationship with her. After I put my bike away, Gemma wanted to go to the oval and have a smoke. 'I'll go to the front and wait for Brian and Jesse,' I said.

'We'll come with you.' Dina turned Gemma around.

'I don't want to,' Gemma moaned.

'We'll go to the oval afterward.' Dina pulled her along.

Brian and Jesse were at the front talking to Adnan. 'There you are!' Brian exclaimed when he saw me. He gave me a smacking kiss. Jesse gave me a peck on the cheek, his dry lips barely making contact.

'Hey cuz.' Adnan kissed me too.

When I turned I was gobsmacked to see Dina giving Brian and Jesse pecks. When she reached Adnan she almost fell into him as she kissed his cheek, holding onto his shoulders and thrusting her hips forward. So much for Tony. Gemma looked daggers at me, like I was responsible for Dina's touchy-feely routine.

'I want a ciggie,' Gemma whined when the hellos were over.

When we got to the oval Dina and Gemma pulled out their packets while Brian scabbed a smoke from Adnan.

'I didn't know you smoked,' I said to Brian.

He eyed the cigarette like he was shocked to find it in his hand. 'I'm more of a social smoker.'

Jesse and I were the only ones who didn't smoke. We stood on edge of the group. 'It's just you and me kid.' Jesse smiled.

'Since we're the only ones who don't think it's fun to suck on a cancer stick.'

'You should try before you judge,' Adnan said, smoke punctuating his words. He offered me his packet.

I pushed it away. 'Thanks, but no thanks.'

'What about you Jesse?' Adnan offered.

'I've got bronchitis,' Jesse said. Adnan returned the packet to his shirt pocket.

Jesse and I moved away from the smokers. 'I read your article,' I reached into my backpack. Jesse had written about teenagers who cared for their ill parents. I stood closer to him and leaned his story on one of my books so I could go over my notes. 'I've only got minimal feedback because it was amazing.' I met his eyes. We were centimetres apart.

'Thanks.' Jesse's minty breath caressed my face.

'Where did you get the idea from?' I asked.

'Someone I know is a carer.'

There was a faint sprinkling of freckles on his nose. He looked adorable. He reached for his story, his hand brushing against mine, and shivers raced up my spine.

***

That night I called Brian and explained Dina's phone call system.

'Are you and Dina best friends now?' he asked, after we'd gasbagged about the day's happenings.

'Shit no,' I replied. 'We're pretending to be friends so our parents don't know what we're up to.'

'Good,' he said. 'Because I thought *we* were best friends.'

'Best friends?' It was like I was in an elevator and my stomach was on the third floor, while my body was on the ground. Weren't we more than friends?

'Well yes,' Brian said. 'I mean Jesse is my oldest friend, but you're the one I feel I can talk to about anything. Don't you feel like that too?'

'I guess—'

'Even though we haven't known each other for long, I feel like we've been friends forever.'

'I do too—'

'I'm glad we're on the same page,' Brian said. 'I feel blessed to have a friend like you in my life.'

'Me too,' I whispered, wiping tears. 'I'd better go. My hour is almost up.'

'Okay, see you tomorrow.'

I hung up, feeling I was weighed down under a cement blanket. I'd been sure that he was as attracted to me as I was to him. There were so many signals. We both felt like we knew each other forever. Usually I was weird around guys, especially guys that I liked, but with Brian it was different. There was nothing I couldn't talk to him about, nothing that was off-limits. But now I was scared to see him again.

***

The next morning at the oval, everyone was already there. Adnan nodded, Jesse smiled as I stood next to him, Dina waved, Gemma flicked her hair and gazed the other away.

'Hello love!' Brian grabbed me into a bear hug, lifting me off the ground. 'Isn't it a beautiful morning?'

As he swung me in his arms I put my hands on his shoulders, my whole body flush with his. I smiled, full of joy. Last night's conversation retreated like a nightmare does after you're awake.

'He's been insufferable,' Dina shouted.

'What's going on?' I asked after he set me on my feet. I tried to dampen my joy. My feelings for Brian were too obvious.

'The party is all set,' Brian handed me an invitation to attend a comic book character costume party.

'Who are you coming as?' Brian demanded.

'I don't—'

He cut me off before I finished. 'Because I'm torn between the Riddler or the Joker.'

'We all know the Riddler is out of your league, Brian,' Dina quipped.

'So you're coming as Poison Ivy?' Brian glared at her. We all laughed. 'What about you Adnan?' Brian continued.

'He'd be a perfect Superman.' Dina's eyes zeroed in on his chest. Adnan smirked. He thrust his chest and stood in the Superman stance with his arms crossed.

'Gemma?' Brian asked as he bummed a ciggie off Adnan.

'Supergirl.' Gemma watched Adnan. Dina's eyes narrowed. Brian coughed on his cigarette smoke. Everyone laughed as he got his breath back.

I relaxed as the banter continued around me. I'd spent all night tossing and turning, nervous about seeing Brian after his 'Just friends' talk, but I'd underestimated how easy it was to hide tension in a group. Each time I met Brian's gaze and felt the connection between us I couldn't believe that he didn't feel the same way. Maybe he needed time to cross over from friends to something more?

'What about Jesse?' Dina asked. 'Who could he be?'

'I know.' Brian came to stand behind Jesse and me, putting a hand on our shoulders and pushing us closer together. 'Peter Parker.'

'He is the perfect Peter Parker.' Dina approached Jesse and looked into his eyes. 'Unassuming, yet has hidden depths.' Jesse held her gaze.

'That's our Jesse.' I put my arm around his waist. 'Full of depth.' Jesse turned and looked at me.

'Maybe I should come as Mary-Jane?' Dina put her hand on Jesse's chest, forcing him to look at her again. 'I'd look good as a redhead.' We stood, like an abstract statue exhibit representing the promise of love.

'Cat Woman is sexier,' Adnan called out.

Dina backed away. 'Cat Woman it is.' She sashayed back to Adnan and Gemma.

The bell rang and we headed to class.

***

Hanging around with Gemma and Dina meant that I learnt more than I ever wanted to know about either one of them. Dina was sneaky. Most of her conversations were bitching about her parents or perving on Adnan because she couldn't talk about Tony. I couldn't figure out if she was really liked Adnan or was using him as cover.

Gemma had a pretty full-on life: she was the oldest of three children and when she was twelve her stepfather died, so she became a second mother to her four and two year old siblings. She also had a boyfriend, Rob, who was twenty and worked as a mechanic's apprentice. They'd been going together for two weeks and he wanted sex.

'It's not as if we're not doing anything,' Gemma said. 'I give him blowjobs—'

'Yuck, that's disgusting,' I interrupted.

'Why? It's a natural expression of love,' Gemma insisted.

'Does he reciprocate?' I asked.

'I couldn't let a guy go down there.' Gemma was horrified.

'So you're the only one expressing your love,' I stirred.

Gemma turned away and spoke to Dina. 'So I give him blowjobs, but now he says it's not enough.' Gemma chewed on her nail. 'I always wanted to wait until I married.'

'So wait,' I said. She was shitting me. We'd been having the same conversation all week.

Dina shot me down. 'Bullshit. You can't marry until you're eighteen. No guy will wait two years.' Gemma watched us, her head moved from side to side as she watched, her mouth hanging open like a clown at Luna Park.

'If he loves you he will,' I said.

'No guy can hold out for that long.'

'Why not?'

'Spoken like a virgin.' Dina smiled.

'Is there something you want to share?' I needled her.

She glared at me before turning back to Gemma. 'I'm sure he'll wait.'

'See.' I grinned at Gemma. 'You should wait.'

Gemma came to school a few days later with red eyes. Dina took one look at her and hugged her. 'You did it, didn't you?'

Gemma nodded and sobbed in earnest. 'He cried and said that if I loved him, I'd do it. So I did.'

I opened my mouth to rip into Gemma about her being conned, but Gemma shook her head at me.

The next day she looked sad and confused. 'We did it again last night and it still hurt,' she mumbled. 'He said there was a bone that had to loosen and then it wouldn't hurt as much.'

Dina and I gaped at each other. 'There's no bone that has to be broken,' I said. 'There's only a hymen, but not all women have that.'

'Yes, there is,' Gemma insisted.

'It shouldn't hurt the second time,' Dina said cautiously.

'How would you know? You're still a virgin.' Gemma was getting agitated and didn't try to hide her scorn. Suddenly 'virgin' had become the worst insult.

Dina stared at the ground.

'Sounds like he doesn't know how to turn on a woman so he's spinning a yarn,' I said.

'What would you know, virgin?' Gemma spat.

Unfortunately more than she would ever know. Because Mum had treated me as her confidante since I was ten years old, and I definitely knew more about sex than I needed. One of the things Mum talked about was how if a woman wasn't turned on, her natural lubrication wouldn't kick in and sex would hurt.

'I know better than to fall for an idiot's fake tears,' I retorted. She was so stupid.

'Neither one of you even *has* a boyfriend.' Gemma sneered.

I opened my mouth, about to let loose about how boyfriends were not compulsory.

'You're right,' Dina interjected, shooting me a glare. 'All that matters is that you're happy.'

Gemma smoothed her hair back. 'I am. I'm very happy.'

When I got home I heard Safet's greasy voice from the living room. Since I'd caught him and Mum having sex I'd avoided him by hiding out in my room whenever he was over. Thankfully he and Mum were spending more time at his house. I dumped my backpack in my bedroom, debating whether I could stay there until he left. But I was starving: waiting wasn't an option today.

"*Merhaba,'* I said as I entered the living room. Dido and Edin were playing chess. 'What's there to eat?' I asked Mum, ignoring Safet sitting at the kitchen table. Mum opened her mouth to chastise me, but thought better of it.

"*Mutuša,'* she said, scarcely containing her irritation at me. *Mutuša* was a baked pancake mixture with chopped potatoes and, in a rare gesture of maternal devotion, Mum served it to me.

'Where did you get the bike?' She nodded through the open back door where my bike was propped against the stairs.

Typical. I'd been riding the bike for a few weeks, but she only noticed it when it was under her nose. 'From someone at school,' I said between mouthfuls.

Mum stopped washing the dishes. 'Did a boy give you the bike?'

'No, I traded it.'

'What did you trade?' Mum asked suspiciously.

I knew where her mind took her. 'I traded my music,' I said quickly.

'You'll have to return it,' she said.

'Sure.' Mum frowned at me like I was a reptile about to strike. 'The minute you start driving me to and from school the way real parents do, I'll return it.'

'Don't speak to your mother that way,' Safet said.

I turned to him and had a flashback of him naked. 'Don't tell me what to do,' I said, as I held onto my stomach, hoping the *mutuša* wouldn't make a comeback.

'Treat Safet with respect,' Mum said, like she was reciting a mantra.

'I give respect to those who earn it.'

'What homework have you got today?' she asked.

'Why? Do you want me to do '*home work'* and clean the house for you?'

'I want to supervise and make sure you do it.'

I realised she was serious and snorted with laughter as I stomped back to my bedroom. Mum washed the dishes, banging the pots and pans until Dido shouted for quiet.

***

The next day I came home to an empty house. So much for Mum supervising my homework. I was in my bedroom when I heard them return. Mum called me and with a grunt I rolled out of bed. In the living room I sat in the armchair and flicked through the channels with the remote.

'We visited your school,' Mum said. Safet sat next to her on the sofa.

'What?' I shouted and turned off the TV.

'After our conversation last night I realised you were right.' She read the paper in her hand. 'You're behind in English and have to catch up.'

'Hold on.' I raised my hand up. 'The two of you— ' I pointed at them '—went and spoke to my teachers.'

Mum squirmed and glanced at Safet.

'You had no right!'

Dido walked in. 'Stop screaming girl.' He took off his coat and hat.

'We're disciplining Sabiha,' Mum said.

'You don't have any rights over me!' I shouted at Safet.

Mum took Safet's hand in hers. 'You need to think of Safet as your father.'

I leaped to my feet. 'He is *not* my father.'

'Nevertheless, Safet and I will be supervising your homework from now on.'

'No you won't,' I was getting louder.

'Quiet!' Dido shouted. 'Bahra, explain.'

Mum was smug. 'Safet and I met with Sabiha's teachers.'

'Sabiha go to your room,' Dido commanded.

'But—' I started.

Dido had gone quiet, but he was all the scarier for it.

I was about to slam my door when I heard Dido speaking. He hadn't closed the sliding door to the living room. I left my door ajar so I could eavesdrop.

'You shouldn't have done that,' Dido said. 'Safet is not Sabiha's father and he should not be involved in disciplining her.'

'But Babo, it's like you said, she has no respect for me,' Mum was moaning.

'Then come to me,' Dido said.

'I didn't mean to step on anyone's toes,' Safet said. 'My daughter would have been her age and I wanted to help.'

'Sabiha has had a lot of people come in and out of her life and she needs the stability of her family,' Dido said.

'When Bahra and I are married things will be different.'

My heart nearly stopped as I waited for his response.

Chapter 12

'When are you getting married?' Dido's voice was so soft I could scarcely hear him.

'In a few months time,' Safet answered.

'Bahra, leave us,' Dido said. Mum tiptoed into the hallway. 'Bahra isn't like other women,' Dido continued. 'She needs someone who understands her special needs.'

'Of course, I understand her condition' Safet said.

'Having children is stressful for any woman her age, but with her illness—'

'Bahra and I have finished with that phase of our lives.'

'Well, if you can take care of Bahra's daughter, Safet, I say any man would be happy to have you as a son-in-law.'

As they reached for each other's hands, I slammed the door and slumped to the floor of my bedroom in disgust. They'd only known each other for two months and now this creep was going to be my stepfather. I was stuffed.

After Safet left, Dido called Mum and me to the living room. 'Your schoolwork has been appalling,' Dido said. It could have been the refrain to a really bad song Mum and he had written. I wanted to explode.

'How the hell am I supposed to do my homework when I have to fetch and carry for you?' My jaw was clenched as I tried not to scream at him.

Dido's eyes narrowed. 'From now on Bahra will be here when you finish school and she will do the household chores so you can complete your homework.'

Mum looked like she'd swallowed a lemon. I smiled.

'And since you will have extra time to study I expect you to get straight A's or you'll get a strap on your hand for each mark you miss.'

My eyes widened. I was at best a C student at the moment. 'But, but,' I stammered. 'That's child abuse.'

'Not where I come from,' Dido said. I wanted to remind him he wasn't in Bosnia, but he was in take-no-prisoners mode.

He wagged his finger at me. 'Remember, I'll be coming to parent—teacher interviews with your mother at the end of the year.'

Shit. Now I had to work like a dog to catch up with my schoolwork or there'd be a scene with Dido at school that I'd never be able to live down.

At seven o'clock the phone rang. Oh, no. I'd been counting the minutes until I could call Brian—now someone was calling for Mum and would tie up the phone.

'Yes,' I said, hoping I could pretend it was a wrong number.

'Sammie?'

It took me a moment to recognise the voice. 'Kathleen?'

'Can you meet me?'

'It's a bit late,' For the train trip to Thornbury.

'I'm in your street,' she said.

I headed to the living room window and tried to peer out discreetly, without Dido and Mum noticing. Kathleen waved at me from in front of my house. I walked nonchalantly back to my bedroom before whispering into the phone, 'I'll be right there.' I hung up the phone and ran out the front door.

'I'm going to the shop to buy some tampons!' I shouted as I slammed out. I knew Dido didn't have a comeback for that.

I grabbed Kathleen into a hug. 'I can't believe you came to visit me.

She pulled her arm out of my grip. 'My boyfriend is with me.' She nodded down the street where there was a red car with two guys standing beside it.

'Since when do you have a boyfriend?' I demanded. She hadn't mentioned anything in the few emails we'd exchanged since the failed birthday lunch. Actually, she hadn't said much at all; she'd mostly sent me annoying chain letter emails and memes.

'Come and meet him.' She walked towards the car.

The guys were watching us like hungry wolves. 'How long have you been going out?' I asked, slowing my steps.

'A few weeks,' Kathleen said. 'His name is Rafael and he's a friend of Francesca's brother.' Francesca was eighteen years old and Kathleen's favourite first cousin. Francesca's brother was twenty.

Kathleen's boyfriend and his mate looked me up and down. As Kathleen introduced me she stood by Rafael's side and he put his arm around her waist.

'You were right,' Rafael said. 'Sammie *is* gorgeous.' His hand drifted to Kathleen's butt and he cupped it proprietarily.

'She sure is,' Shane, Rafael's mate, said, his eyes on my chest.

'Are you up for a night out?' Kathleen asked.

'Um,—' I stuttered.

'We're going to a pub to watch a band.' Kathleen's eyes pleaded with me to say yes.

'I have to ask my Mum—'

Kathleen moved from Rafael and I followed her. 'Since when do you have to ask your Mum for anything?' she demanded.

'Maybe if you talked to me you'd know,' I replied. 'How were you able to go out tonight?' Her parents kept her on a tight leash and in the past I'd been her only chance to slip off the collar.

'My parents think I'm sleeping over at Francesca's.' Kathleen leaned in closer and lowered her voice. 'I really need you to come with us. Rafael wanted to go out without me, but I said I could get a date for Shane.'

'Why didn't you ask Shelley?' I couldn't resist having a go at her.

'Sammie, are you helping me out?'

'What's the big deal?'

Kathleen opened her purse and pulled out her cigarettes. 'I don't want Rafael to think I'm too young for him.' She lit up.

'You *are* too young for him,' I said. 'And he'll find out soon enough.'

'What do you mean?' She puffed smoke at me and I moved out of the way.

'When you don't have sex with him.'

'That's not a problem.' She glanced over her shoulder and smiled at Rafael.

'Kathleen, did you have sex with him?' I demanded.

She turned back to me and nodded, her eyes dull.

'Do you love him?'

She didn't answer.

'Why did you do it?'

'Why not?'

'We were going to wait until we married.' Another pact we'd made when we were twelve.

Kathleen took another drag. 'If I waited I'd make my parents happy.'

She was so stupid. 'Please tell me you used protection,' I whispered, clutching her arm.

'Of course. I've been on the pill for a year and we used condoms.'

She hadn't told me she was on the pill. It was like I was looking at a stranger. 'You broke your promise.'

'So did you.' Kathleen picked up her handbag.

'I never broke my word.'

Kathleen lifted an eyebrow. 'What about telling Shelley? None of us is perfect. Your problem is that you think you are.'

It was like she'd slapped me across the face. My eyes burnt as tears threatened. 'I'm not like that—'

'So *you* say,' Kathleen interrupted. 'But ask anyone who knows you and you'll hear a different answer.' She threw her cigarette on the sidewalk and ground it with her heel. 'So you're not coming?'

I couldn't answer her through the choking sensation in my throat. I stayed on the street and watched her get in the car. Rafael did a burnout as he drove off, the car swinging from side to side and the wheels scarring tracks on the asphalt.

I snuck back to my bedroom through the back of the house, my whole body frozen. I couldn't believe Kathleen had turned on me like that. We'd promised each other to be best friends for life, but in a few short months our friendship seemed to have completely died.

I was supposed to call Brian, but I lay under the doona and covered my head. I couldn't talk to anyone. My mobile beeped a SMS message. I turned away, burrowing deeper under the covers.

How could Kathleen have accused me of such awful things? I didn't think I was perfect. She was so unfair. My mobile rang, but I ignored it. Kathleen hadn't made any effort to be a friend to me since I'd moved to St Albans, yet she was branding *me* the bad friend. The phone diverted to my voicemail and then started up again. I threw the doona off and picked up the phone. 'Hello?' I snapped.

'Why didn't you call?' Brian demanded.

'Because,' I said.

'Because why?' he persisted.

'Because I had a really, really, really crap night.' I lay back on the bed.

'Spill,' Brian's voice was full of glee.

'Okay...' I settled in and told him about Mum speaking to my teachers.

'It's a bit late for the concerned Mummy routine,' Brian said.

'Exactly.' I was pleased that he got it. 'Then Kathleen came by.' I'd avoided talking much to Brian about Kathleen up until now. It kind of seemed in bad taste to talk to your new best friend about your old best friend.

'What's with her?'

'She's got a new boyfriend.' I told him about her plan to set me up with Rafael's loser friend. 'Then when I said no she came down on me like a ton of bricks and said I was a bad friend.'

'Not like she'd know,' Brian said. 'You're my friend and I reckon you're great.'

'Really?' I asked, desperate for reassurance.

'Really,' Brian confirmed. 'You're thoughtful, kind and a great laugh. Kathleen was paying you back.'

'Yeah, I know. She didn't say anything until I said no.'

'See, I told you. Forget about her.'

My mood lifted. Brian was right. Kathleen and I were finished. My friendship with her was in the past, and my friendship with Brian and Jesse was the future.

'Anyway, enough of this depressing crap,' Brian's voice became upbeat. 'Let me give you an update on the party.'

As Brian talked up his plans, Kathleen kept popping into my head. It still felt unreal that our friendship could end so abruptly and stupidly.

***

The next day at school we met up at the oval. 'I've got to talk to you about something,' Dina whispered while the boys stood opposite us. Her eyes shifted. I turned and saw Gemma approaching. 'I'll tell you later,' she said.

Throughout the day she kept trying to get me alone, but Gemma wouldn't let Dina out of her sight. We were in the toilets together at lunch and Gemma was waiting by the sink while Dina and I were in the cubicles. 'Oh no!' Dina groaned from the cubicle next to me. 'I've got diarrhoea.'

'I'll wait for you outside.' Gemma's footsteps echoed as she ran for the door.

I quickly pulled up my pants and held my breath as I burst through the cubicle door. Dina appeared at my side. 'What—' I bleated.

'I was faking.' Dina waved her hand dismissively. 'Gemma can't stand a bowel movement.'

'She's not the only one,' I muttered as I washed my hands.

'I was thinking we'd organise a fake sleep-over and tell our parents we were at each other's house. You can spend the night at Brian's and I can be with Tony.'

'I don't know...' I knew I wanted to go to the party, but I wasn't sure about sleeping over.

'You'd be crazy not to go.' Dina almost vibrated with excitement. 'You can get drunk, smoke, hang out all night.'

I tidied my hair. Dina wouldn't get it even if I spelled it out. I had the chance to do plenty of grown-up things before Mum became an uptight Born-Again Muslim. I'd learnt from experience that grown-up parties were overrated.

At the last party that Mum and Dave threw before they broke up, one of his drunken mates stumbled into my bedroom while I was sleeping and groped me under the doona. I screamed so loud that and Dave and Mum came bursting in.

When they switched on the light his mate was sitting on the bed beside me, dazed, his pants unzipped. 'She wanted it,' Dave's mate said. Dave bashed him in my bedroom while I huddled against the wall. Hearing the noise other party-goers poured into the room and a melée began. The brawl was so bad that cops came and hauled everyone away...

Dina waited for an answer. 'I'll go to the party,' I said. 'But I won't be sleeping over.'

Her face dropped. 'Don't make up your mind yet.' She followed me to the door. 'There's still plenty of time.' She never gave up.

I opened the bathroom door and there was Gemma waiting for Dina like an eager puppy. Dina bit back her questions. It was the only time I was thankful for Gemma's presence.

Brian and I had a free period because our teacher was away. 'Give it a break?' He was still carrying on about his party and I was sick of the topic. I took my juice out and stabbed the foil with my straw.

'Why don't you come as Wonder Woman?' he stared at my hair. 'You can get a dark brown rinse and with your light eyes, you'd be a dead ringer.'

'Puhlease,' I said, between sips. 'I don't look anything like Wonder Woman.'

'Sure you do.' Brian's eyes moved to my breasts.

'You're such a pig.' I slapped him on the arm and crossed my arms.

'What's your problem? We always talk like this.'

I shifted uncomfortably. Of course he was right. We'd talked about circumcision, periods, sperm, masturbation and everything under the sun, but I couldn't help my discomfort at the possibilities Dina raised with her whole stupid sleepover idea. 'I'm not coming to the party.'

'Why?'

'I won't be allowed.' For the first time I was grateful for Mum's transformation.

'But Dina told me the two of you were organising a fake sleepover.'

I coughed as the juice went down the wrong way. I was going to kill Dina.

Brian slapped my back. 'Are you all right?'

I shrugged his arm off my shoulders.

'Just say you're sleeping over at Dina's and stay at my house,' he said matter-of-factly.

'Can't.' I grabbed my backpack. 'If Mum caught me I'd be dead meat.'

Brian put his hand on my arm and stopped me from leaving. 'Sabiha, is something else going on?'

I side-stepped him, losing his hand in the process.

'There's plenty of room in the double bed,' he said.

I jerked back like I was stung.

'Oh...' Brian said knowingly. 'Cause, you know, nothing will happen.'

Oh, so I was a street skank he'd never want to touch.

'I mean...' he stuttered. 'You know we're just mates.'

I walked away.

'Sabiha,' he called, but I didn't stop.

I wanted to kick him. He'd tried to kiss me only a few weeks ago.

He grabbed my arm and turned me to face him. 'What's your problem?'

'What's *your* problem?' I shouted.

He raised his hands in surrender. I backed down, more embarrassed than ever. We'd never had a fight and now I'd ruined everything. I was so confused: I wanted him to like me but I had to admit that I still wasn't sure exactly what I meant by that.

'What's going on?' Brian asked gently. 'It's me. Your best friend.'

My throat choked up and I was blinking back tears.

'If you don't want us to sleep together...'

I flinched.

'You think we're going do more than sleep together?' Brian demanded.

I didn't say anything.

'Sabiha, we've been in a bed together before,' he said, exasperated.

How could I forget parent—teacher night?

'That was daytime,' I said.

He arched his eyebrow. 'You know people can have sex during the day, right?'

'Smartarse,' I replied. I was sick of feeling so horridly embarrassed. It's like there's a baseline to how much embarrassment you can feel in one session and then it retreats like it never existed. 'It's the way Dina talked about the sleepover.'

'You let that slag create this.' He pointed at me and him. 'What the hell is wrong with you?'

'Oh, shit.' I covered my face with my hands. 'I can't believe I freaked out.'

'It's okay.' He hugged me. I stiffened, but this was Brian, my best friend and my body relaxed into him. 'Are we cool?'

'Yeah.'

'Good.' He kissed me on the forehead. 'What are the chances of you coming as Wonder Woman?'

I shook my head.

'What if I died your hair for you?' he persisted.

How could I refuse that offer?

***

Dina called me that night. 'Are you going?' she demanded before I even had the chance to speak.

'Hello to you too.'

'Are you or aren't you?' Dina was getting edgy.

'I don't know yet,' I lied. I wanted her to suffer for stuffing me up today.

'Didn't you and Brian talk?'

'You mean after you spilled your guts about the fake sleepover?' Anger crept into my voice.

'Yeah.' Dina sounded confused.

She was as thick as a brick shit-house. Anything that wasn't about her flew right over her head. 'We talked,' I admitted. 'If we got sprung it would be World War Three. Aren't you worried?'

'Nope. I just want to get a break.' Her voice was full of bitterness.

'Aren't you scared?' I licked my dry lips. 'I mean if you sleep over at Tony's then you and he will ... you know.'

'I've waited for six months because I wanted our first time to be special, and a guy will only be satisfied with blowjobs for so long,' Dina said.

Was I the only one who didn't think sex was the be-all and end-all?

'I know that you're scared,' Dina said. 'But I really need this. I need one night where Tony and I can be with each other like a normal boyfriend and girlfriend.'

Even though her idea of normal was clearly way off mine, I heard the pain in her voice. 'All right,' I interrupted. 'I'll go to the party.'

Dina shrieked and I nearly dropped the phone. 'You won't regret this, I promise. Okay, gotta go,' she squealed.

The dial tone purred in my ear. I returned the headset to its cradle. Dina had a one-track mind leading to Tony. I still had time to call Brian. I picked up the phone and dialled. As I pressed the last digit the uncomfortable feeling I had earlier in the day returned and I quickly hung up. I bit my nail and stared at the phone. I thought I was over this feeling, yet I was still behaving like an idiot. This was Brian. I wiped my sweaty palms on my skirt and called him.

'So, hi Wonder Woman!' Brian exclaimed.

'What makes you think I'm coming?' I asked petulantly.

'Because Dina told me,' he said. 'So are you?'

I held the phone away from my ear. What the hell? She moved so quickly. 'Um...'

'Because you'd look fabulous as a brunette.'

'Okay, I'll do it.'

'We'll put a hair rinse in tomorrow after school. Dina's already done the prep by telling her parents she has to go to the library.'

She was out of control. Pretty soon I'd be opening my mouth and she'd be talking for me. 'I want a dye job, not a rinse.' I'd tried the whole rinse thing and wasn't impressed, plus I actually did fancy being a brunette.

'You sure?'

'Mmm,' I stared at myself in the mirror. 'I want the real deal.' I was imagining my hair as sleek and shiny, a seal's pelt of rich brown.

The next day we snuck out of school at lunchtime and went to a chemist. Brian tried to talk me into a light brown colour, but I got the dye that was one shade off black. After school we went to his house. I sat on a kitchen chair in the bathroom wearing a black rubbish bag as a cape while Brian ran his gloved hands through my hair.

'You should be a hairdresser,' I teased.

'I've thought about it,' he said seriously.

I gulped down my laughter. Thankfully Brian was caught up with my hair. 'How come you changed your mind?' I asked.

'My dad would go apeshit,' he said. 'He thinks that only poofs are hairdressers.'

I squirmed on the chair. 'That's not true. Hairdressing is a type of trade too.'

'Thanks.' He squeezed my shoulder, and a warm glow filled my belly. He'd finished squirting the dye on my hair and was Glad-wrapping my head. I resembled a human condom. He stepped back and admired his handiwork. 'All done.' He slicked back a few errant strands. 'Let's watch TV until it sets.'

Twenty minutes later I bent over the basin while he washed the dye out. As he worked around me his crotch rubbed against my hip. I was never more aware that my best friend was a guy. Kathleen and I had dyed each other's hair heaps of times, but I'd never been conscious of how intimate a thing it was, their hands on your head, their body surrounding you.

Brian lifted a section of hair. 'Oh, oh.'

I forgot about my discomfort. Now I was terrified 'What's wrong?' I demanded.

Chapter 13

'You're kind of patchy,' Brian said. I inspected my hair. Even though it was wet and therefore darker, it was obvious that the brown hadn't covered it completely.

'I told you to buy two packets,' Brian accused.

'I didn't have enough money,' I said between gritted teeth. Instead of the gorgeous, glossy brunette I'd imagined, I looked like my hair was covered in spew. 'I'm up shit creek.' I sat on the edge of the bathtub and covered my head with my hands.

'It's okay,' Brian said. 'You can wear a cap to school and we'll buy two packets of dye and fix it tomorrow.'

I liked his plan, but we still had the same problem. 'So, once again what do I do for cash?'

'Sorry Sabiha! I told you: I used the last of my allowance on decorations for the party. Can't your mother help you?'

I would have to suck up to her and I hated the thought. It was a come-down after my extortion bid. 'I'll have to.'

'Let me dry your hair before you go home.'

I couldn't even enjoy him running his hands through my hair. When I got home Mum stepped into the hall while I was taking off my shoes. Shoes littered the hallway and chatter came from the living room. Visitors, again.

Mum's eyes widened. 'What did you do to your hair?' she gasped.

I touched it self-consciously. 'I dyed it brown.'

She thrust me into the living room. 'Look at my stupid daughter.' Safet was there, and other familiar faces. 'Girls would kill for her long, blonde hair and she does this.' She took a handful of hair and tossed it. The women clucked their tongues and shook their heads like crazy chickens.

'Mum.' I pulled from her grasp.

One of the women squinted at my head. 'It's multicoloured.'

I touched my hair again. 'There wasn't enough dye to cover all my hair.'

'She's still half-blonde,' another woman said, and they all cackled.

I ignored them and turned to Mum. 'Can you lend me money so Dina can fix it tomorrow?'

'No,' Mum went in and sat on the sofa. I left for my bedroom. Mum called me back. 'I'll take you to the hairdresser tomorrow and pay to have it died back to blonde.'

'No, thanks,' I forced a smile. 'It's growing on me.'

In the morning I stared at the mirror. I'd tied my hair into a ponytail so that the patches of blonde kind of resembled streaks. I twisted and turned in front of the mirror. I was fooling myself. I put the cap on and poked my ponytail out the back.

As I ate breakfast the smell of bleach filled my nostrils. I sniffed and saw that the walls were still damp. Mum usually washed the walls with bleach and water once a year to wipe the cigarette smoke stains, but I hadn't seen her do it yesterday.

She burst through the back door. 'Have you finished breakfast?'

'What are you doing up?' She was never awake before eleven a.m.

'I wanted to get a early start.' The back door was open and the Hills Hoist was full of washing. Mum took the dishes from me. 'You don't want to be late.' She'd hadn't seen me off to school since I was in third grade. She glanced at my cap. 'I can still make an appointment at the hairdresser.'

I shouldered my backpack and left.

Brian was waiting for me at the bike-shed. 'How did it go?'

'Mum won't give me any money because she wants me to go back to blonde.' At Brian's blank look I elaborated. 'It's a ethnic thing. They're all try-hard Anglos and only believe that hair dye should flow one way, from brown to blonde.'

'You can always go to the party as Poison Ivy.'

I shook my head. 'I'm not letting her win.'

'What are you going to do?'

'I'll wait.' I'd snuck into her purse and lifted five dollars from the Bank of Bahra this morning. Within a week or two I'd have enough.

'But your hair.' He lifted his hand helplessly toward my cap.

'It'll keep.' I was already sick of people telling me this was a tragedy.

'Okay,' Brian said, obviously unconvinced. We walked to the oval and met up with the rest of the group.

My disguise didn't last the first period. 'Ms Omerović, please remove your cap,' Mr Kumar, my science teacher, commanded from the front as soon as I sat.

'Can I please keep it on?'

He smiled. 'Take it off now or go to the principal's office.' He hated me because I didn't do any homework and I hated him because he was a crap teacher so we were even. I removed my cap. Everyone gasped. 'Perhaps if you paid more attention to science you would have had a better outcome,' Mr Kumar said.

'I was aiming for this look.' I pulled my hair out of the ponytail. The only way to win was to show no fear.

Mr Kumar turned to the whiteboard.

'What the hell did you do?' Gemma whispered loudly.

'Nothing'

'Ms Omerović if you persist in disturbing the class I will have no choice, but to call your mother.'

'She's taken,' I shot back.

There was silence for a second, before the class exploded into laughter. At lunchtime I was the eighth wonder of the world and practically the whole school tracked me down to check out my hair.

'I wouldn't be caught dead like that,' Dina pronounced loudly. People in the next suburb would be over to perv soon.

'I'm not a wuss,' I retorted. Honestly she was the shallowest person I knew. How anyone could believe we were friends escaped me. Dina flounced off, Gemma in tow.

'You're so brave.' Brian said. 'I would have faked pneumonia rather than go out like that.'

I couldn't help feeling disappointed in Brian, but tried to push it away. 'What's the big deal? It's only hair.'

'It's more than that,' Brian got excited. 'Hair is an expression of our individuality.'

'It's just dead cells.' On this subject, it was clear we'd never understand the other point of view.

'Perhaps the question is why you don't think it's important?' Jesse weighed in as the mediator.

'When you have a Mum like mine, public embarrassment is a waste of emotion. When she's sick she can be like a kid and when she's healthy she's not much better, so I don't find this shit,' I waved my hand at the school, 'important.' Staring at Brian and Jesse, I added, 'I only care what people I respect think about me.' Jesse watched me like I was a puppy who'd performed a cool trick. Our eyes locked and I had to look away.

'You really don't care if other people like you or not...' Brian sounded incredulous.

'Not if I don't like them.'

Brian glanced at the buildings behind us. 'We're different.' There was such a naked look of longing on his face. 'I'd give anything for people to think I'm cool, but they know I'm a loser.'

'You are cool,' I blurted. I was already out of my depth. I sought Jesse's support, but he still had that goofy look on his face. 'You dress nicely and your hair is always perfect.' I forged ahead anyway.

Brian smiled sadly. 'No, you're cool, Sabiha. Because you don't give a shit about what those idiots think of you.' He walked away.

'But—' I protested.

'Leave him.' Jesse held my arm. 'He needs to be alone.'

'I didn't want to make him feel bad.'

'He does that himself,' Jesse said emphatically. I propped myself next to him on the table. We sat in silence. Brian was always a buffer and we were hardly ever alone together, so it felt a bit weird. 'He's right you know,' Jesse finally said.

'About what?'

'You are cool.'

There was something in his eyes that made my heart speed up. 'Thanks,' my voice came out in a whisper. His head dipped toward me. I clenched my hands tight on the table and blushed. 'The bell's about to go.' I jumped off the table and bent to get my backpack, hiding my face. After what seemed like forever the bell rang.

Jesse jumped off too and stood so that we were almost touching. We stared at each other. 'Saved by the bell,' he said.

Sprung. My heart was pounding. 'We'd better go or we'll be late,' I said.

He stepped aside and let me lead. As we walked to English class I was excruciatingly aware of him beside me, of our arms almost touching as we walked. I wanted to move away, but was scared and uncomfortable.

I stopped in front of the toilets. 'I'll meet you in class.' I hid in the stall and sat on the toilet seat, my head in my hands. What was I going to do? Somehow I'd stuffed things up with both Brian and Jesse.

When I got to class the teacher was writing on the whiteboard. 'Sorry,' I muttered to Ms Partridge as I passed. Oddly, she smiled back at me, instead of reprimanding me. I sat next to Jesse and avoided looking at him.

'As you all know the *St Albans News* has been running a weekly feature publishing articles from each school in the district,' Ms Partridge said. 'It is with great pleasure that I congratulate two of our very own students, Sabiha Omerović and Jesse James.' The class clapped as Ms Partridge handed us a copy of the newspaper.

I flipped through the paper and found our articles on page thirteen. 'We did it!' I exclaimed. We'd handed in our articles, but the newspaper hadn't notified us that we would be published. I wriggled with joy then gave Jesse a hug. His hands moved to my waist and he pulled me against him. When his body pressed against mine I gasped and met his gaze.

'Congratulations.' He leaned down and brushed his lips against my cheek.

'To you too,' I whispered, letting go.

His hands moved from my waist slowly, a lingering caress through my T-shirt.

After class, I packed up my bag, my whole body off-centre, my head floating separate above my body. I snatched glances at Jesse who was surrounded by students congratulating him. He caught me looking and smiled at me. I nodded and rushed to the bike shed. I unlocked the padlock in record time and only after I'd wheeled the bike off school grounds did I feel I could breathe properly.

I didn't know what was happening between Jesse and me, but I didn't like it. We were friends and had to stay that way. Friendships were thin on the ground and I couldn't jeopardise them with pointless flirting.

When I got home my legs trembled from the pedalling. 'Mum,' I yelled as I burst through the back door.

Mum ran from the living room. 'What's wrong?'

'I got published!' I handed her the newspaper. 'Read it, read it!' I jumped around her.

'What's the noise?' Dido came into the kitchen, Safet beside him.

Mum opened the page and held it up for him to see. 'Sabiha got published in the newspaper.'

'Good, good,' Dido said.

'What did you write about?' Safet asked.

'About the building of the mosque.'

'Congratulations,' he said.

'I'm very proud of you.' Mum hugged me. I followed her into the living room. While they drank their coffee I sat on the floor and watched TV. 'I'll frame the article so everyone can see when they come to visit,' Mum said.

'I'll take a copy to the mosque tomorrow,' Dido said. 'Show everyone how my granddaughter is promoting Bosnians.'

I smiled. The phone rang and I picked it up. 'Dido, it's Adnan for you.' I held out the phone.

Dido hung up after a few minutes. 'Put it on *The Price is Right,*' he demanded.

I switched channels. 'What's going on?'

'Adnan's on TV.' Dido peered at the screen.

We all watched the television in silence. He was the third guest to get a chance to compete for the prize. 'We hear you've led an interesting life,' the host asked. 'Your family came to Australia from Bosnia?'

'Yes, Larry,' Adnan spoke into the microphone. 'My family had to leave Bosnia as refugees and we came here when I was a child. We lost our house and both my parents couldn't get jobs in their field here and now work as cleaners to put me through school.'

'What would you like to win?' Larry asked.

'A car of course.' Adnan grinned into the camera.

'I think we can help with that.' Larry gave him a cheeky smile.

'That's right, Larry,' the voiceover guy broke in. 'Adnan you're playing for a new car.' The camera panned to a shiny blue car. A model in a sparkly gold dress waved her arm and flashed her teeth.

'We're playing the grocery game.' Another model stood behind a fake cash register. There were five items on a stand. A bag of Edgell frozen peas, a Cadbury chocolate tray, a can of Friskies cat food, Impulse deodorant, and a can of Heinz beans. 'To play this game, Adnan, you can buy any of these items, but you need to spend a minimum of $10.00 and no more than $10.50,' the host explained. The figures appeared on the register just in case we didn't understand the sophisticated maths. 'If you succeed, the car is yours! And what a prize it is.'

The studio audience went crazy, yelling at Adnan and exhorting him to buy their lucky combination of items. He didn't look at the audience. 'The chocolate, please,' Adnan said cooly. The model rang it up. The register flashed $6.50 on the display screen. 'Deodorant.' The register flashed $8.55. 'Cat food.'

The register hit $10.10 and the theme music played. 'Congratulations Adnan. You've won yourself a car.' Bits of confetti fell from the ceiling. The model in the gold dress led Adnan to the driver's seat of the car. The camera moved to a close-up of him. 'Adnan will be competing for the chance to win the showcase on the other side of this commercial break.'

'Look at what my grandson did!' Dido shouted. He tried calling Auntie Zehra, but their phone was engaged.

I groaned. How big would his head be now... After the break he and the woman who won a holiday stood behind two desks.

'The showcase you're competing for is between $52,000 and $53,000. The person guesses the closest amount receives the showcase.' The host opened an envelope and read the amount, which then appeared on the television for the viewers to see.

Adnan and the woman took turns guessing the price of the showcase, while the host indicated if it was higher or lower. I sat on the floor biting my knees as Adnan inched closer to the correct price. 'Please, please,' I prayed. 'Please don't let him win.' When Adnan missed out by $10 to the woman I sighed my relief, while Dido and Mum shouted their disappointment. 'Thank you,' I whispered.

The phone rang and Dido answered. A big grin broke out on his face. 'That's my grandson Adnan. The movie star of our family. He's going to do well for himself.'

I folded up the newspaper with my article in it and went to my bedroom. The phone rang all night and Dido kept answering, his voice full of joy as he expounded on his grandson's qualities.

At school the next day Adnan was greeted like a celebrity. 'They taped it a month ago and I was waiting for the episode to air,' he explained.

'You were so lucky,' Dina said.

'Luck had nothing to do with it,' Adnan said. 'I went three times before I was picked to appear as a contestant. It took me that long to figure out how the system works.'

'What system?' Brian asked.

'They want people who have an interesting story. One time I told them I was an orphan, but I think that was too sad for them, so I pulled it back a bit.'

'You deceived people,' I said.

Adnan lifted an eyebrow. 'I gave people a story they wanted to hear.'

A mob gathered around him. Everyone wanted to touch him as if his good luck would rub off. I grabbed my backpack and left. Someone called my name and I turned to see Jesse running toward me.

'Was your Mum happy about the article?' he asked.

'For a whole five seconds, until Adnan the movie star made his debut appearance.'

'They're all hoping they're getting a ride from him.' He glanced over his shoulder and so did I. The crowd grew. 'Once they realise there's nothing in it for them they'll back off. There's no way Adnan will spoil his car with that rabble in it.'

'So, was your family happy about the article?' I asked.

'My sister got me a cake. It was all right.'

'That's so kind,' my voice was high-pitched as I tried to cover up the thickness in my throat.

'There's light at the end of the tunnel,' Jesse said.

'What?'

'No one will be talking about your hair anymore.'

Jesse and I had lunch under the elm tree in front of the car park. It was the first time we'd hung out together alone. We talked about books we liked and shared opinions on the storylines of our favourite TV shows. 'Why is this the first time it's been only the two of us?'

Jesse carefully peeled back the Gladwrap from the other half of his sandwich. 'I got the feeling that you wanted to be alone with Brian.'

I winced. 'Brian and I are just friends,' I exclaimed, putting my sandwich down. 'Nothing more.' I put my hand on his arm.

'Really.' Jesse stared at my hand. I went to remove it, but he put his hand over it and held it. 'I'm glad to hear that.'

I froze, seeing the same expression on his face as when he'd tried to kiss me. 'I want us all to be friends,' I rambled, throwing words between us in an effort to diffuse the strange energy that had sprung up again.

He smiled and once again he was the Jesse I was used to. He patted my hand and let go. 'We're friends.'

I breathed out my relief. 'What character are you going to be at Brian's party?'

He frowned. 'I don't know.'

'What about Zorro?'

'Maybe. I've heard that cowboys always get the girl,' Jesse smiled.

The weird energy returned and I laughed again.

By the end of the week Adnan's popularity had subsided and things had almost returned to normal.

'Are you fixing your hair?' Brian glowered at my head.

'I've been collecting the small change from Mum's purse, but I think she's twigged. The last two mornings her purse was missing from her handbag.'

'The party's in two weeks and you can't go like that.'

He was right. I had to do something or I wouldn't go to the party. Even I had my boundaries. Plus I was getting sick of hat-hair from wearing my cap all day.

***

That evening, I was watching TV while Mum and Safet drank coffee. Mum was looking at me. 'What?' I asked.

'Do you really want to walk around like that?' She inspected my hair with disgust.

'Does it bother you that much?'

'Of course not. But you need to learn a lesson.'

'And what exactly is the lesson?' I demanded.

'That you have to listen to your mother,' Safet said. He was one dumb parrot, repeating everything Dido said.

'That you can't do whatever you like,' Mum cut in before I could counter Safet.

'Hello?' I waved at her. 'It's my head, my hair.'

'You need to respect your elders,' Safet said.

If I heard that line again I was going to find a weapon and use it. This time I chose to ignore him. I turned back to the television.

'I know that it's hard,' Mum said. 'Kids at school must be making fun of you.'

I patted my hair. 'Everyone at school thinks it's cool.' Mum was refusing to help dye my hair brown, but now she was worried about people's opinions—this could only work to my advantage.

'We should get going,' Safet said.

'Where to?' I asked.

'Murat and Suada's.' Mum put on her shoes.

'Cool. I'll come.' They were visiting Dina's parents and I'd figured out how to put my plan into action.

'Don't you have homework?' Mum asked.

'Nothing that can't wait.'

'Here's your cap.' She waited for me to run into my bedroom where I grabbed the bundle of Darko's letters from under my bed.

As Dina's parents greeted Mum and Safet, I hugged Dina and let her in on my plan. Her eyes widened and she hissed, 'You're crazy.'

'Go along or I'll ditch the sleepover,' I warned her.

Even though Dina's parents had money, décor of her house was just a grander version of ours. The true display of Dina's parents' wealth was the special 'guest' living room. It was hardly ever used, as no guest was special enough for it. In it was a L-shaped leather sofa, shiny black wall units and a huge TV that Dina wasn't allowed to turn on. They did all their entertaining in the rumpus room at the back of the house.

Dina did the good daughter routine and helped her mum prepare the coffee and bring out the sweets. When Dina put down the plate of dried meat and sweets, I salivated. Bosnians all tried to outdo each other in feeding the visitors, but God forbid a kid should help themselves to anything. You had to take food stealthily, only when your parents gave you the nod of approval, eat one thing at a time, and not go back for seconds.

When she'd finished serving, Dina sat on the floor beside me. 'Are you sure this will work?'

'Watch and learn.' I waited for my chance. It didn't take long.

Chapter 14

'My Dina is an excellent student. She's hard working, modest, knows how to cook and clean. She'll make an excellent wife,' Suada said, looking at her as if she were admiring a prize-winning dog.

Dina kept her eyes on the carpet, a small smile on her face. You had to look modest as the Bosnian version of high-noon took place: these two mothers had each other in their sights as they fired brags about their children.

'My Sabiha,' Mum said, and I knew this was my cue. I took off my cap and waited. '... is a great writer,' Mum continued. 'She got published in the local newspaper.'

Mum was saying nice things about me and I was being a bitch. I reached for my cap, but it was too late. All eyes were on me.

'Bože sačuvaj!' Dina's mum exclaimed, her hand on her chest as she stared at my head like I'd grown horns. 'What's wrong with her hair?' she asked.

Dina was silent so I nudged her.

'Mum, can I do my hair like Sabiha?' Dina asked.

Suada looked like she was about to have a heart-attack while Mum gaped like a fish on dry land. 'Don't even think about it,' Suada said. 'You should get it fixed,' she said to Mum.

Mum nodded. She couldn't tell Dina's mum about her ultimatum because it was unheard of for a kid to refuse a parent's command.

Dina and I sat quietly for a while and waited until we were no longer the topic of conversation. 'We're going to my room to do homework,' she whispered to her mum. She closed the bedroom door and turned on her radio. 'What was that about?'

'Mum won't pay for it to be dyed brown so I'm convincing her.'

Dina shook her head in disgust. 'Next time keep me out of your stupid schemes.' She lay on her bed.

I wasn't feeling too crash hot about the success of my plan. 'My Mum thinks I'm a talented writer.'

'It's not as if she could say you're talented at anything else.'

'Cow,' I muttered under my breath. Dina was falling asleep. 'Hey,' I prodded her.

'Leave me alone.' She pushed my hand away. 'I was talking with Tony until three in the morning and I'm buggered.' She snuck the phone into her room and called him after her parents were asleep.

I slapped her arm. 'Wake up, I need a favour.'

Dina turned on her side without answering.

'I need you to translate my Mum's love letters.'

She turned back, peering at me from under her arm. 'Who are they from?'

'She had a Serb boyfriend before she married my Dad.' I waved them under her nose. There were only five so it wouldn't take her long.

She snatched them from my hand and opened the first envelope. 'Interesting.' She went for a second envelope.

I snatched the letters back. 'What does it say?' I said urgently.

'He's telling her... he doesn't want her to give up her family to be with him.' She paused and frowned. 'That they should take it slow and her father will accept him in time.'

'Fat chance,' I muttered. There was no way Dido would accept a non-Muslim son-in-law. Dina held out her hand for another letter. I handed her the second one in the bundle. This time I only gave her one letter at a time.

'I think your Mum suggested they run away together,' Dina said after she finished the second letter. 'But Darko is saying he can't abandon his mother and sisters. Without his income they can't survive because his father is dead.'

As Dina read the letters we were able to piece together Mum and Darko's story. They were madly in love and Mum was willing to do whatever it took to be together, but Darko was afraid of Dido. Dido was well-known in their town and put pressure on Darko's employer to fire him. Without a local job Darko had to move to Germany for work and in his last letter he told Mum to find another partner.

Dina lay back on her side. 'Now let me sleep.'

As I returned the last letter to its envelope I noticed the date on the envelope. Darko broke up with Mum one month before my parents married. Did she marry my Dad on the rebound?

Suada called Dina, who groaned as she swung out of bed. Everyone was gathered by the front door. I yawned, relieved the torture was over and pleased that I'd finally got the dirt on Mum.

When we arrived home I went to the bathroom to brush my teeth. I was walking into my bedroom when Mum stopped me. 'Get your hair fixed tomorrow,' she thrust a note at me. 'I'll make an appointment so you can go after school.'

Seeing the $50 in my hand, the fog of fatigue cleared. 'Mum—'

'I don't want to hear it.' She pushed past me.

At school I showed Brian the money. 'Mum's paying for me to get my hair fixed properly.'

Brian lifted my ponytail. 'Get it trimmed too.'

'I don't think I should spend all the money.'

'It's not that much more.'

I didn't say anything. Living on a pension meant that, when Mum wasn't manic, she watched every cent. Her giving me the money to get my hair fixed professionally was a big deal and the least I could do was give her change. 'I'll see.'

***

Refika was a Bosnian hairdresser who had opened a proper salon in a backstreet of St Albans. She lifted strands of my hair. 'Tsk, tsk,' she admonished. 'You tried to do this yourself?'

I nodded shamefully.

'Do you want to go back to your natural hair colour?'

I shook my head and fingered a hank of the dark brown hair colour on her swatch. 'This is what I want.'

Refika squinted at my head. 'It would look better if we stripped it back to blonde.'

I shook my head. I knew Mum put her up to it and I wasn't falling for it. 'Brown.'

'Do you know how many women pay a lot of money to make their hair blonde?'

'If you can't do it...' I walked to the door.

Refika pulled me to a stop by yanking my arm. 'Edo,' she called. A young man emerged from the backroom. She pushed me into a chair. 'Make this,' she ordered Edo, and caressed the hair I'd chosen on her swatch.

Edo had shoulder-length brown hair. As he mixed the dye he rolled up his sleeves, showing off his muscled forearms. He threw the cape over me and sectioned my hair, the gypsy hoops in his ears glinting. 'Gay,' I thought, disappointed.

'Do you go to school?' he asked, his accent revealing him as a new arrival.

'Yes, what about you?' I asked, trying to figure out his age.

'I did one year of English school and now I go to hairdressing school.'

I nodded. 'Why did you decide to be a hairdresser?'

'I wanted to work instead of going to school for years and years. At least this way by the time I'm twenty-one I'll finish my apprenticeship.'

'Bingo.' A bell rang in my head. He was seventeen. He met my eyes in the mirror and smiled back. He was flirting with me. So much for the gay theory.

'Do you live around here?' he asked.

I nodded. 'In Wooley Street. You?'

'Clive Street.'

My heart sped up. 'That's a few streets away from me.'

'What do you do for fun?'

I was about to say nothing much, but stopped myself short. 'I write. I had an article published in the local newspaper.'

'Did you get any money?'

'No.'

'Bend your head.' My hair flopped forward and hid my face as he put dye in the back sections. 'I don't see the point,' he said.

I moved my hair out of my face so I could see him through the parting. 'Have you ever been published in a newspaper?'

He shook his head.

'Well then.' He dyed my hair in silence. I wanted to smack my head into a wall. Why did I have to be so touchy? I cleared my throat. 'What do *you* do for fun?'

'Go to the movies, play computer games.' He put the timer on the mirror-stand in front of me. 'I'll be back soon.'

'Cute, isn't he?' Refika asked me when Edo went into the storeroom.

'He's okay.' I'd play it cool.

Refika let out a piercing laugh. 'Business has doubled with young'uns like you.' She winked at me when Edo came back in. I picked up a magazine, hoping to hide my perving.

When the timer went off, Edo led me to the sink and washed my hair. I sighed as I leaned back in the chair. This was my favourite part. Edo rubbed at my head and I shuddered as he tugged on strands of hair. 'We're finished.' He walked back to the cutting chair.

Already? I hesitated before following.

When he finished snipping my hair he used the blow-dryer and my hair curled in a sleek-brown bob, exactly the way I'd imagined when Brian and I had begun.

He pulled off the cape with a flourish and I followed him to the counter.

'That's $51.50.'

My heart started racing. I handed over the $50. 'Sorry. I'm short,' I whispered, mortified.

'It's okay.' Edo winked. 'You can buy me a drink the next time we see each other.' He handed me the receipt.

I smiled weakly. when you're poor you don't want anyone to see you're poor.

When I got home Mum was watching TV. I sat on the sofa and waited for her to say something, but she ignored me.

'Have you been to Refika's lately?'

Mum didn't answer.

'There was this guy there, Edo, an apprentice hairdresser.'

Silence.

'He's seventeen.' I tried to sound nonchalant. 'It's the funniest thing, he lives in Clive Street.'

We watched TV for a few more minutes. 'What does he look like?' she asked.

I held back my smile. She was hooked. 'Wavy shoulder-length brown hair, beautiful green eyes, five foot ten, well built.' The words shot out of me in one breath. Mum's face was neutral, as if we were discussing the weather.

'I should get my hair cut too,' she said, her eyes on the TV. 'I haven't had it done since the *zabava*.'

I bit back a grin. We sat watching TV for another half an hour, then I kissed her on the cheek and took the phone.

'Where's the change?' Mum asked.

I took a deep breath and turned. 'I don't have any change.' I stroked my shiny hair. 'He put in treatment and trimmed it.' I waited for her to explode into her usual rant about money not growing on trees.

'Your eyes stand out more.'

I didn't know what to say. Once when I was ten years old we were in a milkbar and I'd asked for change to put in a jar for needy children. 'We're needy too,' was her retort. I never asked for change again.

'I'm ringing Dina.' I sidled out the door.

'You'll never guess what happened to me,' I screeched when Brian answered.

'I know you didn't buy a Calvin Klein shirt,' Brian said.

Sometimes he was such a girl. 'I met the cutest guy,' I announced.

'Do tell.'

For a moment my good mood deflated at his matter-of-fact tone. *We were friends*, I reminded myself. After I told Brian Mum's reaction about spending all the money I added, 'I think if I told her I was knocked up, she'd smile and start planning the wedding with this guy.'

'You need to use this. You could get your hair dyed every colour under the sun. All you have to do is tell your Mum it's the only way to spend time with Edo.'

'I can't milk Mum for money like that. She lives off the pension.'

'So?' Brian said.

I told him how much Mum got a fortnight. 'We barely have enough money to buy groceries and pay our bills. If Dido hadn't helped pay off the house, when he sold his property in Bosnia, and we had to pay rent, we'd be in poverty.' Sometimes Brian could be so thick.

'I didn't realise.'

'Now you know why it's such a big deal that my Mum *isn't* making a big deal about the money.'

'She's really desperate for you to be with a Bosnian. What does he look like?'

I described Edo. 'He was wearing hooped earrings and a black T-shirt with red suspenders.'

'I hate to tell you—' Brian started.

'He's not!' I interrupted.

'He so is,' he said.

'So not.'

'So is.'

'So is not.'

'So is.'

'So not.'

'How do you know?' Brian demanded.

'A girl knows.'

'Aha,' he said, sceptical.

'He flirted with me,' I burst out in frustration.

'Because he wants a return customer.'

'You are so beastly!' I hissed.

'Beastly right.'

'Edo is definitely not gay.'

'I need to get a haircut myself.'

'I'll make an appointment for you tomorrow after school,' I said. 'You'll owe me an apology big time for being such a prick.' I hung up. 'Mum,' I yelled when I burst into the living room. 'Can I ring Refika at home now?'

Mum had emptied the kitchen cupboards and was cleaning every shelf. I picked up the address book and flipped to R. 'Sure, but you'll look desperate,' she said with a pained expression.

'It's not for me.' I wrote down the number. 'B—,' I remembered my ruse with Dina. 'Dina wants it.'

'Is that a good idea?' Mum asked. 'What if she likes him too?'

I was about to say that Dina had a boyfriend, but swallowed the words back in time. It was a hassle keeping track of lies. 'We have different tastes.'

Mum nodded as she cleaned. 'Be careful. Girlfriends can be devious.'

She was so on the money it was scary.

The next day I walked Brian to Refika's after school, my certainty about Edo's heterosexuality ebbing with every minute. An hour later he came back to the cafe where I was waiting, trying not to be desperate.

'So not gay,' he said.

'I told you so,' I said as relief flooded me.

'What's our plan?' Brian rubbed his hands together.

I frowned. I didn't know what I'd expected, but it certainly wasn't for Brian to be so eager to set me up. I'd hoped that when he saw Edo as competition, he'd step up, tell me he cared about me as more than just a friend.

'I'm not sure,' I muttered.

***

When I came home from school Mum walked in front of me three times before I noticed her smug look and her newly permed hair. 'You got a new hairstyle!' I exclaimed.

'Oh, that.' She touched her hair. 'Yes, I did.'

'Okay, spill.' I gestured my hand in a 'gimme' motion.

I'd thought about lying to Brian and telling him Mum found out nothing about Edo, but I had no choice but to continue with Brian's mission.

Mum didn't say anything.

'If you don't want to talk.' I headed for the door. 'I have homework.' My hand was on the door when she stopped me.

'His father is Serbian and his mother Bosnian,' Mum said.

As if I cared?

'Usually the children follow the father's religion, but then again Edo and Halida—that's his sister—are both Bosnian names.'

'Whatever...' I made a gimme gesture again, prodding her to move on.

'These things are important Sabiha,' Mum pronounced. 'If the two of you became serious you need to know what his religious beliefs are.'

'Mum,' I whinged. 'I haven't even had a proper conversation with the guy and you're already marrying me off.'

Mum frowned and finally continued. 'They're originally from Prijedor and were in Austria as refugees before getting their visas here.' She was telling me nothing I was interested in.

I tuned her out until one word snapped my attention back. 'Girlfriend?' I asked.

'They went to high school together and she's still in Bosnia.' Mum patted my hand. 'They haven't accepted that they won't see each other again.'

'Mmm...' I rubbed my lips. This was my out with Brian. If I told him about Edo having a girlfriend we could put this whole mess behind us.

'Okay, interesting Mum. Gotta call Dina.' I kissed Mum on the cheek and headed for the door.

'There's more,' Mum sighed.

I winked at her. 'I want to save it for later.'

***

'Most guys would have moved on,' Brian said when he answered my call. 'It means he knows how to love. Now we have to get him to love you.'

'Oh my God, Brian. Since when have you been such a romantic! I'm not sure—'

'Come on, Sabiha. No guts, no glory. Anyway I thought you really liked him?'

'I do—'

'Leave it to me. First, proximity,' he said. 'We need to plant Dina as a mole into his group and then you'll make your move.'

'This sounds complicated.'

'Slow and steady is the way to go,' Brian said.

'Since when are you the dating expert?' I stirred.

'I'm a guy aren't I?'

'Yes, but—'

'How many boyfriends have you had, Sabiha?'

My first 'boyfriend' was Michael. He was Frankie's neighbours' son. We fell into hanging out together while I was living with Frankie, during the episode when Mum had a nervous breakdown and was admitted to hospital.

Michael was awkward and socially underdeveloped, otherwise he never would have committed the cardinal sin. Dear, clueless Michael asked me out directly.

We were in his living room watching *Grease*. 'Will you go out with me?' he whispered in my ear.

I was engrossed in the movie and murmured my assent. It was only when his sweaty palm pawed my hand that I noticed his blissful face. There was only one thing to do.

While Michael didn't adhere to the going out protocol, I followed the breaking up protocol and sent Kathleen to do the deed. She came back teary-eyed and refused to tell me what happened.

My first official boyfriend was Joshua. He was the Casanova of our high school. Everyone knew Joshua. He was friends with the Nerds, the Skinheads, the Headbangers, the Emos, the guys who were into sports *and* the ones who were into cars. He had developed a suave routine by latching onto girls who were new to the school. The girls he asked out overlooked his spotty face and pudgy body because they saw a ticket to being accepted.

Joshua followed high school protocol. Our relationship began with hello, developed over lingering glances, and was confirmed with whispered conversations between our best friends who passed on messages, until it culminated into the official asking out.

It happened at lunchtime, under the walkway between buildings. He waited at one end of the walkway, his best friend Dean stood beside him like the best man, while the rest of his friends gathered behind like groomsmen. I stood at the other end, Kathleen beside me, Shelley behind me.

A crowd gathered at the possibility of a spectacle. We walked towards each other and met in the middle. 'Does Sabiha want to go out with Joshua?' Dean asked Kathleen. Kathleen repeated the question in a stage whisper, as if I wasn't standing right next to her.

'Yes,' I answered, staring at the ground.

Dean stepped towards us and took my arm, thrusting me at Joshua. We walked to the oval for the official consummation, our friends following behind and cheering. When we were hidden behind bushes Joshua put his hand lightly on my waist. I stood in a ditch. I stretched onto my tiptoes and we kissed.

His breath was minty fresh. He kept a toothbrush and toothpaste in his locker. My breath smelt of the hotdog and chocolate milk I'd eaten for lunch. We mashed out lips together, opening and closing our mouths like fish gasping for water.

Every few seconds, we tilted our heads in the opposite direction, our lips never breaking contact. I heard the shouts of kids playing on the oval and the giggles of our friends. I opened my eyes and saw one of them peering at us. My calf cramped and my leg trembled.

Dean came around the bushes. 'Fifteen minutes.' He tapped his watch. 'You've made a new record.' Joshua clutched me tighter against him. Furtively I wiped the spittle from my mouth with my sleeve. 'You can't wipe off someone's kiss,' Dean said.

Embarrassed I dropped my arm and turned away from him. It was like I was wearing a clown mouth. Joshua bent his head and kissed me again. Two days later I sent Kathleen over to break up. All the novels I read talked about kisses being romantic or hot or steamy. I never heard about a slobbery kiss where your mouth dried up because your combined saliva ended up on your face. Joshua moved onto the new exchange student.

And don't even get me started on the unofficial would-be-boyfriends that I stalked...

'I'll call Dina.' I was defeated. All I could do was follow Brian's instructions and hope I'd eventually find an exit strategy.

Her phone kept ringing and ringing. She had call-waiting and was probably talking to Tony. She finally answered, with terse hello.

When I explained the plan Dina said: 'You want me to befriend him, be your spy and informer, then casually introduce you so you can hang around with Edo.'

'Yes,' I said.

She hung up.

Chapter 15

I called Brian back. 'Dina's not with us on this one.' For once Dina's self-absorption worked in my favour.

'Doesn't she see the beauty of the plan?'

'Evidently not.' I rubbed my ear, still ringing from Dina's hang up.

'Did your Mum find out anything about his interests?'

'Wait...' I ran to the living room. 'Okay, great news.' I panted from my sprint back to the phone. 'He's going to the movies at Highpoint this Saturday.'

'Your Mum, the private investigator.'

'If only.'

'I'll check the sessions and we'll fine tune our plan tomorrow at school,' Brian said.

'Si, El Capitán,' I teased.

I was carrying the phone back down the hall and heard Edo's name. I slowed. 'You shouldn't be encouraging Sabiha's interest in that boy,' Safet murmured. 'Mevluda said his father is a gypsy.'

That's what I thought the first time I met him. I couldn't wait to tell Brian. I stepped back from the door.

'You could ruin the child's life with those rumours,' Mum said.

I stopped dead.

'You'll ruin Sabiha's life if you let her pursue this boy.'

'He's Muslim,' Mum said.

'No, he's not. If his father is a gypsy then he's taken on a Muslim name to make things easier for himself in Bosnia, but make no mistake, he's no Muslim. Gypsies follow no god,' Safet said.

Gypsies had always sounded romantic to me and Mum had told me how they lived in former-Yugoslavia. They were nomads and travelled with a horse and carriage from town to town, usually following the local fairs where they worked. I loved to fantasise about them in their colourful outfits and old-fashioned carriages, the men tall and swarthy like Edo.

But Mum said they were seen as vermin because they were known to beg and steal. The rumours were that they stole children and maimed their own so they could get money from begging. They were the bogeymen Bosnian mothers used to keep their kids in line.

'It has to be his name,' Mum said. 'They wouldn't let him into the country without proper papers.'

'Anyone can pass themselves off as a refugee,' Safet's voice was angry now.

I tensed, waiting to see if their argument would escalate.

'This is the first time Sabiha has liked a Bosnian boy.'

'Then put her into an Islamic school. She'll meet only Muslim boys,' Safet's voice calmed again.

'She'd never go...' Mum sounded despondent.

I smiled. At least she knew which fights she could win. Next thing, the front door slammed and Mum yelled out: 'Don't go.' The car revved and Mum moaned.

This day was getting better and better. First I met a cute guy and now there was trouble between Mum and Safet.

***

I was waiting for Brian at the front of the school, so we could organise our Edo—stalking at Highpoint on Saturday. Mum was in on the plan and she was letting me get out of *mejtef*. Her willingness to do anything that manoeuvred me with a Bosnian was scary.

When Brian arrived we checked the movie sessions on his phone.

'Definitely *Juno*. I've heard it's a great movie.'

'Did you forget we're staking out Edo?' Brian insisted.

'So?'

'No guy would see *Juno* unless he was on a date. He'll either be watching *American Gangster* or *The Bourne* movie.' He tapped his finger on the session times.

'*The Bourne* one wouldn't be bad. Matt Damon's hot.'

'Earth to Sabiha.' He pretended to knock on my head. 'Now we have to guess what session he'll see.'

Jesse stood in my line of vision. 'Are you going to the movies?' He dropped his library bag on the ground.

I straightened and signalled Brian to keep quiet. 'We don't know yet,' I said. I was so focussed on my plan to make Brian jealous, I'd almost forgotten about Jesse's near kiss.

Brian shifted without looking at me. 'We're staking out Sabiha's new crush.'

As he spoke it was like I was watching a train collision, helpless to prevent it. Jesse blinked rapidly.

'You want to come?' Brian was still scanning the sessions on his phone. 'We're seeing *The Bourne Supremacy*. You can help provide a cover for us.'

'No,' Jesse said. 'I've seen it. ' He turned and walked away, his shoulders hunched.

'You shouldn't have told him.' I slapped Brian's shoulder.

'Told him what?'

'That we were going to the movies.'

'Why?' Brian asked.

I stared at my feet in confusion.

'What's the problem?' Brian kept flicking through session times.

I bit my lip. Jesse and I had that conversation about being friends so I didn't owe him anything. Right? If that was true, why did I feel so guilty about the possibility of hurting him?

'Best stake-out time is the afternoon session.' Brian tapped his screen.

At lunchtime we went to the oval. Jesse sat on the other side of the group, reading his book. I sat in the middle: Adnan and Brian one one side, Gemma and Dina on the other, and I switched between the two conversations.

'Did you see the match highlights on SBS?' Adnan asked.

'I watched the whole thing,' Brian said.

'Wicked.' Adnan slapped Brian's knee.

'I've got it on tape. Come after school and watch it.'

'Great!' Adnan punched him on the arm.

'I thought we were going to the library,' I said.

'We'll go tomorrow,' Brian replied.

'He gave me a necklace.' Gemma held the chain away from her throat for Dina to inspect. 'It's eighteen-carat gold.'

'It's pretty,' Dina said unconvincingly.

I leaned closer and saw that the gold paint gone from one of the links, revealing the metal underneath. I grinned at Dina. She tried not to laugh.

'We're moving in together,' Gemma said. 'He's saving money for the bond and rent.'

I caught Jesse looking at me. He returned to his novel, hunching down so he wasn't visible behind Adnan. I shrank back too.

The next day Jesse, Brian and I, set off for the library. We were walking toward the station when a car slowed to a crawl and followed us. The window rolled down and Adnan's face appeared. He pushed his sunglasses down his nose. 'Want a lift?'

'Sweet ride,' Brian shouted as he admired Adnan's car from *The Price is Right.*

Adnan nodded smugly.

Brian jumped into the passenger seat and caressed the dashboard. 'This is sick, mate.'

Jesse opened the back door for me. 'Thanks,' I muttered as I slid across the backseat.

After Jesse got in, Adnan took off. 'Where to?'

'Sunshine library,' Brian said.

Adnan turned into St Albans Road. 'You'll have to give me directions.'

While Adnan and Brian talked in the front, Jesse and I stared out our separate windows as if our lives depended on it. Adnan's sharp turns made us jostle on the backseat like bottles in a crate.

'Here we go.' Adnan screeched to a halt. 'It's a shame you're busy, Brian,' he said as we got out of the car. 'I'm hooking up with my Bosnian mates for a soccer game at Footscray footy ground. We could use your ball skills.'

Brian pulled his leg back inside and closed the door. 'You don't mind do you?' he yelled through the open window.

Jesse and I stood on the footpath and watched as Adnan drove off, Brian's arm waving out the side. Too scared to look at Jesse, I stared down the street.

'I don't think he's coming back,' Jesse said.

'I can't believe he did that,' I whispered.

'That's Brian for you,' Jesse said wryly. 'Always on the lookout for something better.'

I followed Jesse into the library, dragging my feet. I was going to kill Brian. After we'd borrowed our books, Jesse and I walked to the station. 'What did you get?' I asked him, desperate to fill the silence.

'The usual.' Jesse hitched his backpack higher on his shoulder. 'What's the name of your new crush?'

His expression was neutral. OK, he was just being an interested friend. 'His name is Edo.'

'I hope it works out on Saturday,' Jesse said.

During the train ride he went on about homework. I held up my end of the conversation with monosyllabic responses, but I was out of sorts. I must have been wrong about him liking me. I was so stupid. I'd avoided him when there was no reason for it. I was seriously deluded, imagining both Brian and Jesse liked me more than as a friend. What was wrong with me?

When the train pulled up at St Albans I mumbled a quick goodbye and leaped out as soon as the doors opened. I was almost at the gates when someone called my name. I turned and saw Edo standing at the ticket office window. He was wearing jeans and a white shirt under his black leather jacket, his hair slicked into a ponytail.

'Where are you off to?' I asked.

'City.' He nodded east. 'We're going to a club on King Street.' The notorious street where anyone with a fake ID could get into a club. There were always reports of a stabbing or fight there. 'What about you?' He nodded at my backpack.

'Just came back from the library.'

'They told me at English school that the best way to improve my English was to read, or get an Australian girlfriend.' He winked, then looked away.

I turned and saw a bunch of guys approaching. 'I nearly left without you,' Edo shouted at his mates.

'What's your hurry?' one of his mates shouted back.

'The girls will wait,' another added.

Edo disappeared into the throng as they hugged and slapped each other's backs. I waited on the sidelines for him to say goodbye, but he walked off with his friends.

I turned and met Jesse's sympathetic blue eyes. My stomach churned. That was twice in one day that I'd been an idiot in front of him.

'You forgot it.' My jacket was neatly folded across his arm.

'Thanks.' I swallowed back tears as I took the jacket from him.

'You okay?' Jesse asked.

I clenched my teeth to stop from crying. 'Sure.' He handed me a tissue. I forced myself to meet his eyes. 'Thank you.'

'I'll see you at school.' He walked off.

When I got home Mum was checking the mailbox at the fence. 'What's wrong?' She ripped open an envelope, the word 'overdue' stamped on it in red on the sheet of paper inside.

'I bumped into Edo at the train station,' I told her.

She crumpled the envelope.

'He snubbed me.'

Mum walked me to the house. 'I'm sure he didn't mean it. English isn't his first language after all.'

I took off my shoes. 'He knew exactly what he was doing.'

'You should give him a second chance.'

'No,' I snapped.

'There aren't many nice young Bosnian boys,' Mum urged.

'Don't you get it?' I shouted. 'He's an arsehole and I don't want anything to do with him.' I slammed my bedroom door.

***

The next day I waited until Maths in fourth period to talk to Brian alone. 'Thank you so much,' I hissed when I sat next to him. I'd been stewing all night. 'You ditched me.'

'What's the big deal?' he asked. 'You were with Jesse.' He opened his books. 'Anyway the two of you are the bookworms. I just go along for the ride.'

'You left me alone with Jesse,' I wailed.

'Is this about him liking you?'

'He likes me?' I squeaked.

'Of course,' Brian said. 'Everyone knows.'

Jesse liked me. He really liked me. I broke into a smile.

Brian peered at my face. 'Do you like him?' he asked.

I forced my face into a serious expression. 'No.' I shook my head until I was dizzy. 'I don't.' What was I doing? Was I just happy to be flattered?

'Then it's no big deal,' he said.

***

Friday night I was watching *Home and Away* when Mum walked in front of the TV to peer out of the window. 'Can you quit that?' I asked. She'd been fluttering up and down for the past hour.

'Sorry.' She sat on the sofa. Two seconds later she was up again, twitching the curtain as she checked the driveway. 'He should be here by now.' She glanced at the clock and back out the window.

'Call him,' I retorted.

'I don't want to be pushy.' She sat down again.

'If you don't, I will.'

'You wouldn't dare.'

'Try me.'

She took the phone into the hallway. 'He's not coming,' she said when she returned a few minutes later.

'Good riddance,' I muttered.

'What did you say?' She stood in front of the TV.

'Move.' I tried to look around her.

She snatched the remote control and switched off the TV. 'What did you say about Safet?'

'Good. Riddance.' I pronounced each word slowly.

'You've chased him off,' she whispered.

'You're better off without him.' I tried to take the remote, but she wouldn't let go. She threw it against the wall. It hit with a thud, the plastic splitting open. For the first time I noticed the look in her eyes and goose-pimples rose on my skin. How could I have missed it?

'Stop!' Dido yelled from the kitchen where he was watching the second TV.

'It's always you!' Spittle shot from her mouth and she slapped me on the face.

I froze, my body going into lockdown.

Her hand swung back and hit me again, this time landing against the side of my head, on my ear. Dido rushed into the living room and grabbed Mum, pulling her away from me.

'She did it, she did it!' Mum shouted as she tried to break from his hold. 'She always ruins everything.' Tears and snot dribbled down her face.

'Sabiha, go to your bedroom!' Dido yelled as he held Mum. 'Sabiha, Sabiha!'

I couldn't move.

Mum tore out of his arms. He jumped between us and shoved me away.

My legs worked again and I ran from the room. I looked over my shoulder and saw them go down on the sofa in a tangle of arms and legs. When I got to my bedroom I locked my door and leaned against it. I expected her to break it down. My cheeks and left ear ached. I grabbed my pillow and cried into it, not lifting my head until I was faint.

This was my fault. I had suspected she wasn't taking her medication, but I let her convince me otherwise and now it was the time of reckoning. I was ten years old the last time Mum stopped taking her medication. She hooked up with a guy who claimed he was a *hodža*, but he wore regular clothes and only knew one Arabic prayer that he repeated over and over like a chant.

He made holy water by putting tap-water in a bottle and dropping in folded pieces of paper that he'd written Arabic prayers on. He cleansed our house by chanting as he walked through every room, splashing water on the furniture.

The fake *hodža* gave Mum the bottle and told her to drink it three times a day and pray after each drink. In return Mum gave him a fifty-dollar note. When I told Frankie about the *hodža* she said he was a quack. Muslims didn't believe in holy water or superstition. It was against God.

A month later Mum got the sickest she'd ever been. It ended when she locked us in a bedroom and the police had to break in and drag her away. From then on I supervised her meds, but I'd become complacent. My own dramas took precedence and I'd assumed Dido would be a stabilising influence.

You'd think by now I knew the signs when Mum was getting sick, but somehow every time it happened it was a punch to the gut. Some parents are heavy-handed and lay into their kids like it's a world championship event and they're competing for gold. Other parents think that kicking the shit out of their kids to ease their frustration is their right; and then there were parents like Mum.

Mum hated physical violence. When I was a kid an ex-boyfriend slapped her. She crouched on the floor like a grenade went off, while I tried to kick him. I guess her passive nature made me the aggressor in order to protect us.

So when Mum hit me all the little signs I'd been ignoring came together. Tonight I'd seen in her eyes that she was walking the tightrope between sanity and the place where the alien invaders held her hostage.

In the morning I examined her pillbox. The punch to my gut became a cannon ball. Dido walked in and I showed it to him.

He took the pillbox from me. 'I'll talk to her.'

'I want to be there.'

He sat at the kitchen table.

'You don't know what it's like when she's sick.' My voice was doing a Minnie Mouse imitation as I fought back tears.

Dido nodded. 'When you come home from *mejtef*.'

I didn't know whether he was being for real. I thought about ditching *mejtef* and staying home so he didn't cut me out, but that would set him off.

His face looked like it was in spasm. A sure sign he was fighting his temper. He nodded.

***

When I came home from *mejtef* Dido and Edin were playing chess. I poured myself an orange juice and checked the pillbox. The meds for Saturday were still in there, along with those for the last three days.

'Did you talk—'

'No—' Dido cut me off and made his move on the chessboard.

'Where—'

'Milkbar.' He gave me a shitty look.

'Okay, okay.' I made myself a sandwich and took it into the living room. As I ate I stared at the door, waiting for Mum to come home. When she walked in ten minutes later, the bread in my mouth became cardboard.

Her eyes were glowing. She had that far away look on her face like she was listening to a conversation only she could hear. She glanced at the clock. 'I have to pray.'

'Aha!' Dido's war cry signalled he'd won the game.

'Again?' Edin asked.

'Tomorrow.' Dido walked Edin out. When he returned he sat on the other end of the sofa.

'She didn't take any of her tablets today,' I said.

I went cold as we heard her praying. At first her mutterings sounded like gibberish, but my ears pricked up and I recognised the odd word here and there. She was mixing English, Bosnian and Arabic words.

'Turn on the television,' Dido said, passing me the remote.

She was one step from returning to the loony bin. When she'd finished praying she came into the living room. I waited for Dido to speak, but he was smoking his cigarette like it was his last on earth. Coward.

'Mum—' I started.

'Bahra.' Dido gave me a dirty look, but he spoke to Mum like she was his five year old daughter again.

Chapter 16

'Have you been taking your tablets?' Dido asked.

'I don't need them anymore.' She smoothed her skirt.

'Why?'

'All I need is to pray.'

'If you don't take your tablets you'll get sick,' Dido said gently.

Mum shook her head vehemently. 'I pray to *Allah* and I won't get sick.'

'And *Allah* hears your prayers, but he created medicine so it helps you.' Dido nodded to me. I handed Mum the glass I was holding and put the pills into her hand.

She chucked them into her mouth and swallowed in one gulp. 'I'm going to lie down,' she said and left the room.

'She needs to see a doctor.' I lowered my voice. We had a regular doctor Mum used to see when we lived in Thornbury, and she still had repeat scripts left over from him, but since we'd moved to St Albans she didn't see anyone.

'She'll be fine.' Dido shook his head.

'Didn't you hear her praying?'

'If she believes it helps her then perhaps it does.'

'Last time she didn't take her meds it ended with the cops surrounding the house and knocking her out with tranquillisers,' I bleated.

'We'll see.' Dido rolled another cigarette. 'Leave it to me.'

He seemed to think a miracle was in the making and after sixteen years of illness, Mum would wake up and be normal—all because she prayed. I walked past her bedroom. She was lying on her bed and I shuddered at the malevolence in her burning gaze.

Dido assumed that because Mum started taking her tablets everything was all right, but I knew better. She needed to go to the doctor to get the dosage adjusted or she could still tip into crisis. I needed to get help. There was only one person who understood what Mum was going through.

***

I left home Sunday morning while Dido and Mum were asleep. I'd propped a note on the fridge saying that I was spending the day with Dina. When I called and woke her, Dina was furious, but when she realised she got an extra day with Tony while I undertook my rescue mission, she was more agreeable.

I arrived at Frankie's at eight a.m. It was too early, but she'd understand. This was an emergency. There was a time when I was a regular visitor and used to come and go as if it was my own house.

I took a deep breath and knocked. There was no answer so I knocked a few more times. Finally I heard footsteps padding on the floorboards in the hallway. The door opened. Frankie was wearing a T-shirt, her hair was dishevelled. 'Sammie, what are you doing here?' Her voice was slurred.

'I need your help,' I said. 'It's about Mum—'

Frankie shot up from her slouched position against the doorway. 'She's not with you is she?' Frankie demanded, her face clearing of sleep.

'No,' I said.

'Good, good...' She relaxed again.

'She's not taking her medication,' I said.

Frankie frowned. 'That isn't good,' she muttered. It was Frankie who called the police last time.

'I need you to talk to Dido. He's not taking it seriously. He thinks she's going to recover like *that.*' I snapped my fingers.

'Sammie, I'd like to help,' Frankie said.

I breathed a sigh of relief.

'But I can't involve myself in someone else's family business.'

'You *are* family,' I said.

Frankie shook her head with a pitying look. 'No, Sammie, I'm not.' She reached out and put her hands on my shoulders. 'Your Mum and I were friends, but when she moved to St Albans she chose to have a life that I'm not part a of.'

'Frankie, who's there?' a male voice shouted from inside.

'No one.' Frankie called out, pulling the door closed behind her. 'I've got to go—' Frankie began when the door wrenched open behind her.

'Who the hell shows up on a Sunday—' he stopped mid-sentence. It was Dave, wearing boxer shorts and nothing else.

Frankie and Dave watched me anxiously. Numbness washed over me. So this was why she couldn't help me. No wonder, when she was sleeping with her ex-best friend's ex-boyfriend.

'Sammie, believe me, we didn't start seeing each other until after your Mum and Dave broke up,' Frankie said.

As Frankie talked, I joined the dots. Now I knew who she had a date with the last time I dropped by unannounced, and why her friendship with Mum had gone into deep freeze.

'Your mother doesn't know,' Frankie said. 'And considering her vulnerable state it's best if she doesn't find out.'

'What's going on with Bahra?' Dave asked.

'I have to go.' I stepped off the porch. 'I'm sorry for interrupting...' I ran out of words. 'I'm sorry.' I turned and headed for the street.

'Sammie, wait!' Dave called. I slowed my steps, about to turn around. I knew Frankie wouldn't leave me hanging.

'Let her go,' Frankie said. 'We can't help her now.'

I sped around the corner and out of sight from the house. I didn't know where I was heading until I got there. The one person who had always comforted me. As I stood at Kathleen's gate, the front door opened. My heart lifted. Kathleen must have seen me.

Shelley closed the front door behind her. She was wearing a dressing gown over her pyjamas and held a black garbage bag. Her body stiffened when she saw me.

'Sammie, what are you doing here? I know Kathleen doesn't want to see you.'

'Bullshit!' I pushed the gate open. 'You're telling lies again.'

'No, I'm not.' Shelley dropped the rubbish bag on the ground and opened it. She pulled out a shiny piece of nylon. 'See, we had a birthday party for her.' She held up a Happy Birthday banner. 'And she didn't invite you.' She returned the banner back to the rubbish bag. 'I know it's difficult for you to accept, but friendships change, people move on.'

Seeing her pity, something inside me snapped. 'You lying bitch.' I shoved her. 'You're loving this!'

She stumbled back, quickly righting herself. 'You're the one who refused—'

'What do you mean I refused?' I shouted. 'Was this the birthday party you were inviting me to?'

Shelley turned her face away.

'How could you?' I opened the gate, determined to see Kathleen.

'I tried inviting you. You have only yourself to blame.'

'No, you're the one to blame.' We stood nose to nose. She panted like a dog as her asthma kicked in, her soft puffs of breath hitting my face. 'Kathleen only keeps you around because she feels sorry for you,' I grunted.

She took the inhaler from the pocket of her dressing gown. 'Maybe she keeps me around because I'm not a selfish bitch like you.'

I pushed her again and she dropped the inhaler on my foot.

'Watch it!' She was scared now. 'Or I'll get my cousins Sharon and Karen to come by your house again.'

I stopped, all the pieces of the puzzle coming together. 'The Twins are your cousins?'

She nodded jerkily. 'Yeah, and they'll bash you again. All I have to do is make the call.'

A red mist swept over me. My ears popped and all sound faded. I saw each strand of Shelley's hair lifted in the wind and then everything sped up in a blur. When I came back to myself Shelley was lying on the ground, her hands clutching her stomach, her eyes wide with panic as she fought to breathe.

I tried to run away, but my legs felt shaky and my stomach heaved like I'd swallowed a large oily fish and it was swimming in my guts. She grunted behind me, trying to call out, but I started to run, my balance wobbly like a toddler's. When I heard the ping of metal under my feet as I hurtled away, I didn't look down but forced my legs forward faster.

I reached High Street and crossed, feeling the press of air as a car whizzed a few inches from my body. Horns blared, cutting through my panic. I slowed down and half walked, half ran, images of what I'd done in front of me: my hands pushing Shelley and her falling backwards in slow motion, turning in the air and landing on her side.

While she was on the ground I had kicked her, grunting as my foot connected with her stomach, my toes jamming into her soft flesh until I hit her ribs and my foot bounced back out. She'd jerked on the ground with each kick, her hands clutching her belly as she tried to protect it, her mouth open like a black hole in her face while she screamed noiselessly.

I fell onto the grass and vomited up my breakfast. At Flinders Street station I found the toilets and hid in a cubicle. I covered my mouth with my hand and muffled my sobs. What had I done? I'd bashed Shelley, the one person who had it in for me. All she had to do was contact the police and I was stuffed. I remembered my foot hitting her inhaler as I'd escaped and Shelley's red face as she writhed on the ground, fighting for breath.

What if no one found her and she kept writhing on the ground in silence, as her chest constricting? What if I'd killed her? What if she died on Kathleen's front lawn and the police was after me for murder? I got out my mobile and called Kathleen's house phone.

'This is Melissa, Shelley's sister,' I said when Kathleen's mum answered. 'Can I talk to Shelley?' I made my voice high-pitched and hoped she wouldn't recognise me.

'I'll get her,' Kathleen's Mum said.

I exhaled and hung up. I wasn't a murderer. But just as quickly my relief faded: if Shelley was alive she'd dob me in to the police. I was definitely stuffed.

When I got home I lay in bed for the rest of day, alternating between depression and terror. I wanted to call Kathleen, but Shelley had probably given her side of the story. Anyway, this was the last nail in the coffin of our friendship.

Frankie was supposed to be Mum's best friend, and Kathleen mine. It was as if our life in Thornbury was a temporary aberration: Kathleen and Frankie had resumed their lives as if we'd never existed.

***

On Monday morning at school Brian and Jesse were waiting when I arrived at the oval. 'Hello, Miss Sunshine,' Brian sang out, buzzing like he was a battery-powered appliance. 'It's only six days to my paaar-ty!' The closer it got to the party, he became more obnoxious he became.

'Yeah, I know.' I was incapable of faking cheer. I'd spent the whole night awake, an invisible clock ticking away the minutes of my freedom: any minute the police would knock on my door and take me away in handcuffs.

'Geez, did someone die?' Brian asked.

'I've got stuff going on,' I said. 'Can we talk tonight?' I needed to get advice, to figure out if there was anything I could do to avoid jail.

He frowned. 'I'm not sure...' He was distracted now, waving to Adnan and then he walked off.

I lifted my hand to my face, I was about to cry. Was I such a terrible person that I couldn't keep any friends? I tried to wipe my cheeks discreetly so Jesse didn't see.

'Sabiha, are you all right?' he asked.

The sympathy in his voice was my undoing. A sob built in my chest. Not here, not now, not in front of Jesse. I ran for the toilet blocks. I'd rather be a coward than be pathetic. I got as far as the Arts class doorway before I crumpled and covered my face in my hands and wept.

Something dropped to the ground next to me. I peered through my fingertips and saw it was my backpack. I was pulled to my feet and Jesse held me.

'It will be all right,' he murmured, his hands rubbing my back.

Our cheeks were pressed together and stubble scraped my skin. I'd always thought he was chubby under his loose clothing, but now that we were cheek to cheek, I realised I was wrong—his solid build was the most soothing thing I'd felt in ages.

I leaned back so I could breathe. He lifted his hand and brushed my hair behind my ear, before wiping a tear from under my eye. My breath caught in my chest at the tenderness of his gesture. Lately it seemed like all the people who were supposed to care about me turned away instead; yet here was Jesse, whom I'd treated terribly, showing he cared with his every gesture.

'Tell me what's wrong.' He reached into his pocket and passed me a hankie.

'I'm going to jail,' I wailed as I blew into his hankie.

'What the...? Start from the beginning,' Jesse commanded.

I blurted my story.

'I don't think you have anything to worry about,' Jesse said.

'Haven't you listened to what I just told you?'

'Sabiha.' Jesse put his hands on my shoulders, forcing me to look at him. 'If she goes to the police then it will come out that her cousins bashed *you*.'

'Oh...'

'See...' Jesse stroked my arm. 'I told you everything would be all right.'

I shook my head, remembering my original problem. 'No, it's not' I avoided his gaze. 'My Mum's getting sick again.' I was on the edge of tears again.

Jesse reached over and took my hand in his. 'What's wrong with your Mum?'

By the time I told him everything, the bell had rung. 'Are you okay to go to class?' he asked.

I nodded.

When the bell rang for recess, Jesse walked me to my locker and Brian followed. After we swapped our books Jesse took my arm and led me down the corridor. 'Aren't you coming to the oval?' Brian asked.

'Not today,' Jesse said, without breaking his stride. We sat under the elm tree and I told him the rest of my drama. As I talked and talked, Jesse's blue eyes met mine, his attention never wavering. Nobody looked at me like that and it was intoxicating. He made me feel like I mattered. 'I'll see you in History,' he said as we went our separate ways for third period.

I had science with Gemma and Dina. 'Are you and Jesse going out?' Dina asked, as I sat on the seat that she'd saved for me.

'No.' I pulled my notebook out of my backpack. 'As if. He's just a good listener.'

'What's going on with you two?' Gemma leaned over Dina to talk to me.

'Nothing,' I said pointedly.

Dina and Gemma were curious and usually I enjoyed tormenting them, but all I wanted was for them to leave me alone.

We all ambled to the oval at lunchtime, but our huddle was out of whack.

'What's with you and Jesse?' Brian asked.

'He's being a friend.'

'Looks to me like he's more than a friend.' His tone was snide. His eyes shifted. I'd lost his attention and I knew without looking behind me that Adnan was approaching.

'Not that you'd know what a friend acted like.' My voice was full of sarcasm.

'What do you mean?' Now Brian was defensive.

'Maybe if stopped being so impressed with Adnan you'd know,' I snapped. Brian looked shocked. I moved away from him and went to stand by Jesse.

When I arrived at school on Tuesday, Jesse was waiting for me by the bike rack. 'I talked to my sister about your mum.'

'Why?' I asked.

'Sarah's a nurse and I thought she might be able to give us advice about what to do.' He handed me a few sheets of paper. 'You need to read it.'

The heading on the first page was 'Symptoms of Bipolar Disorder.' I stood reading the handout as he waited next to me. When I finished a few minutes later, I gaped at Jesse in wonder. 'This description fits Mum to a T,' I exclaimed. 'I've always known the name of her illness but I've never really understood it.' I sat on a bench next to the bike rack.

'Now I can see there were signs all along. She did all these things.' I read from the paper. '*Spending money recklessly, hyperactivity, high energy levels, inappropriate behaviour, mystical experiences.* It's just that we didn't know.'

The first clue was her hyperactivity and her staying up into the early hours of the morning cleaning the house over and over. The second clue was the way she spent money like water and bought unnecessary things. Considering what a natural tight-arse she was, any excessive spending was clearly pathological. Then there was her sudden generosity. When she was in the grip of illness, whenever someone came to visit she'd hand them a gift, usually something we owned. Once she'd even given away her sewing machine.

The people with a conscience would take it so they wouldn't hurt her feelings, and then return it later. Those without a conscience took it with a disbelieving smile. And arseholes took her gifts and pointed out other things that would be of use to them. Once we went without a toaster and a kettle for a month until she scraped enough money to replace them. In her frenzy of spending and gift-giving Mum also forgot to pay the bills.

Then there were the physical changes, only visible when she was so far gone. Her eyes glittered, the pupils shrinking so that the bright green of her iris glowed. Scratch marks appeared on her body: the nerves made her twitchy and itchy so that she scratched herself until she bled. And she couldn't talk. It's like her tongue got too thick for her mouth.

But the worst part was that when you met her eyes—there was fear. It was like there was a part of her brain still aware, but she couldn't stop herself. Sometimes the aliens would lose control, for just a second, and I'd see my real Mum, but soon enough they repossessed her.

I hated the way people treated her when she got sick. Most got angry and told her off, as if she could stop what she was doing. Others treated her like the village idiot and egged her on for their amusement. And there were a few who'd see beyond the alien invaders and realise that somewhere deep inside, my Mum was still there, and they'd treat her the same—like she had a few too many drinks at a party and they'd have to wait for her to sober up.

And me, well I pretended there was nothing wrong. Somehow, despite all the times I'd experienced it, I closed my eyes to what was happening. I was always terrified that my life would unravel when she got sick. I couldn't face it, so I pretended everything was okay and I closed my eyes to all the warnings, until the event that punched me awake.

'Why didn't she tell me?' I felt betrayed. 'If I'd known I could have watched over her.'

'She probably didn't know herself,' Jesse sat next to me, our legs pressed together. 'Sarah told me that a lot of people who come from overseas don't know how to translate the medical jargon. My sister included contact details for the CATT team.'

Jesse flipped the handout to the last page. 'You know the Crisis Assessment Treatment Team, that professionals or family members can call in an emergency.'

'I don't think I need to. Mum seems to be taking her medication again.' I'd been checking it every day and there wasn't a miss since Dido and I had talked to her. Calling the CATT team would be I was dobbing Mum into the authorities. I couldn't betray her like that.

'Okay...' Jesse folded the handout and returned it me. 'It's there if you do need it.' As I took it, our hands touched.

'I can't believe you did this.' I was embarrassed as I remembered all the things he'd done for me, and yet I'd given him nothing. I held his hand.

'That's what friends do,' Jesse said, gripping my hand.

His eyes telegraphed that he wanted more than friendship. Gratitude overwhelmed me. I leaned in. Jesse's eyes widened.

Chapter 17

'Hey, lovebirds,' Brian called out as he approached. He caught of the paper in my hands and he snatched it. 'What's this?'

I grabbed the pamphlet back. 'What do you care?'

'Of course I care,' Brian said. 'We're friends.'

'Yeah, right,' I muttered under my breath.

'Sabiha, what's going on?' Brian asked.

'If you were a *real* friend you wouldn't have to ask that question,' I shot back.

'What does that mean?' Brian demanded. 'I *am* a real friend.'

'A *real* friend cares about what's going in your life.' I gestured at Jesse. 'A *real* friend doesn't dump you as soon as something better comes along.'

'A *real* friend would understand that you have a life and can't be at their beck and call twenty-four seven,' Brian said.

'A *real* friend would sense when you're in need.' I stood and we were facing off.

'A *real* friend would tell you something was going on instead of taking pot-shots,' Brian shouted.

'Enough.' Jesse stood between us.

'He's the one who—'

'She—' Brian and I spoke over each other.

'Cool it!' Jesse shouted. 'Brian, we've been friends a long time.' Jesse placed his hand on Brian's chest. 'You do sometimes get caught up in new things and forget about everyone else.'

Brian stared at the ground and kicked a pebble with his shoe.

Jesse turned to face me. 'And Sabiha, you can't expect people to guess when something is wrong. You have to tell them.'

'I guess,' I said, chastened.

'Now are you two making up?' Jesse asked as he looked from one to the other.

Brian made a face.

I sucked in my lips to stop a smile.

'All right, Dad.' Brian grabbed Jesse into a hug.

'Get off me!' Jesse tried to push Brian's arms off. Watching them grapple I burst into laughter and grabbed hold of Jesse's arm. Brian threw his arm around me and pulled me in so that I was between him and Jesse. Jesse laughed, his chest against my back while Brian was pressed up against my front.

'Oooh an orgy.' Dina said as she and Gemma came around the corner, Adnan following.

'We need one more girl for this orgy!' Brian grabbed Dina's arm and pulled her into the circle. We laughed at Dina's giggles as Brian tried to pash her. Our laughter was infectious and Dina started up too.

'Let her go!' Gemma beat her hands against Brian's back.

'There's room for you too.' Brian turned to Gemma.

'Yuck,' Gemma exclaimed as she stopped hitting him.

The bell rang and we all moved away from each other, suddenly self-conscious, straightening our clothing as we headed to class.

Brian walked beside me. 'I'm sorry for not being there for you,' he said.

'It's okay.' I felt lighter than I had in days.

'I'll call you tonight,' Brian said. 'Cross my heart.'

Brian kept his promise and I brought him up to speed over the phone with everything that happened.

'That's some heavy shit,' he said when I'd finished.

'Yes, it is.' I was lying on my bed staring at the ceiling.

'How are you feeling now?' he asked.

'Better. I think Mum is turning a corner.'

'And it's definitely over with Kathleen?'

'Definitely. Shelley would have told Kathleen her version of our fight—with me as the villain.'

'I agree with Jesse,' Brian said. 'Shelley won't go to the cops because it would expose her cousins.'

'Yeah, I s'pose...' I'd been thinking about it: Shelley and I were at a stalemate. Now that I knew it was her cousins who had bashed me I wanted to press charges to get Shelley in the shit, but then she could press charges against me.

'Sounds like you're better off without either them in your life. That whole threesome thing sounds toxic.'

'Mmm,' I murmured, wondering if there was a secret Jesse and I shared, that Brian wasn't privy to. But I had to assume that my new threesome was a whole lot better than my old one, or else I was truly the worst judge of character ever.

'The great thing is you've got the party to look forward to,' Brian announced triumphantly. 'Only four more sleeps.'

'Fifteen minutes.' I looked at the clock.

'Fifteen minutes for what?' Brian was confused.

'You lasted fifteen minutes before bringing up the party.'

'Wasn't it time to shift the conversation from this depressing shit to something fun? Of course, I'm happy to keep talking about your mum—'

'No, no,' I interrupted him.

'If you're sure...' Barely leashed excitement crept into his rising intonation.

'I am.' I needed something to look forward to.

'Okay, I'm picking up our costumes tomorrow.' I couldn't dress at home because Dina and I were faking sleeping over at each other's house, so Brian was keeping my costume at his place. I just hoped things weren't getting too complicated.

***

The rest of the week flew by. The gang hung around together at school and all our conversations were about the party.

On Saturday I caught a bus to Brian's house. 'Sabiha.' He looked surprised when he opened the front door. 'You're early.'

I tapped my watch. 'It's five o'clock.'

'Already?' Brian lifted my wrist and checked the time. 'You can get dressed in my parents' bedroom.'

A man walked up the footpath behind me. 'Here!' He tossed bags of ice to Brian, who introduced me to his brother Greg.

'Sorry, it's a bit crazy right now,' Brian said as he carried the bags to the kitchen. 'Go get ready.'

I walked hesitantly down the hall and into his parents' bedroom. I sat on the bed—the one I'd be sleeping in tonight. Comfortable. My costume was hanging on the door. I took out my make-up from the backpack.

After twenty minutes of applying make-up, I examined myself in the mirror and smiled. With my dark hair, light eyes and red lipstick I made a respectable Wonder Woman.

I was way ahead of schedule. I'd allowed two hours for getting ready, forgetting that it usually took that long because Kathleen and I would do each other's hair and make-up, giggling and carrying on as we planned our night.

'Enough already,' I grumbled as I sorted my bag. That phase of my life was over. I found Brian in the bathroom putting beer in the half-full bathtub. 'What do you think?' I crossed my arms in the Wonder Woman signal.

Someone whistled behind me. I spun around. Greg had appeared holding a slab of beer. 'You look amazing.' His eyes were on my chest.

My costume was probably a size too small and the corset top pushed my breasts up so that they nearly hit my chin. 'Thanks.' I crossed my arms over my bulging boobs.

Brian took the box from Greg. 'Get out of here.' He slapped him on the back.

'Do you think it's too much?' I asked.

'You're supposed to be Wonder Woman.' Brian sat on the edge of the bathtub and put the beer cans in the icy water. 'There's no such thing as too much.'

'What do you want me to do?'

'All done.' He crushed the empty box. 'I'm getting ready now.'

I followed him to the bedroom. He closed the door and reached for his fly. I turned away.

'Actually,' Brian said over the rasp of his zipper. 'Do you reckon you could go around and see how Jesse's doing? He should be here by now. I bet he's freaking out.'

'I can't go out like this.'

Brian opened his wardrobe and handed me a trench coat. 'Wear this.'

I bundled myself up and walked down the street slowly. I wasn't sure whether it was a good idea to see Jesse. Since the day he'd been my shoulder to cry on we hadn't been alone. When I reached his house I kept going. I'd just walk around the block to kill time until Brian dressed.

A woman called my name. I turned and saw Sarah, Jesse's sister, running after me. 'This is our house.' She grabbed my arm and tugged me down the driveway.

'I was just going to—'

'Shhh...' Sarah put her finger over her lips. 'Jesse's trying out his costume. You can surprise him when he comes out.' She pulled me through the front door. The living room was dark and cluttered. The walls were covered with stripy wallpaper and the carpet was dark and shaggy.

'Sit.' Sarah pushed me onto the brown sofa. 'I'll get you a drink.'

'Sarah,' I heard Jesse yell. 'What the hell have you done?'

'Come out here so I can see!' Sarah shouted back as she handed me a glass of orange juice.

I took a sip and nearly choked when Jesse entered the living room. He was wearing a Zorro costume. It was a size too small, too. The shirt had a deep V that showed his muscled chest, while the pants moulded to his legs. He definitely wasn't chubby after all. He'd bulked up with muscle and the costume certainly revealed it.

'Sarah, I hope this is your idea of a joke.' He was looking at his boots and didn't see me. He lifted his head and blushed. So did I.

'Doesn't he look great, Sabiha?' Sarah went up to Jesse and pinched his arms. 'Everyone can see his muscles.'

'Um, yeah, he does.' I sipped my drink.

'I'm *not* going like this.' Jesse pushed her hands away.

'Jesse...' A feeble voice called from the back of the house. 'Come here, please, so I can see you?'

Sarah laughed and pushed him towards the door. 'Go show Mum how hot you are.' Jesse grumbled under his breath as he left. 'Bring Mum out here so she can meet Sabiha,' she called out. Jesse broke his stride and gave her a look that I couldn't read. 'It'll be fine,' she urged. Sarah sat down next to me. 'I'm glad he's had you to talk to. The two of you clicked because you have so much in common.'

'I guess we do.' I was surprised Jesse told her about my reading habits.

She shook her head. 'Kids can be so cruel when you have a mother who's different.'

I stiffened. Before I could say anything, Jesse came back into the living room, pushing a wheelchair. Sarah introduced me to their mum.

'Jesse has told us so much about you,' the woman said, her small voice incongruous with her large body. She reached out her hand to me, the dimpled rolls of fat on her arm shaking as she held it in the air.

Jesse's whole body language was a portrait in pleading. Did I look the same when I introduced people to Mum? 'Nice to meet you too.' I clasped her hand, my fingers sinking into the folds of her flesh.

'I'm getting changed,' Jesse said.

'Into what?' Sarah was panicking. 'You haven't got another costume.'

'Peter Parker,' Jesse said smugly.

'No!' Sarah howled. 'Tell him he looks great, Mum.'

'You look very handsome, Jesse,' Mrs James said. 'Do you think so?' She turned to me.

I examined Jesse from head to toe. 'That's a great costume,' I pronounced.

'They got to you,' he said.

I shook my head and smiled.

He relaxed and looked at me approvingly, finally registering what he could glimpse of my own skin-tight number, visible through the partially open trench coat. Only this wasn't the same chest-ogling as Brian's brother. 'Okay, you win.' Jesse lifted his hands in surrender.

Mrs James smiled at me gratefully. Sarah headed for the TV cabinet. 'Photo time.' She held a camera.

'Oh, no,' Jesse groaned.

'Yes, yes!' Sarah shouted as she pulled me off the sofa and pushed me toward Jesse. She watched us through the viewfinder. 'Take off that trench coat,' she commanded.

Jesse's eyes widened at the sight of my outfit revealed in all its body-hugging splendour. Why the hell had I let my vanity get the better of me? The smaller costume was a mistake.

Sarah snapped a few photos. 'Okay, put your arm around her,' she instructed.

Jesse's arm curved gently on my waist.

'You do the same,' she said to me.

Tentatively, I hooked my fingers through his belt loop, feeling his back, taut under the thin shirt.

'You look fabulous.' Sarah continued snapping.

We relaxed and I sunk against him. His hand firmed around my waist.

'Okay, look at each other,' Sarah said.

His blue eyes were steady on me. Even though I'd seen him every day at school for the past three months, this was the first time I *really* saw him.

'It's okay.' He nudged his head toward Sarah. 'I didn't charge the battery.'

Sarah smacked the camera. 'Damn, it's finished.'

'Told you.' Jesse smiled and let go of me.

Trying to retain the sensation on my skin, I placed my hand on my waist where his hand had been. 'We'd better get going,' I said.

'It's only six o'clock,' Sarah said. 'Go and wait in Jesse's room until it's time for the party. That way you can make a grand entrance with your costumes.' She pushed us away from the front door and down the hall.

'But we should help Brian,' I protested.

Sarah cut me off. 'Greg and his mates have done plenty of party set-ups.' She closed Jesse's bedroom door behind us.

More and more bewildered, I stood in the middle of the room, staring at my feet.

'Would you like to sit down?' Jesse pushed his office chair toward me and I sat down obediently. His bedroom was neat as a pin. The single bed was made and the floor tidy. 'Thanks,' he mumbled as he sat on the bed.

'What for?'

'For being nice to my mum.'

'Why didn't you tell me?' I asked, remembering that Sarah had assumed I knew.

He shrugged. 'She has hypothyroidism. Her thyroid doesn't produce enough hormones and her metabolism is slow. It doesn't matter what she eats or what she tries to do, she's obese.'

I wondered if my voice sounded as raw when I spoke about Mum. 'Has she always been in a wheelchair?'

'Just in the last couple of years. It's difficult for her to move otherwise.'

'I still wish you'd told me... It would have made a lot of stuff a lot easier...' He shrugged again and I knew better than to push it. I examined his room. 'How did you get hold of so many books?' Three tall bookshelves took up a wall.

'You have one glaring omission.' I gave him a stern look. 'You don't have any of Stephenie Meyer's books.'

Jesse laughed. 'They're under the bed.'

'That'd be right.' I turned back to the shelves. 'I know you secretly love them even though you pretend you hate vampire stories.'

'Have you read this one?' He stood behind me, his arm reaching for a book over my head, his voice a whisper against my ear. He handed me *Wuthering Heights* by Emily Brontë, his hand floating around my shoulders so that he was almost embracing me.

I shook my head and my hair brushed against his face.

'You'd like it. It's a gothic romance.' His breath fanned my hair.

Our eyes met. His cheek was right next to my mouth. He inclined his head and his lips gently brushed mine, like the caress of a feather. He waited. He was giving me the chance to back away. I leaned in and kissed him. His hands came to rest on my shoulders and he pulled me to him, the book pressed between us like a chaperone as we kissed. He lifted his head. As the glow of the kiss faded I was awkward again.

I didn't know how to stand against him or where to put my hands. He rubbed my arms and leaned down. I thought he was going to kiss me again, but instead he planted a soft kiss on my cheek and stepped away.

'You want to listen to music?' He moved to the computer on his desk.

I nodded, not trusting myself to speak. To buy time I read the back cover of the book. 'Sounds like my sort of novel.' It was described as a vindictive, passionate love story set amongst the wild Yorkshire moors.

'You can borrow it if you like,' Jesse said.

'Thanks.' I glanced at my watch. 'Perhaps we'd better forget the music; we should go.'

He nodded and held the bedroom door open.

Sarah kissed my cheek as I entered the living room. 'Have a great night.'

'Come again,' Mrs James said.

As we walked, our hands brushed against each other. His fingers gently tugged mine. I didn't look at him as I clasped his hand. Music blared from Brian's house.

Jesse stopped.

I turned to look at him.

His eyes were questioning and he was about to speak.

'Let's go, silly.' I tugged him toward Brian's house. I didn't know what he wanted to say, but I knew whatever it was, I was way too confused to hear it.

I knocked on the front door and Brian opened it. He was wearing a lycra green suit covered with black question marks. I dropped Jesse's hand and hugged Brian. 'You look amazing!' I yelled. 'Don't you think, Jesse?'

Jesse smiled. 'Yeah, he sure does.'

'I didn't think you had it in you.' Brian clapped Jesse on the shoulder. 'I thought for sure you'd chicken out and come as Peter Parker.'

'I'll put this in my bag.' I held up *Wuthering Heights* and headed for Brian's parents' bedroom. I closed the door quickly and leaned against it. I broke into a sweat as the urge to run and scream built and built. What had I done? What had possessed me to kiss Jesse? I stared at my reflection in the mirror 'What the fuck are you are looking at?' I demanded, my sneering face ugly and twisted. I slammed out of the room.

Brian was in the kitchen. 'What do you want to drink?'

'That.' I pointed at the Baileys.

I didn't drink alcohol and had never been drunk. I'd had heaps of opportunities whenever Mum and Dave had a party. Kathleen loved sleeping over on those nights. She'd sneak into the party and bring back alcohol to my room. I'd tried drinking with her, but the taste put me off. That, and watching how people turned into idiots when they got drunk.

But tonight I wanted the feeling of carelessness Kathleen described when she got drunk. I wanted the oblivion of forgetting everything. I wanted to forget Mum, Frankie, Kathleen, Shelley, and Jesse. I wanted to forget all the betrayals and the things I'd stuffed up.

He unscrewed the top for me. 'Do you want milk?'

'I want it straight.' I took it from him and skolled from it. The warmth hit my stomach and my stiff muscles loosened instantly.

'Go Sabiha.' Brian exclaimed when I handed him the back the bottle.

'Another please.' This time he half-filled a glass and, sipping my drink I walked into the living room to see Batman, Robin, Spider Man, and a Hulk had arrived. Some of the party-goers were wearing regular clothes, but most were in costume. Jesse appeared beside me, but even his presence didn't break my buzz. I finished my drink. 'You want me to get you something?'

'I'm good.' He held up his Coke.

'You're such a geek.' I examined the drinks on the kitchen table and decided on ouzo next. When I returned to the living room there were a few people swaying to the music. Gemma walked in wearing a Supergirl costume and, before I had a chance to hide from her, she headed my way.

'Where's Dina?' She looked around.

'She'll come by later,' I lied. Since Gemma didn't know about Tony, my job was to bluff Gemma. Dina would murder me if anyone found out she was spending the night at Tony's.

'Here you go, babe.' A man in a Superman costume handed Gemma a glass.

'How cute.' I took a sip from my glass to hide my smirk. Clinging onto the guy's arm, Gemma introduced him as Rob and made the same googly eyes Mum made at Safet. Rob's eyes were glued to my chest. Usually a look like that made me hunch into myself, but now I pushed my chest out further and leaned in. 'Not tonight, honey.' I winked. 'Tonight I'm Wonder Woman.'

Brian was dancing to 'Push It' by Salt N' Pepper. I loved this song. I approached him from behind and curved myself around him. He turned his head. When he saw it was me, he flipped and we ground our hips against each other as we mouthed the words. I don't know how long I danced for, but my mouth was parched. I stumbled into the kitchen and was slurping down orange juice and vodka when Jesse materialised next to me again.

'How are you doing?' he asked.

'I'm having a blast,' I shouted, leaning against him. I'd seen him on the edge of my vision while I was dancing and each time I'd turned away. As I gazed into his eyes now I couldn't remember why I'd been avoiding him.

'With or Without You' by U2 was playing and I swayed as I sang. Jesse took the glass from my hand and returned it to the table. He lifted my arms and put them on his shoulders. He sang in my ear as we slow-danced. I was giddy with happiness. I leaned back in his arms and closed my eyes, enjoying the feeling of hanging in mid-air. He pulled me up and I opened my eyes. All the things I'd tried so hard to forget came back as I stared at his face.

Now, with each word Bono sang, a layer of my happiness faded, as if I was slowly waking from a deep sleep. Jesse's hand gently caressed my face. My heart raced under the weight of expectation and hope in his eyes.

Chapter 18

'Don't do that.' I pushed his hand away.

Jesse tried to pull me back. 'I don't understand.'

'Just don't do it!' I shouted. His face filled with hurt and I reached for the vodka. 'Just don't like me, okay.' I added orange juice and headed for the living room.

I skolled the vodka and put the glass on a lamp table, then drifted out to the dance floor. I gyrated with the crowd, the alcohol coursing through me. I thought I was floating, when suddenly a man's hands pulled me against the front of his body. Assuming it was Brian, I pushed my backside into his groin. Hands cupped my breasts. I wasn't dancing with Brian.

The man turned me to face him. I was dancing with Rob. He pulled me against him, his erection on my thigh. I put my hands on his arms trying to move him away, but he didn't budge. I struggled to get free.

'That's it babe,' he whispered against my ear. 'That's so good.'

I slumped and closed my eyes. My knees gave out and he held me up. He kissed my neck and I moved my head. 'Don't, please,' I whimpered. He ignored me. 'Stop it!' I tried wrenching away.

'You bitch!' Fists hit me in the back and I was drowning in a cloud of red satin. 'He's *my* boyfriend.'

Rob let go and I dropped to the floor. Gemma tried to kick me, but her cape got in her way. Her hands tangled in my hair and she yanked. Rob grabbed her and tried pulling her back.

'Fucking bastard!' She let go of my hair and hit him.

As he dragged her away, I crawled in the other direction, pushing through dancing feet. I pulled myself up against a wall and used it to walk to the kitchen. I was pouring Jack Daniels when Jesse appeared at my side.

'Sabiha, are you all right?' He held my arm and peered at my face in concern.

'I'm bloody marvellous.' My tongue was thick in my mouth.

He took the glass from me. 'You've had enough.'

'No, I haven't.' I hit his arm and reached for the glass.

'Everyone having a great time?' Brian shouted as he walked in.

'I am!' I shouted back and grabbed Brian. 'It's a great party.' I kissed him on the cheek.

'You want some?' Brian asked as he poured himself a drink.

I reached for the glass. 'Fucking oath.'

'She's had enough.' Jesse pushed between us.

Brian took a sip of the glass Jesse had put down. 'It's a party.'

I took the glass off him. 'I'll drink to that.'

'She can barely stand.' Jesse grabbed the glass out of my hand.

'Don't be a bore,' Brian said. 'I'll keep an eye on her.' Someone called his name and he turned in the other direction. 'Hey, Adnan.' He hugged him. 'I didn't think you'd make it.'

'I came when the party started.' Adnan rubbed my hair. 'Hey cuz. So are you a prostitute or Wonder Woman? I can't tell the difference.'

'Ha, ha,' I sneered, brushing his hand away. I felt dizzy. Jesse helped me onto a kitchen chair. I pushed him away. 'I'm fine.'

Brian and Adnan laughed and left the room. Jesse knelt beside me. 'Are you going to be sick?'

'No.' I shook my head and the dizziness intensified. Jesse handed me a glass of water. 'Thanks.' I handed him back the empty glass. 'I feel better now.'

'You need to ease up.' Jesse held a wet washcloth against my forehead.

'I'll be fine.' I took the washcloth from him. 'Brian will take care of me.'

'You need to understand one thing.' Jesse squeezed my wrist. 'Brian takes care of himself first, last and always.'

'No, he doesn't.' I tried to pry his hand away, but his grip didn't ease up. 'He's my best friend.'

'He's been my best friend longer,' Jesse said.

My ears filled with static and I didn't hear anything he said after that. It was Kathleen and Shelley all over again.

'Did you hear me?' Jesse shook me.

I pushed him away. 'Mind your business.'

'Fine.' He threw off my hand. 'You win.' He turned and left, making his way through the crowd.

I collapsed back onto the chair, then stumbled to the bathroom. When I opened the door there were two figures kissing in the darkness. 'Sorry.' I pulled the door closed and went to Brian's bedroom. Slumped on the bed, I closed my eyes, my head spinning and spinning and spinning. Something jostled me. I opened my eyes and saw Brian sitting beside me.

'Are you okay?' He held my hand.

I nodded, but stopped short as my head began to ache. 'I guess.'

My eyes filled with tears and I covered my mouth. He lay down beside me and I curled against him. He caressed my hair and whispered in my ear. I was crying so hard that I didn't realise he was saying sorry over and over.

'It's not your fault.' I cupped his cheek. 'I'm the one who stuffed up and kissed him.'

'You're crying because you kissed Jesse?'

I wiped my face.

Brian sat up. 'I thought—'

I sat up and rubbed his back. 'What?'

'Nothing, it doesn't matter.' He lay down again and pulled me with him. 'So, you and Jesse?'

I nodded and settled my head on his chest. 'Have you ever kissed someone and it felt like heaven?' I listened to the beating of his heart.

'Yes,' Brian said.

I lifted my head. 'Who was she?'

'It's not important.' He pushed my head back on his chest. 'Are you and Jesse together?'

'Nah.' I remembered Jesse's face and my heart started pounding again.

I yawned, and as I moved my head, my face rubbed against Brian's. His beard tickled my face and it felt so nice, I did it again. 'Mmm,' I murmured.

I opened my eyes. Brian was gazing at my lips; his eyes were heavy-lidded. He moved his head closer and kissed me, his tongue tasting of cigarettes and Jack Daniels. Jesse's kiss was gentle and tender, but Brian's kiss was carnal and determined.

He moved on top of me and held himself on his arms, his lower body pinning mine to the bed. As his hips thrust against me, the zipper of his jeans rubbed between my legs and his groin pressed between my thighs. His hand went down my top and he gently squeezed my breast. He stopped as abruptly as he'd started. His breath was heavy over my own panting.

'Sorry.' He kissed my forehead. 'I had to know.' He lay on his back and covered his eyes with his arm.

'Know what?' I asked as I leaned over him. 'Know how this feels.' I kissed him, my hand moving between his legs. As I touched him he hardened against my hand. There was one part of me floating above the bed, shocked at what I was doing. I hadn't even gone to second base with a boy before. The other part of me was thrilled at my daring.

'No, Sabiha.' Brian put his hand on mine and tried to move it away. 'Stop.'

I met his eyes. 'Do you really want me to stop?' My hand was still moving up and down.

I started lowering my head—perhaps Dina and Gemma were right about blowjobs. I'd never imagined doing something like that—at least not until I was in a serious relationship—but I wanted to be close to Brian.

He pulled me back up and cupped my head as he kissed me, pushing me back on the bed. I groped to undo his zipper and put my hand down his pants. As I held him in my hands I was surprised at how soft his skin was. His hand covered mine and he pushed it up and down in a stroking motion. His forehead was pressed against mine and he moaned as warm liquid covered my hand.

I must have fallen asleep because I woke up to his arms squeezing me tight as his chest heaved. It wasn't until his tears dripped on my neck that I realised he was crying.

'I'm sorry, I'm sorry, I'm sorry,' he whispered between sobs.

I wanted to ask what was wrong, to comfort him, but I was so tired I couldn't move.

In the morning I was alone in the bed. I pushed myself up, feeling woozy and nauseous. What had I done last night? I was never getting drunk again. It wasn't worth the agony and humiliation. When I stood my head pounded. I carried my backpack into the bathroom and had a shower. When I got out I heard dishes clattering. I hesitated. How was I going to face Brian after what we had done the night before?

'Sabiha, is that you?' Brian called out.

'Yes.' I shuffled into the kitchen, my eyes on the floor.

'You want some?' He held up two slices of bread.

'Ta.' I sat on the kitchen counter.

'Drink this.' He handed me orange juice.

I wanted to heave when I remembered all the vodka and oranges I'd drunk the night before. He put the toast in front of me and handed me butter and jam. After I'd eaten the toast my stomach settled. I relaxed, pleased that everything was okay between Brian and me. 'I'll help you clean.'

He took the sponge from my hand. 'You'd better get going. Dina called and she'll be home by midday.'

What had happened? She'd made a big deal about me not going home before three o'clock so she could spend Sunday afternoon with Tony. 'Okay.' I lifted my backpack and waited for him to turn. He did, slowly. I kissed him on the lips. He didn't pull away, but he didn't kiss me back either.

'I haven't brushed my teeth yet,' he said in response to my questioning look. He put his arm around my waist and led me to the front door. He lowered his head and I pursed my lips for a kiss. His lips landed on my cheek.

'Maybe I should stay.' I stopped walking. 'We need to talk about Jesse and what we're going to tell him.'

'I can't now. I have to clean up before my parents come home.' He gestured down the hallway. 'We'll talk to Jesse tomorrow.'

At least I wouldn't have to face Jesse alone. Brian had cried after we'd messed around—he must feel guilty about Jesse. But I'd never had doubts about liking Brian and now I finally had the chance to be with him. My mistake had been to kiss Jesse. I'd been vulnerable and I let his attentiveness sway me.

There was no one home to answer my knocking. I used the spare key and went to my room. As I lay in bed with my eyes closed I kept seeing flashes from the night before. Whenever Jesse's face appeared, I was filled with shame. If only I hadn't let him kiss me. I pushed him out of my mind and concentrated on Brian, remembering our night together. It had finally happened and we were officially together.

I waited all day Sunday to hear from him. Whenever I tried calling, his phone was engaged. I started feeling the first inkling of concern.

***

On Monday morning I headed for the oval. Dina and Gemma were waiting. 'Slut!' Gemma headed for me like a bulldog on the attack.

Dina stepped between us. 'Stop it.' Dina pushed her away. 'Is it true?'

'What?' I frowned at her.

'Did you come onto Rob?' Dina asked.

'I saw her!' Gemma shouted.

'He came onto me,' I mumbled.

'Fucking liar!' Gemma was crying. 'He would never do that.'

Dina held Gemma's arm. 'Ease up.'

'No.' Gemma threw Dina's hand off and pointed at me. 'Either you believe me or you believe her.'

'No, Gemma.' Dina held her hand up in a placating gesture. 'Either I believe Sabiha or I believe Rob.'

Gemma's mouth gaped open. 'You're taking that slag's side.'

'I'm not taking sides,' Dina said. 'I'm trying to be fair.'

'You ethnics stick together. Rob told me not to trust you.'

Dina stepped back as if she'd been hit.

'Stop it,' I snapped at Gemma.

'What else did Rob say?' Dina asked, her voice sharp as cut glass.

Gemma turned her head, realising she'd crossed a line.

'Come on, Gemma. Since Rob is such an expert I want to hear all about myself,' Dina baited.

Gemma jabbed her finger at me. 'This is all your fault.'

'No, it's not.' Dina knocked her hand away. 'It's our fault.' She put her arm across my shoulders. 'We're lying ethnics.'

I thought Gemma was going to back down. Her eyes blinked like she was about to cry, but then she squared her shoulders. 'Rob *was* right,' she spat out. 'You can only be friends with your own kind.'

Dina threw Gemma's backpack down the oval. 'Find your own fucking kind!'

Gemma scurried to pick it up and ran off, bumping into Adnan as he walked toward us.

'What was that about?' he asked.

Dina flashed me a look of caution. 'Nothing at all.' She gave him a huge fake grin.

Brian came over. I ran and kissed him on his lips. 'What did I miss?' he asked.

Adnan watched, doing his macho 'head of the family' act as I pulled Brian's arms around me, daring Adnan to say anything.

I closed my eyes and burrowed into Brian's chest. The bell rang. 'I need to talk to you at lunchtime,' I said. We urgently needed to figure out what to say to Jesse. I did *not* want to be responsible for messing up their friendship.

'Sure.' Brian headed to class.

I dawdled. First period was English with Jesse. He looked at me as if he didn't recognise me. I walked to the back of the class, haunted by his stony face.

At lunch Dina and I met at the front of the school. After fifteen minutes Brian was nowhere to be seen. 'I'm going to check the oval,' I told Dina.

Dina pulled out a *Cosmo* magazine. 'Whatever.'

I spent ten minutes checking all the soccer groups. When I ran back, Dina was still on her own. 'He didn't turn up?' I gasped.

Dina shook her head. 'Are you sure he's not avoiding you?' She licked her finger and flicked the page. 'He didn't seem excited to see you this morning.'

It was exactly what I'd been thinking. 'Even if he is,' I admitted. 'It's only because Adnan is being a prick.' It was the only reason I could think of for Brian's behaviour. After all, Brian had come on to me after he'd found out I kissed Jesse. That meant he liked me. 'Right?' I asked Dina after I'd repeated my theory.

'Who knows what goes on in the minds of men?' she asked bitterly. 'Maybe now he's got you, he doesn't want you.'

'Brian wouldn't do that,' I denied, trying to convince myself as well.

The bell rang and Dina put her hand on my shoulder. 'Take it from someone who's no longer surprised by the idiocy of men. Be prepared.' Her eyes were full of pain.

I should have asked her about her weekend, instead of being so self-obsessed. Now I'd neglected her, too. I slowed my steps. I had Psychology and was spending two periods with Jesse. Could this day get any worse?

We'd been working in pairs for a few weeks and, of course, I was partners with Jesse. As everyone matched up, Jesse headed over. I stared at the table. He dropped his folder on my desk. I flinched.

'I've followed up those articles in the library,' he announced as he sat down and read through his notes in a monotone voice. I could feel his distaste at being close to me. 'Is there anything you have to add?'

'Um, no...' My voice was barely above a whisper.

He grabbed his folder and went to stand, but changed his mind. He dropped the folder on the desk again and turned in the chair so that he faced me. 'I want to know why you did it?' Jesse demanded.

I couldn't meet his eyes. 'It just happened—'

'Cut the crap,' Jesse interrupted. 'Why Brian of all people?'

'What do you mean?' I looked up. 'You know I've always liked Brian.'

'Yes, but he's had the talk with you,' Jesse said. 'So I don't understand why—'

'Yes, we had the talk.' I was getting angry. While I knew that I'd treated him badly, he didn't have the right to tell me who I could or couldn't be with. 'He was the one who kissed me. He was the one who changed his mind about us being more than friends.'

'He kissed you?' Jesse asked.

'Yes,' I said. Jesse stared out the window behind me, a perplexed look on his face. 'Jesse I'm sorry about what happened between us,' I said. 'I shouldn't have lead you on when I always had feelings for Brian.'

'Have you talked to Brian since Saturday?' Jesse asked.

'We haven't had a chance—'

'This is a mess.' Jesse put his hands through his hair. 'Sabiha, you must know that Brian is—'

'Class, please face the front,' the teacher said.

Jesse sighed in frustration and returned to his desk.

***

I hesitated before I knocked on Brian's front door. I'd waited for him after school. When he didn't show up I'd walked up Main Road and, before I knew it, I was in his street. 'Just do it.' I psyched myself up and knocked.

His brother Greg opened the door. 'Brian's friend right?' I nodded. 'He's in his bedroom.' He showed me through.

I knocked before pushing the door open and then froze, trying to make sense of what was in front of me. Brian and Adnan were frantically pulling up their pants; their hair was mussed and their cheeks flushed.

'What—' I started to ask, but Adnan rushed over and pulled me into the bedroom.

Chapter 19

He closed the door and pushed me onto the bed, his hand covering my mouth. 'You will *not* tell *anybody* what you just saw.' He squeezed my jaw so hard I could barely breathe.

Brian pulled him away. 'She won't tell anyone.'

'How do you know?' Adnan shoved him. Brian fell into the wall. 'I knew I shouldn't have come to your house.' I thought he would kick Brian. Instead he pulled on his jacket and headed for the door.

'Don't leave like this,' Brian said, following him. 'Please Adnan,' he begged, as he kissed his neck.

There was triumph in Adnan's eyes. I turned away, filled with sickening disbelief: he hadn't been possessive of me this morning, but of Brian. I jammed my hand over my mouth, stifling my sobs. They made suckling noises as they kissed.

'I'll see you tomorrow,' Adnan murmured.

The door closed and I was alone with Brian. He sat next to me on the bed. 'How long?' I asked.

'It was there from the beginning.' He lit up a cigarette. 'But it didn't happen until the party.'

I remembered the two figures I'd seen embracing in the bathroom. 'It was you.' I turned to him. 'You were kissing in the bathroom.'

His eyes were wet with tears. He took a puff of his cigarette, but didn't look at me as he nodded.

'Then why did you kiss me?' I asked.

He exhaled and finally met my gaze. 'I had to know for sure if I was gay.'

I closed my eyes. How could I have been so stupid? He'd all but told me after he kissed me, but I hadn't listened. 'You used me,' I whispered.

What we'd done together now overwhelmed me with shame. We hadn't gone all the way, but we'd done more than kiss.

'Don't play innocent,' Brian said. 'You knew all along.'

I kept shaking my head.

He pulled my face to his and put his forehead on mine. 'Yes, you did.' He moved my head so that I nodded. 'You used me too.'

I opened my eyes. 'No, I didn't,' I whispered.

'I stopped.' He smiled bitterly. 'You kept going.'

I pulled away and ran for the door.

'Will you tell anyone?' he asked.

I hesitated, my hand on the doorknob as I turned to look at him. His back was to me, his shoulders hunched in misery, and a wispy cloud of cigarette smoke floating around his head. I wished I'd never found out. There was no way I could ever tell Auntie Zehra what I'd seen today. I'd destroy their family. Adnan was the golden child on whom they hung all their hopes and dreams on. I left without answering.

I walked out of Brian's house in tears and saw Jesse heading toward me. Why did he always have to see me at my lowest point?

Jesse took my arm and walked me down the street. 'So Brian told you he was gay?'

'When did he tell you?' How come I was the last one to find out?

'I always knew he was gay.'

'Well, I didn't,' I said flatly.

'Will you be okay?' he asked, before I had a chance to get angry.

I nodded. He made me feel worse by being nice to me. He should hate my guts after what I'd done to him. 'I'd better get going.' I edged down the road.

'Okay,' Jesse said softly.

All I wanted was somehow to go back in time: I wouldn't have gone to Jesse's house and kissed him, I wouldn't have got drunk and come onto Brian and I wouldn't know Adnan's secret. I wanted to go back to my state of innocence.

The house was silent when I got home. I walked into the living room and stopped abruptly. Mum and Auntie Zehra were sitting on either side of Dido. Mum had one arm around Dido's shoulders and Auntie was patting his knee. Safet was smoking by himself on the other side of the sofa.

'You heard...' Mum hugged me. 'I know it's sad, baby.' Her touch made me want to bawl again. The phone rang and Mum answered. 'The *dženaza* will be tomorrow at the *džamija* at one o'clock,' she said when she hung up.

The funeral will be at the Mosque... I gulped. What? Who'd died? My head hurt from crying, but I didn't have time to indulge my emotions any more. I had to find out what had happened or all the lies I'd constructed over the past few months would implode.

Mum headed to the kitchen. 'I'll make coffee.'

'I'll help.' I followed her. 'So the funeral is tomorrow?'

Mum nodded as she filled the kettle with water. 'You know Muslims bury their dead within twenty-four hours.' Mum patted my arm. 'It would be nice if you comforted Dido.'

Now I was getting somewhere. It had to be Dido's relative. Didn't he have a brother in Germany...?

'Give him a hug, tell him how sorry you are.'

I peeked at Dido in the living room. His mouth gaped open as he sobbed. I'd only ever hugged Dido once, when he first arrived to Australia and we met him at the airport. Since then our relationship had been based on strict avoidance. I had no idea how I'd hug him or what he'd do if I did.

'It's so terrible for the family.' Mum shook her head as she prepared the tray.

My stomach dropped. Shit. So it wasn't anyone in our family... 'How did it happen?' I was praying for another clue.

'He had a massive heart-attack a few hours ago. Died instantly.' Mum picked up the tray and walked into the living room. 'Turns out he'd had high blood pressure for a while.'

I remained seated at the kitchen table.

'Bring the sugar!' Mum called back to me.

I handed the sugar bowl to Mum and hesitated, working out where to sit. Mum gave me a stern look. I shuffled over to Dido and sat next to him, leaving a space so our legs weren't touching. Mum frowned at me.

I lifted my arm and held it in the air, then gently lay it down on his back, feeling the knob of his spine. I held it there, his heat warming my palm. When he didn't flinch I rubbed his back. He let out a loud moan and I stopped, paralysed, thinking I'd hurt him.

He grabbed hold of my free hand and curled his fingers around mine. 'It's too much.' His eyes squinted shut and tears trickled down the deep creases of his cheeks. 'It's too much pain.'

'How are Suada and Murat dealing with the news?' Auntie Zehra asked. Uh oh...why was Auntie Zehra asking about Dina's parents?

'They're taking it hard. Edin was the only family she had left.'

Edin was dead. Dina's grandfather, my grandfather's chess buddy, almost a permanent fixture in our house. He'd been here only yesterday. Now I was crying too. There was fear in Mum's eyes when she looked at Dido and, for the first time, I faced the fact that one day, possibly soon, Dido would be gone. I'd spent all this time wishing him out of my life and imagining the joy I'd feel; yet now that the possibility existed, I was petrified.

'How's Dina?' Mum asked.

'Okay... I mean, as good as she can be,' I amended, realising how callous I sounded. I was supposed to have been studying with Dina at the library.

It didn't seem possible that Edin could be fine one day and gone the next. If it wasn't for Dido's gasping sobs I would have thought it was a dream. He took shuddering breaths, his hot tears landing on my hand. I leaned on his shoulder and held his hand tight.

Closing my eyes, I pictured Dido and Edin the way they were yesterday, frowns on their faces and cigarettes clamped between their teeth, as they stared at the chessboard. Images swam before my eyes: Brian and Adnan kissing; Jesse's face when he saw me with Brian; Kathleen's face as she walked away from me. Sobs broke from my throat. Dido hugged me.

Auntie Zehra handed us each a tissue.

'You're a good granddaughter.' Dido kissed my cheek, his beard scraping my face. 'The funeral's at one o'clock?' he asked as he took his *fildžan* from the coffee table.

Mum nodded.

I put my hand in the crook of his elbow and he patted it absently as he drank his coffee. 'Can I come?' I asked. I needed to find a way to stay out of school. I couldn't face Brian and Adnan after the recent revelation.

'We'll be going to Suada's house after the *dženaza*.' Mum took a sip of coffee. 'I'm sure Dina would appreciate your company.'

'I'm going to see how she's doing,' I mumbled, and took the phone to my bedroom. When Brian's mother answered the phone, I hung up. I'd automatically rung his number. This time I got Dina's number right.

Her hello was thick with tears. 'Are you okay?' I asked.

'Uh, uh...' She hiccoughed between sobs. 'I've got to get water.'

Just then there was a knock at our front door. I opened my bedroom door and saw Adnan taking off his shoes. I slammed the door shut and turned the lock.

Dina was back on the line. 'Sorry,' she murmured.

'Listen,' I spoke softly in case Adnan was listening. 'Do you want me to come over?' Silence greeted my offer.

'Actually—' Dina began. As I waited for her rejection I tried to think of an alternative to get out of the house. '—that would be great.' Was I mistaken, or was she sighing with relief?

'Okay, I'll be there in a few minutes.'

I opened my bedroom door and called for Mum. 'Can you drive me to Dina's?' I asked when she came to my room. 'She's really upset.'

'I can do it.' Adnan's head appeared over Mum's shoulder.

I made a begging face at Mum.

'Thank you, Adnan.' Mum patted him on the shoulder.

'No—' I almost shouted.

Mum jumped.

'—Suada needs to talk to you about something,' I finished in a rush.

Mum reached for the phone in my hands.

'In person. It's something *really*, really important and she doesn't want to talk on the phone.'

'All right, I'll get my keys.' Mum walked off.

'I'll come with you,' I said loudly, trying to push past him. Once Mum was in the living room, I'd be on my own with him. His malice throbbed in the air like a second heartbeat.

'Mum!' I called.

He didn't budge.

She stopped and Adnan finally let me pass. 'What is it?' Mum asked irritably.

'Sorry.' I grabbed hold of her arm and held on as we walked to the car.

Dina answered her front door. Her eyes were bloodshot and her face was splotchy. Her mum was walking like an old woman, each step carefully measured and her whole body hunched.

'Suada.' Mum hugged her.

I reached out gingerly and placed my arms on Dina's shoulders, holding my cheek close to hers. She rested in my arms. 'Let's go to my room,' she said.

'I'm really sorry about your grandfather.' I closed the door behind me and moved over to her.

Dina stood by the bed and placed a toy teddy bear in a cardboard box. 'Me too.' She turned to the wardrobe and rifled through the hangers.

While her back was turned I bent down to the box of knick-knacks and picked out a photo of her and Tony. She snatched it from my hands and tore it into pieces.

'Did you break up?'

She didn't say anything as she closed the box flaps and sealed it.

I sat next to her on the bed. 'What happened?'

Tears leaked from her eyes. I put my arm around her, expecting her to shrug it off, but she leant her head on my shoulder. When she'd finished crying I handed her the tissue box from her bedside table.

She wiped her face. 'His parents want him to find a good little Macedonian girl, and he caved,' she wailed, folding over and clutching her knees as she cried.

I moved in to her and hugged her. When my back started hurting from holding her up, I lay on the bed and pulled her with me. My arm fell asleep under the weight of her head. We both dozed.

She sat up, clutching her head. 'Shit, my head hurts. What's happening with you and Brian?' She examined herself in the mirror and fixed up her hair and face as she spoke.

'We are so over,' I said.

'So you found out he was gay?'

'How did you know?' I spluttered. 'Did Jesse tell you?' I was filled with rage at my own blindness. Had that bastard told everyone that I was an idiot?

'No...' Dina brushed her hair. 'I always knew.'

'How?' I demanded.

'There were signs.'

'Like what?' I demanded. Was I the only person who hadn't received the 'Gay Radar' memo?

'He doesn't chase after girls the way most boys did. He always cares about the way he looks. He wears make-up. Stuff like that.'

'That doesn't mean anything,' I said. 'Guys can be into those things and not be gay.'

'You're right, but didn't you have a feeling?' Dina asked. 'I always felt like I was hanging around with a girlfriend when I was with him.' Dina put her brush down and tied her hair back. 'Most guys check out girls, even Jesse, but with Brian there was always this nothingness. I never felt that stirring in my stomach that you feel when you notice a guy checking you out.'

Shit. I sat up on the bed. Of course.

I'd always been uncomfortable receiving guys' attention. It brought back memories of Dave's mate who'd tried to molest me. I'd never told anyone, but on the night of the party at our house I had flirted with Dave's mate. I'd revelled in his lascivious attention. He'd said that maybe he would sneak into my bedroom during the party for a proper introduction. I'd giggled and said that I would wait, imitating the way women flirted on television, unaware that my naivety might be misinterpreted as worldliness.

Ever since that night I'd freeze when a man looked at me in the same way. But with Brian that feeling was absent. Because he hadn't seemed to treat me that way and, because I felt safe with him, I had allowed myself to imagine us being together as boyfriend and girlfriend. How deluded and mixed up could you get?

'I'm such an idiot,' I moaned.

'Well, yeah,' Dina said. 'It was visible from an aeroplane that Brian was gay, but don't be hard on yourself. We all make bad calls.'

I thought of Jesse and my hands clenched into fists and my toes scrunched down onto the soles of my feet. What had I done? Even Blind Freddy would have seen it: I liked Jesse and that's why I'd always felt uncomfortable with him. My old guilt about Dave's mate meant that every time there was a connection between Jesse and me, I'd shied away. Somehow I'd never twigged and now it was all too late; I'd ruined everything.

There was a knock and Mum's head poked around the door. 'Sabiha, are you ready to leave?'

I reached over to Dina. 'Sorry again about Edin, Dina… I'll see you tomorrow. Mum and I are taking Dido to the *dženaza*.'

Dina pulled me into hug at the door. 'Thanks,' she whispered into my ear.

'And don't get too stressed about Tony, either,' I whispered back and smiled at her.

The next morning when we reached the *džamija* the car park was full. Dido got out of the car and I went to follow. 'No, Sabiha,' Mum said. 'We have to wait here.'

'Why?'

'Only men go to Muslim funerals.' She nodded outside the window.

I peered out at a group of men huddled at the back of the mosque. It was a windy day and their hair and clothes billowed in the wind. There were no women in sight. Just then a hand waved from a car door not far from us.

'There's Dina and Suada,' I said, pointing.

'Let's join them,' Mum said.

Dina stepped out of the passenger seat and Mum sat next to Suada, while Dina and I sat in the back. Dina's eyes were red-rimmed and swollen. 'How are you doing?' I took her hand in mine.

'All right…' Dina squeezed my hand. Suada cried and Mum hugged her. After a few minutes she pulled herself together. The silence in the car was punctuated by sniffles.

'What's that?' I looked over to where the men were gathered around a large box was draped with the Muslim flag, its green background and a white moon and crescent emblem clearly visible even at our distance.

'The body's in there,' Suada said from the front seat. That was probably more than enough information for me at that point, but she went on to explain how instead of a coffin, a box is made from slats, to transport the body to the graveyard where, draped in its shroud, it's then taken out and laid into the grave.

When she finished explaining, Dina and I peered at each other with disgust. I was so getting cremated.

The *hodža* left the *Mosque*, his white hat a contrast to his black beard and billowing black robe. Suada rolled down the window and we listened as he spoke. 'Please form three rows.' He gestured and waited as the men shuffled into the rows, and then nodded. 'Edin Ćengic was a true believer and during his lifetime he completed his pilgrimage to *Mecca*, the highest duty according to the five pillars of Islam. Edin was—'

A mobile phone rang. The men shifted from side to side, eying each other. Two Arab men stood in the front row, their three-piece suits, bushy beards and black hair marking them as strangers among the jean and T-shirt-garbed crowd. One of the Arab men took the ringing phone from his pocket. When he'd finished the *hodža* asked him to turn it off, enunciating each English word.

'Who are they?' Dina asked.

'They're from the Islamic Society,' her Mum said. 'They do our funerals.'

The *hodža* ran his eyes over the mourners. 'Edin would have been happy to be honoured by so many. In the *Hadith* it's written that if forty men attend the funeral of a Muslim and pray to *Allah* to send the deceased to *dženet*, then *Allah* will grant that wish.'

I counted the attendees. Adnan was in the front row holding Dido up. There were nearly eighty men. I'd heard about the *Hadith* from Dido and I wasn't buying it. But Dido certainly did which is why he'd mention it to any male visitor to ensure he had the requisite number of attendees at his funeral—guaranteeing his spot in heaven.

The *hodža* turned to face Mecca, the direction the casket also faced and lead the prayer. We all bent our heads in the car. I pretended to pray, peeking at Dina until it was over. The ceremony finished ten minutes later when the *hodža* announced that the procession would go to Springvale cemetery where the burial would take place.

'I didn't realise we had to drive to Springvale,' Mum said. 'I don't think I have enough petrol.'

'It's okay,' Suada said. 'Your dad can go with Murat.' Dina's parents drove separately so Dina and her Mum could return home and prepare for mourners coming to pay their respects.

We'd just pulled into Dina's driveway when two cars parked on the street behind us. Over the next hour it was like a revolving door. Since the men were at the funeral it was the women who came over, offering their condolences to Dina's Mum. I ran backwards and forwards, helping Dina serve food and wash the dishes, gossip swirling around me.

'Do you know Safet Kadić?' I overheard a woman ask another as I stacked plates next to them. 'He used to be a Professor of history at Prijedor.' I glanced over and saw the speaker was a woman who wore a *šamija* covering her hair.

'He went to the funeral,' a second woman replied.

'His wife has been trying to find him since the war ended,' the *šamija*-covered woman said.

'His wife is dead,' the second woman said, echoing my thoughts.

'No, they got separated after the war and she's been living in Germany with their two daughters. She got his address from the Australian embassy, but her letters weren't answered.'

Fear cut through me. Mum couldn't take this now. I searched for her in the crowd. She was sitting next to Auntie Zehra and Suada, intent on their conversation.

'Hurry up.' Dina was beside me. 'We're running out of plates.'

'I have to talk to my Mum,' I gasped.

Dina nudged me. 'Not now.'

Reluctantly, I went to the kitchen and helped Dina wash the dishes. By the time we'd finished, the *šamija*-covered woman was standing in front of Mum. Mum's face was white and Auntie Zehra had her arms around her, holding her up. I ran over and took Mum's other arm.

'Let's go.' Auntie Zehra frogmarched us out of the house.

Everyone was quiet as we passed, but as soon as we were out of the room the conversation started up again, like a bunch of hissing snakes. Auntie Zehra helped Mum into the car. She buckled her seatbelt like she was a child.

'It's not true, it's not true!' Mum bashed her head against the window as Auntie Zehra drove us home.

'What did he tell you?' Auntie Zehra asked.

'She's dead. She has to be dead.' Mum was working herself up into a frenzy. I caught a glimpse of her glittering eyes in the rearview mirror.

'Of course he'd say that,' Auntie Zehra said. 'He's riding the gravy train and if he has to kill off a wife and two kids to buy a ticket, he'll do it.'

'Shut up, shut up, shut up!' Mum screamed as she covered her ears. Auntie Zehra met my eyes in the rearview mirror and I shook my head.

'No!' Mum shouted as Auntie Zehra turned into our street. 'I want to see Safet!'

'It's better if we wait at home.' Auntie Zehra pulled into our driveway and parked behind Mum's car. 'We'll call him and he'll come over.'

Mum threw the car door open and ran to the carport.

'What is she doing?' Auntie Zehra yelled as leapt out after her.

'Move your car!' Mum shouted as she got into her own car.

'Bahra, calm down.' Auntie Zehra could have been trying to placate a raging toddler.

Mum reversed, heading straight for Auntie Zehra.

Auntie threw herself back and fell onto the bonnet of her car with a thud.

Mum it the brakes inches from her sister's body and the smell of burnt rubber filled the air. Auntie Zehra stood shakily. 'Are you crazy?' she shouted.

Mum's car lurched forward again.

'Move your car!' I yelled at Auntie Zehra.

Auntie Zehra jumped in the car and reversed, while Mum revved her engine. Mum's burst down the driveway and sped off, swerving down the street.

'Get in the car. We're following her.' Auntie Zehra commanded, rolling down her window.

'She hasn't been taking her tablets,' I sobbed.

'God protect us,' Auntie Zehra whispered.

When we arrived at Safet's, Mum was pacing up and down the footpath in front of his block of flats. Auntie Zehra approached—it was like Mum was a stray cat who could lash out in self-defence. 'Let's wait in my car, Bahra.' She ushered Mum over while I went to our car and took the keys from the ignition.

We waited for an hour, the tense silence broken only by Mum popping her knuckles. Then she saw Safet's car coming down the street. He'd barely come to a stop when Mum yanked the driver's door open.

'Did you know she was alive?' she cried.

'What's with you?' He frowned as he undid his seatbelt. Safeta was in the passenger seat.

'Sevda Muratović,' Auntie Zehra said.

Safet's head spun around.

'She was your neighbour in Prijedor.'

His eyes were fixed on Auntie Zehra's face.

'She says your wife is alive.'

His sister fidgeted in the passenger seat and he gave her a harsh stare.

'You didn't know, did you?' Mum implored.

'Of course not—' Safet got of out of the car and held Mum.

'Sevda said your wife wrote to you,' Auntie Zehra interrupted. 'That the Embassy gave her your address.'

'I never received any letters from her,' Safet retorted, his head muffled in Mum's hair.

'Sevda says she wrote five times and the letters weren't returned.'

Mum lifted her head from Safet's chest. 'He didn't get the letters,' she barked.

'Why don't we go inside?' Safet stroked Mum's back as he walked her to his flat. Safeta went ahead and unlocked the door.

'It's not appropriate for my sister to be alone with a married man,' Auntie Zehra said.

Safet stopped walking. 'I'll, of course, be legally rectifying that.'

'And your daughters?' Auntie asked.

He turned. 'I'll always be their father.'

'Being a parent is more than just a word. I'm sure Bahra would agree.'

Mum rushed at Auntie Zehra. 'He's not Esad. He's nothing like Esad.'

I blinked back tears at my Dad's name. This was getting ugly.

'While I will meet my obligations to my daughters, my life is with Bahra.' Safet reached Mum's side and put his arm around her.

'By obligations you mean you'll give money so your wife can support your daughters.'

'Of course.' Safet's hold tightened on Mum.

'That will be difficult to do without a job.'

'Stop it! We've already worked this out with Dido!' Mum shouted.

'And Bahra's pension will only stretch so far.'

Mum's arm arced back and she whacked Auntie Zehra across the face. Auntie Zehra nearly toppled to the ground. I ran to her side.

'You've already chased away one man I loved, I won't let you do it again!' Mum yelled.

Auntie looked at Mum, shocked. When Mum was healthy she wasn't capable of hitting anyone.

While Auntie Zehra was struck dumb, I pointed at Safet. 'He's lying. He knew his wife was alive.'

'Shut up.' Mum headed for me. 'I'm trying to find you a father, but you're an ungrateful little bitch.' For the first time in ages, I was scared of my mother. Of the emptiness in her eyes, as if she were possessed.

'Come on, let's go.' Safet pulled Mum toward the flat.

'I curse the day I fell pregnant with you!' Mum shrieked, her voice disembodied as the kid in *The Exorcist*.

Her venom took my breath away. My legs were trembling; I was certain I'd fall down, or be struck down by this witch my mother had become.

'She doesn't mean it.' Auntie hugged me. 'Remember, she's sick.'

I grasped her arm as we walked back to her car.

Safet's sister turned around to us. 'My brother isn't a bad man,' she said. 'They were getting divorced anyway.'

It took Auntie three tries to get the key in the ignition. 'What was Mum talking about when she said you chased off the man she loved?' I asked as we drove home.

Auntie's lips tightened. 'When we were young I told Babo about her seeing her boyfriend, Darko. Dido managed to get him fired from his job, and she never saw him again.' She kept looking straight ahead.

'But Auntie,' I cried, 'how could you do that?'

'I have no regrets at all, Sabiha. Your mother married a Bosnian, and you wouldn't be here otherwise.'

The love letters I'd found had been full of passion and now I understood why there was so much tension between Mum and Auntie Zehra, and why Mum sometimes acted like she hated her sister. How could she *not* feel resentful, even after all this time. 'Mum didn't love my Dad, did she?' I murmured.

'Of course she did,' Auntie's response was immediate.

'She married my Dad one month after Darko left.' I knew in my heart now that Mum hadn't married my Dad simply on the rebound, but because she wanted to punish her family.

Auntie pulled up in our driveway. 'She was angry with all of us after Darko. Your father came from Australia looking for a bride and she saw it as her chance to run away.' I stared through the windscreen. Auntie put her hands on my face and turned my head toward her. 'But she learnt to love him.'

I bit my lip. 'She never wanted me.'

Auntie slapped my arm. 'Of course she did. Every mother loves her child. They're a gift from God.'

I pretended I believed her *clichés*, but I knew differently. Every time Mum looked at me she saw the life she'd missed out on with the one man she truly loved.

I pretended to be sick the next day and didn't go to school, not that anyone noticed. Mum was still at Safet's and Dido hadn't moved from the sofa since Edin's funeral the day before. While I sat stunned in front of the TV, there was a knock at the front door. Two police officers stood on our threshold. Fucking Shelley.

Chapter 20

'Does Bahra Omerović live here?' asked the police officer, his name tag identifying him as Constable Twist.

I shook my head. 'She's not home.'

'Is there an adult we can speak to?'

'Not really. My grandfather doesn't speak English.' I wiped my sweaty palms on my jumper.

'May we come in?' Constable Twist persisted.

I held the door open for them and shouted for Dido. When they entered the living room he sat up on the sofa, confused. 'They want to speak to you,' I told him.

He pushed the blanket off and smoothed his hair. 'What do they want?'

The officers looked concerned. 'Call an interpreter please, Constable,' Constable Twist said to his partner.

The other officer turned away as he used his mobile.

'Why aren't you at school?' Constable Twist asked.

'I'm sick.'

'Call the Department of Human Services, too,' he said, turning back to his sidekick, who nodded while he talked.

'They're calling an interpreter.' I pulled him into the kitchen and tried to tell him about the Department of Human Services, but I didn't have the words to explain what a caseworker does and how much power they wielded. It was the DHS that had put me in a foster home when I was little and Mum became sick. It was only when Frankie came into our lives that I'd been safe from their clutches. If Shelley pressed charges then they'd take me away again.

'Call Zehra and tell her to bring Merisa,' Dido said.

'I'll call my Aunt,' I told the officers.

'Does she speak English?' Constable Twist asked.

I shook my head. 'My cousin does.'

Auntie Zehra came straight away. Merisa was at work, but Auntie said she'd called her to come home. The police officers retreated to their car to wait.

'What are they doing here?' Auntie Zehra watched them from the window.

'They're here because of me.' I burst into tears and told them about bashing Shelley.

'Oh Sabiha.' Auntie Zehra held me against her.

'They're bringing the government,' Dido said hoarsely. 'They can take her away.'

'Allah protect us...' Auntie sat on the sofa and pulled me with her so that I was between Dido and her. She plucked a tissue from the tissue box and wiped her eyes. 'We won't let them take you away.'

The police officers returned an hour later with the interpreter in tow. We stood. I held tightly onto Auntie and Dido's hands.

'Bahra Omerović was taken into custody this morning at ten a.m.,' the Constable Twist declared. 'She was discovered wandering in Sunshine Shopping centre disorientated and belligerent. She's been admitted to Sunshine Psychiatric ward.'

My legs gave way and I dropped onto the couch while the interpreter translated for Dido and Auntie. Auntie gasped and covered her mouth with her hand. Dido sobbed.

There was a knock on the door and Constable Twist led in a woman. 'This is Janet Woods, a caseworker with the Department of Human Services.'

I went cold. I knew exactly what was going to happen now. It was a story that had been played out before. They were taking me away. Auntie and Dido argued that they were my family and could take care of me, while the caseworker explained DHS procedures. I had to be taken into care while they evaluated whether my Auntie and Dido were suitable carers.

Ms Woods asked me to pack my things. I tried to leave, but Auntie wouldn't let me go. Constable Twist held her back while the other police officer led me to my bedroom. My mind was frozen. I opened my drawers, but I couldn't get anything out. Ms Woods came in and sifted through the drawers, stuffing the backpack with clothes. She took me by the arm and led me out the front door.

Merisa pulled up in the driveway. 'Sabiha, what's going on?' she asked.

I couldn't speak. Behind me, I heard Dido's sobs and Auntie comforting him.

I kept walking. I'd learnt never to look back because that last glimpse would haunt me. They put me in the police car and Ms Woods sat in the back seat next to me. I closed my eyes and leaned my head against the seat. I don't know how much time passed before the car stopped. Ms Woods helped me out of the car and into a house. A woman bustled to open the door and started chirping at me.

'Sabiha will be staying here for a few weeks,' Ms Woods spoke for me. 'Martha will be taking care of you.'

After she walked back to the car Martha closed the door behind me. 'What would you like to do now?

I stared at her blankly.

'Maybe a lie down.'

I followed her into a bedroom.

'This will be your room while you're staying here.' Martha took the backpack from me and put my clothes away. 'I'll leave you until dinner.'

I lay on the bed and closed my eyes.

***

The next day the caseworker came back to fill me in on my future. As the foster home was somewhere deep in the eastern suburbs, and the court date when my care would be decided was in two weeks time, I chose not to go to school. Ms Woods told me that I would definitely be placed with a family member so I could return to my old school.

She asked if I wanted to visit Mum. I shook my head. I remembered the hatred in my mother's eyes at our last confrontation, the venom in her voce when she told me that she'd never wanted me, and I felt tired again. Even though I'd slept for twelve hours I craved sleep and the oblivion it offered. After Ms Woods left I returned to bed. My days passed in a in a blur of sleep and daytime television.

She returned the following week and took me to visit my family. When the car pulled up in Auntie Zehra's driveway I couldn't get out. Auntie came to the door and led me into the house like an invalid. She sat me down at the dining table and brought out food. I felt as if I was drifting in and out of consciousness. She and Dido talked to me, but it was like their words were coming from inside a tunnel. When I went to respond to their questions, I couldn't make my mouth move.

They left me alone and went to the living room to talk, Merisa acting as a translator for Ms Woods. Snatches of their conversation drifted to the dining room.

'Sabiha's depressed,' Ms Woods said.

'She needs to be with her her family,' Merisa translated for Auntie Zehra.

'Bahra is asking about her. When can Sabiha visit her?' Dido asked.

'Whenever her mother is mentioned she retreats even more,' Ms Woods said.

'Sabiha, Sabiha, Sabiha,' someone kept calling.

I lifted my head from the plate of *pita* I'd been staring at, its spiral shape mesmerising me.

Adnan sat on the chair next to me. 'You're not telling anyone, are you?' he asked, his eyes on the living room door. 'You'd just hurt everyone.'

I stood to leave.

He stood too and gripped my arm. 'Not that anyone would believe you.' He studied me like I was a specimen at a museum. 'You've gone crazy like your mother.'

My arm flesh was pinched between his fingers. As the pain pierced through the fog in my head, a flicker of anger lit into my stomach. I met his gaze and while he stared at my face, I lifted my knee and drove it into his groin. The soft flesh squashed under my kneecap and I kept pushing his balls into his torso. Those fight lessons he'd given me finally paid off. He leaped into the air, letting out a whimper.

'Is everything all right?' Auntie asked from the doorway.

I sat and took a bite of *pita*.

'I was just checking on my cuz,' Adnan said. Auntie nodded and retreated back into the living room. Adnan limped from the kitchen, sweat covering his face as he fought not to make a sound.

Later, I sat on the sofa surrounded by Auntie, Dido and Ms Woods, each of them looking at me with wary concern.

'We want to talk about your future while your Mum is in hospital,' Ms Woods said. 'Your Auntie wants you to live with her.'

I shook my head violently. Auntie looked like she was going to cry. I couldn't tell her about Adnan. 'I want to go home,' I forced out, my voice like a rusty pipe.

'You can't go home,' Ms Woods said. 'There's no one to look after you.'

I looked at Dido.

'Your grandfather is old and needs help himself.'

Ms Woods kept asking me questions. She mentioned Frankie. I lay on the couch and closed my eyes. Someone covered me with a blanket and patted my hair. I smelt tobacco and knew it was Dido's hand gently caressing me. I heard them talking as I drifted in and out of sleep.

'I can stay with Dido and Sabiha,' Auntie said. 'My children are adults and Merisa can take care of the house while I live in Bahra's home.' It was a solution of sorts... even in my befuddled state, I knew I could endure it. I grunted acknowledgement from the couch.

***

Two weeks after I'd been taken away, Ms Woods drove me back home. Dido and Auntie Zehra waited for me on the porch. 'Welcome back,' Auntie said as she embraced me. Dido held me, his raspy beard scratching my face. He'd aged ten years in two weeks.

I walked through the house, haunted by Mum's presence. Auntie had moved into her bedroom. She'd packed up some of Mum's clothes so she could use one side of her wardrobe.

'She's doing better,' Auntie said when she found. 'She's been asking for you.

I touched Mum's hairbrush.

'She misses you.'

I snatched my hand back from the hairbrush and went to my bedroom. Auntie had cleaned it and changed the bedding, but my things were still in their place.

Auntie drove me to school the next day. When she pulled up I held onto the doorhandle, paralysed. All the things I'd avoided thinking about while trying to sleep myself into a coma were waiting for me on the school grounds. 'There's Dina!' Auntie waved at her.

Dina opened the car door and smiled at me. 'It's okay. I'll look after her,' she told Auntie.

'I'll be here to pick you up after school.' Auntie drove off, beeping her horn.

We sat on the picnic table and Dina chatted. I kept looking around, not wanting to be ambushed by Brian or Jesse. I didn't know what I'd do when I saw them, but running seemed like a good option.

'How's your Mum?' Dina asked.

I shrugged. I hadn't seen my mother since the confrontation at Safet's. While I knew I couldn't hold her responsible for what she'd said then, I also knew that when she was sick she said all the things she would normally keep inside. I couldn't help but believe there was some truth in her words and I didn't know if I could forgive her.

'I tried texting you,' Dina said.

'I know,' I replied. I'd received messages from her and Jesse while i was in the foster home. 'Sorry, I didn't want to talk to anyone.'

'That's okay. I can catch you up on all the gossip.' Without waiting for a response, Dina launched into it, instantly more animated. 'Well... Gemma moved out with Rob. She got an apprenticeship to be a pastry chef and isn't coming to school anymore.'

'Have you and Gemma talked?' I asked, now curious.

Dina shook her head. 'Not since our fight on the oval. And I think Brian and Adnan had a fight because they're not hanging out anymore. Do you know anything about that?'

I shook my head. Adnan was a cold-hearted bastard. He'd ditched Brian so no one would find out about them. As much as I hated Adnan I couldn't hurt my aunt and destroy our family by revealing Adnan's secret.

'Adnan has a girlfriend. Her name is Tanya and she's Greek,' Dina continued.

I almost smiled as I thought about what Auntie would do if she found out her precious son was dating a *vlah*. It was something to keep in mind for the future.

Dina went silent.

'Tony?' I asked.

'He's going overseas with his Mum. He's denying it, but I reckon they're going to find him a wife.' I covered my hand with hers. She gripped it tight and leaned into me.

'Hello.' I stiffened as I recognised Jesse's voice.

Dina wiped her face with her hands. 'I've got to go to the bathroom.'

Jesse walked to the front of the table. 'How are you?'

'Okay,' I whispered, terrified, my eyes on the ground.

'I collected your English homework.' He handed me an envelope.

When I pulled out a few sheets I saw that he'd collected notes from all my classes, even the ones we didn't share.

'Why did you do this?' I crushed the envelope in my fist. 'After what I did to you.'

'You didn't do anything to me.'

'What do you mean? I led you on.'

'No.' Jesse's gaze didn't waver. 'I let you.'

There had always been softness in his eyes when he'd looked at me; but since Brian's party it had gone. There was only so many times a person could take rejection before their feelings scabbed over to protect them.

'I always knew you didn't like me the way I liked you.' Jesse sighed and put his hands on the tabletop. 'I thought that if enough time passed...'

My eyes were mesmerised by his hand. It was only centimetres from mine. All I had to do was take it in mine. He'd look at me and he'd know what I was feeling. I wouldn't have to say anything. While he looked away my hand inched toward his, my breath caught in my chest as I got closer.

'But that's not important anymore.' Jesse took a step backwards and my hand landed in the empty space where his had been.

I willed him to look at me. I knew that he'd recognise what was in my eyes.

'Do you want to talk to him?' Jesse asked.

I followed his gaze to the school building and saw Brian peering at us from the corner. When he saw we were watching, he ducked back. I hesitated, desperate to tell Jesse that my feelings for him had changed, but the words kept sticking in my throat.

'He wants to apologise about what he did,' Jesse said, misinterpreting my silence, still looking at where Brian had been.

'Okay,' I said. Now wasn't the time. I'd have to find a way to tell him later.

Jesse signalled for Brian to come over. 'I'll leave you guys to talk,' he said.

'Hi...' Brian appeared next to me. 'I'm sorry—'

'I'm sorry—' We spoke at the same time and both stopped abruptly.

'Why are you sorry?' I asked him.

'For kissing you.' His hair was mussed, while his normally immaculate clothes were wrinkled. 'I only kissed you because I thought that if there was anyone I could not be gay for, it would be you.'

'Oh...' I murmured after a few seconds of silence. I didn't know whether to be happy or angry.

'Why are you sorry?' Brian asked, his face was creased in puzzlement.

'For kissing you,' I said. 'I guess I always knew on some level you were gay, but I never allowed myself to acknowledge it... so I confused the friendship chemistry we had for boyfriend, girlfriend chemistry.'

Brian drew circles with his finger on the picnic tabletop. 'You know I love you, Sabiha,' he said, his voice choked. 'You're my best friend.'

I reached out and took his hand in mine. 'I love you too.' Before I knew it we were holding each other as we both wept.

A group of kids passed in front of us. Conscious of their stares, Brian and I moved away from each other. He got out his handkerchief and wiped his face, before folding it over and passing it to me. 'So we're okay?' he asked.

'Yes.' I gave back the handkerchief after I'd wiped my face.

'Are you and Jesse okay?' Brian asked, nudging his head in Jesse's direction.

Jesse and Dina were waiting for us. 'Looks like he's forgiven me,' I said.

'That's what you do when you love someone.' Brian kissed the top of my head.

In every class, either Jesse, Dina or Brian sat next to me and blocked the staring and whispers that started up when I entered the classroom. I waited for a chance to talk to Jesse, but the group stuck together. I realised that while I'd been gone Dina, Jesse and Brian had bonded without me.

Maybe I wouldn't have to say anything to Jesse? Maybe over time we'd be able to hang out together and it would be effortless and natural, the way it was before I stuffed things up.

At lunchtime we sat at the front of the school, on the picnic bench again. Adnan passed by with his new girlfriend. Brian sat up straight, straining forward as he waited for Adnan to look our way. Adnan ignored us. Brian slumped. Dina took his hand.

'At least I have you,' Brian said, looking at us around him. 'My Sassy Saints.'

'Say what?' Jesse asked.

'We're from St Albans and we're sassy. Sassy Saints.'

'It's perfect,' Dina said, hugging Brian and me, while Jesse leaned against Brian.

As I listened to Dina talking to Brian and Jesse, I couldn't believe how things had changed. I'd spent ten years thinking of Kathleen as my best friend, yet I'd known nothing about her, but I now knew all of Jesse's, Brian's and Dina's darkest secrets and they knew all of mine. We'd all started hanging out together pretending to be friends, and somehow along the way the pretence had became a reality.

I'd once complained to Frankie about Mum not being a good mother. Frankie told me that Mum tried to be the best parent that she could be and that I shouldn't judge her for all the things she did wrong, but instead look at all the things she did right. I'd finally got it.

Since we'd moved to St Albans I'd spent all my time complaining about about the things I'd left behind, and hadn't noticed what I'd gained. I had a real family. I had a grandfather, an aunt, an uncle and cousins. They weren't perfect, but they were here to stay.

Auntie Zehra came to pick me up from school. 'Let's visit Mum,' I said as I buckled my seatbelt.

Glossary

Allah Arabic. God

Babo Bosnian. Dad

Bože sačuvaj Bosnian. Colloquial, God save

Ćevapi Bosnian dish of skinless sausages served in bread with sliced onion

Dido Bosnian. Grandfather

Dimije Bosnian traditional garment, variation of harem pants

Džamija Bosnian. Mosque

Dženaza Arabic. Funeral

Dženet Arabic. Heaven

Džezva Turkish. Coffee pot

Fildžan Turkish. Small demitasse coffee cups. (singular) ***Fildžani*** (plural)

Hadith Arabic. Oral traditions relating to the words and deeds of the Islamic prophet Muhamed

Hodža Bosnian. Priest

Hurmašice Bosnian dish of buns made from cornmeal and baked in sugar water

Qur'an (Kuran) Arabic. Islamic holy book

Maslanica Bosnian dish of pastry layered with cheese and butter

Mecca Arabic. Islamic holy city in Saudi Arabia that Muslims face when praying

Mejtef Bosnian. Islamic classes for children

Merhaba Arabic. Welcome

Muhamed Bosnian spelling for the Prophet Mohammed who received messages from God that formed the *Kuran*

Mutuša Bosnian dish of pancake-like mixture with diced potatoes, baked in the oven

Oklagija Bosnian. Rolling pin—a long stick the length of a broom handle

Omarska Serb-run concentration camp in which Bosnians were imprisoned

Pita Bosnian dish of pastry filling formed into a spiral shape

Ramadan Muslim religious holiday in the ninth month when Muslims fast

Šah Mat Bosnian. Checkmate

Šamija Bosnian. Headscarf covering hair

Salaam Aleykum Arabic greeting. Peace be unto you

Vlah Bosnian. Unbeliever

Zabava Bosnian. Party

Zeljanica Bosnian. Spinach pita

Zdravo Bosnian. Hello

Sabiha's Dilemma

BONUS

Jesse's Story
Sabiha and Jesse's Booklist
Adnan's Showcase Graphic
Mutusha Recipe
Songs featured

Sign up to my newsletter for bonus gifts

https://www.amrapajalic.com/my-newsletter.html

Alma's Loyalty

CHAPTER 1

Alma's Loyalty Chapter 1

I was in my room completing my homework when my mother called me. I bookmarked my Maths textbook and walked down the hallway, hearing a conversation in progress. We had visitors, a regular event in our household.

I entered the living room and saw my parents on the couch, with a trio I'd never seen before.

'This is my daughter Alma.' Mum made the introductions in Bosnian. 'This is Arnesa and her husband Nermin, and Arnesa's mother Enisa.'

'*Bože sačuvaj,*' Arnesa said, which meant God Forbid, her mouth formed an O in surprise as she scrutinised my face. 'She looks exactly like Sabiha.'

'Who is Sabiha?' Mum asked.

'Esad's other daughter,' Arnesa said. 'We saw Bahra a month ago in Melbourne.'

I didn't understand what this stranger was saying. My father had another daughter? I looked at my mother for help.

'Esad doesn't have another daughter,' Mum said.

'Yes, he does. Sabiha, from his first marriage with Bahra. She is the spitting image of her father and sister.' Nermin nodded to me.

My legs felt weak. My father was married before? I turned to my father, hoping to get confirmation this was all a lie. His face was white.

'Alma, return to your room,' Mum commanded.

I walked down the hall, hiding in the alcove so I could eavesdrop.

'How could you not know?' Arnesa demanded. 'Bahra was four months pregnant when you moved to Hobart.'

There was an awkward silence before Mum jumped in. 'Bahra told him the child wasn't his.'

'Aren't there tests to find out?' Arnesa said. 'After all, you both know that she wasn't of sound mind.'

'Do you have Bahra's phone number?' my father asked.

'Of course,' Nermin said.

I heard the ping of a SMS. Nermin must have sent my father the phone number in an SMS.

My father passed in front of the hallway and went to his study, closing the door behind him with finally.

'My apologies. Maybe we should reschedule this visit,' Mum said, walking our guests to the front door.

I inched down the hallway and closer to the study. Mum closed the front door after our guests and walked to stand in front of the study door to eavesdrop with her back to me.

Dad initially spoke in a regular voice and then shouted, 'You should have told me she was my daughter.'

Mum opened the study door. Dad was staring at his phone with a distraught face, tears streaming down his face. 'What am I going to do now?' He fell into Mum's arms, his sobbing rending the air.

Beep, beep.

I opened my eyes, staring at the glaring white ceiling before me. I lifted my arm and hit the snooze button, discombobulated that I was reliving the most traumatic day of my life in my dreams again. Even though it had happened three months before, I always woke up from this dream with the same feeling of betrayal and shock.

I dressed, trying on half a dozen outfits before settling on jeans and a black-and-white striped stretchy top. My new school had no uniform, and I'd debated long and hard about what to wear. Mum's advice was black pants and a white shirt. 'It's a good idea to be smart casual,' she'd said, but I was afraid that was too formal.

I went to the bathroom, washing my face and looking at my frightened green eyes in the mirror. I tried to tell myself that everything would be alright, but if I had learnt anything up until this point, it was that things can always get worse.

I practiced my smile in the mirror until my cheeks were sore. It was important that it looked careless and natural, a mask that I could hide the quiet terror filling me. I stretched my lips wider and pushed my cheeks deeper into my face. That would have to do. It was the first day of term three and I was beginning my third school in year 10.

'Alma,' my little sister Sanela called out my name as she pounded on the bathroom door.

I opened the door, and she rushed in like a tornado. She got her hairbrush from the drawer and handed it to me. I sat on the edge of the bathtub and brushed her hair, while Sanela stood between my legs brushing her Barbie's blonde curls, her little five year old hands finding it difficult to manipulate the tie around the doll's ponytail.

I looked at the clock. Mum was due home soon from her night shift as a nurse. She usually came home before we had to leave for school.

'Done.' I breathed out a sigh of relief. I still had to do my hair and check my outfit one last time before breakfast.

'Now do Barbie.' Sanela thrust the doll toward me.

'I don't have time.' I stopped when Sanela looked at me with pleading brown eyes. It was quicker to tie the doll's hair into a makeshift ponytail than argue. 'Here.' I gave the doll back when I finished.

I carefully brushed my blonde hair back, ensuring that it parted directly in the middle, then stood in profile and smoothed down my top.

My younger brother Ali appeared in the bathroom doorway and met my eyes in the mirror. He and Sanela took after Mum with their brown hair, brown eyes, and round faces. 'Dad's waiting.'

He didn't need to say anymore. I knew Dad was tapping his watch, his patience straining. As a doctor, he was used to being the one who set the schedule.

'Get your backpack,' I ordered Sanela and went to my bedroom to do the same.

As we walked down the stairs, I looked through the round window that was at eye level across from me. Through it I could see the street outside, the roofs of the housing estate we lived in, filling the horizon like little matchbox houses. They all looked alike with their square bricked walls, carefully manicured lawns, and precisely placed plants.

We'd moved to Melbourne three months ago, and I still yearned for our house in Hobart. We'd lived off the beaten track with tall trees hugging our house, cocooning us from the rest of the world. I used to look out the window for hours, my eyes following the leaves as they danced in the wind. Now I averted my gaze from the ugly view that confronted me and continued down.

Dad tried to convince us that the move would be an adventure. He'd given us *carte blanche* to buy whatever we wanted at furniture shops, after our disastrous attempts in transplanting our old furniture: the delicate wrought iron pieces and white wood furniture that looked so perfect and quaint in our brick cottage but had looked wonky and cheap against the multicoloured feature walls.

'It's no good.' Mum had covered her face with her hand. 'This McMansion defies good taste,' she'd said, her tone full of spite. She'd never been enamoured with the charms of our new home, but she'd been worn down from leaving her family behind and fallen prey to Dad's enthusiasm for space.

Mum had wanted to pack our old furniture in storage, but Dad said we couldn't afford the fees, so we'd sold them at a garage sale. I thought I'd had bad days until then. Among the contenders for the title was the day that I found out about his other daughter, and the day that we moved to Melbourne and I was confronted with the monstrosity that was to be our new home.

'It's got four bedrooms so you don't have to share anymore,' he'd sounded like the eager real estate agent when he showed us around the McMansion.

'But I want to be with Alma.' Sanela grabbed hold of my skirt and tried to burrow into my body.

Even though sometimes I had wished for nothing more than my room, there were too many changes too soon. I wanted things to slow down, but life was fast forwarding at super speed.

'You're big enough to sleep by yourself,' Dad replied to Sanela off-handedly and continued the tour.

But in the end the winner of the *Worst day of my life* was the day of the garage sale when Dad sold every trace of our former life to strangers for pocket-change. As each piece of furniture was sold to an eager bargain hunter, I felt like I was being robbed of a childhood memory.

When we hit the bottom of the stairs, the front door burst open and Mum rushed in.

'Mummy,' Sanela exclaimed with pleasure, holding out her arms.

'*Srce moje.*' Mum picked her up, their dark, glossy hair intermingling together as she kissed her, calling Sanela her heart.

'Let's go.' Dad headed for the front door, briefcase in hand.

Our parents insisted we speak only Bosnian in the house so we maintained our fluency. Mum was much stricter about the rule and ignored us if we spoke English.

Sanela's stomach rumbled.

'Did you eat breakfast?' Mum looked at the clean sink and pushed past Dad. 'Let's fix that,' she said as she rifled through the kitchen cupboards. 'Sit.' Mum pointed to the stool with the wooden spoon she was holding.

As I watched Mum expertly flip eggs and put bread in the toaster, my father's burning gaze drilled a hole in the nape of my neck. Usually I was the one who made breakfast when Mum worked, but this morning I'd spent half an hour changing outfits.

'I'm going to be late,' Dad said, still standing by the doorway.

'Alma, your father will drive you,' Mum told me.

I coughed as the orange juice I was drinking went down the wrong pipe. I'd avoided being alone with Dad since I was expelled from my last school.

'And I'll drive Ali and Sanela,' Mum continued.

My new high school was in St Albans near Dad's medical centre, while Ali and Sanela's schools were closer to home in Sydenham.

When Mum served breakfast, I gulped the eggs down without chewing, only to stop abruptly and cover my mouth as the gooey texture of the scrambled eggs triggered my gag reflex.

'Don't rush.' Mum shot an annoyed look at Dad. He retreated to the living room.

When we finished breakfast, Mum pulled out our lunch bags from the fridge and handed them out. We walked out of the front door and I followed my siblings to Mum's 4WD. Ali got in the backseat and rolled down the window.

'Come on Alma.' Sanela tugged me toward the backseat.

'Alma isn't coming with us,' Mum said gently. 'Daddy will drive her to school today.'

'But who's going to wait with me until school starts?' Sanela was on the verge of tears.

Sanela was in prep and was anxious by herself. I used to stay with her at her primary school until her friends arrived, then undertook the fifteen-minute walk to my previous school, a private all-girls school.

'You'll be all right.' I knelt in front of her and cupped her cheek. 'Your new friend Heidi will wait for you at school.'

Sanela hugged me, her little arms clinging to my neck. She was born when I was ten and I reckon I'd nearly changed almost as many of her nappies as Mum had.

'Let go of your sister now.' Mum grabbed hold of Sanela's arms and gently tugged her away.

'Nooooo,' Sanela shouted, holding tighter.

I took a deep breath and blinked back my own tears. 'You won't be alone.'

'I'll stay with you,' Ali said.

'See.' I made my voice upbeat. 'Ali will stay with you.'

Sanela looked uncertainly between Ali and I. 'Promise,' she demanded from our brother.

'I promise.' He took Sanela's other hand.

'You'll be fine,' Mum said to me with a fake smile stretching her lips, while Ali strapped Sanela into the booster seat. 'You'll make lots of friends.'

As Mum hugged me, I hid my face in her hair, wanting to be a little girl once again and believe in every platitude, but I knew she was just as nervous as I was. I was embarking on a whole new adventure at my first co-ed public high school. Either of those would have terrified me. The two together and I was paralysed.

'Don't forget I'll pick you up after school at Dad's work.' Mum pecked me on the cheek and briskly got in the driver's seat.

I waved as the car reversed out of the driveway. The 4WD was parallel to the house and Sanela's pressed her face against the glass window when Dad turned on the ignition to his car. I aborted my waving and jumped into the passenger seat.

We reached the end of the cul-de-sac and Mum's 4WD turned left, while Dad turned right. I watched through the back window until Mum's car wasn't visible anymore.

I looked ahead again, suddenly aware of the silence in the car. The last time I'd been alone with Dad was when I got expelled three days ago and he drove me home, his body taut with seething silence.

Dad took a right turn and cleared his throat. 'There's something I need to talk to you about,' he said, switching to English. He'd lived in Australia for nearly twenty years and had the faintest tinge of an accent when he spoke.

I turned to look at him and clenched my fists. He was going to give me the blasting I'd been waiting for. It was almost a relief after the silent treatment of the past three days. I grabbed hold of the car door handle and fantasised about pulling it open, throwing myself out of the moving car and sliding across the asphalt, my skin peeling like a banana. Surely it couldn't be more painful than what was about to take place in the car.

'It's about your new school.' Dad paused.

I took a deep breath, realising I hadn't exhaled since he first spoke.

'I'm really excited,' I lied. I was full of trepidation about what it would be like to go to a public school. The kids in public schools were rough, and I was told that public schools had less discipline. 'It's got a fantastic academic record.' I recited the facts and figures I'd memorised from repeatedly staring at the school enrolment information.

'It's not that.' Dad waved for me to stop. 'You'll know someone at your new school.'

'Mum told me,' I interrupted again. Mum worked the phones after they enrolled me, calling around the Bosnian community until she tracked down a student who went to the same school. 'Dina Hasanagić.'

'Could you please let me finish?' he snapped.

I hunched into the passenger seat, his words like a slap to the face. My fingers jumped to my mouth, my teeth connecting with enamel, before I remembered myself and sat on my hands.

'I'm sorry.' Dad put his hand through his hair, messing his carefully combed hair.

He was nervous. My stomach clenched harder.

'Your sister goes to St Albans High.' Dad turned to look at me.

'No, she doesn't,' I automatically replied. 'Sanela goes to—'

I abruptly cut out. He was talking about his other daughter. My body lurched as if our car hit a pothole, but the road before us was smooth as glass. It was the same feeling I'd had when I found out about our supposed sister from Dad's first marriage.

After my parents made the family announcement about my father's other daughter, everything sped up. Dad went on a trip to meet his first-born and came back with a job offer and real estate pamphlets in tow. My parents fought over the proposed move. Mum didn't want to leave her extended family who were all within a fifteen minute drive, but in the end it was inevitable. Dad had always wanted to move to Melbourne in order to be more involved with the Bosnian community and have access to greater professional opportunities, and when he found out he had a long-lost daughter, he gained greater familial priority.

Before I knew it we were packing and moving to Melbourne. Dad's attempt to atone for his inadvertent years of neglect were thwarted when Sabiha refused to have contact with him. I wanted to ask him if he knew before they enrolled me. I wanted to shout and scream, but years of habit taught me to keep my lips zipped and my eyes on the floor.

'I know you're probably thinking that I wanted you to enrol at St Albans High because of Sabiha, but that's not true,' he said, as if he'd read my mind. 'It truly is the best school in the area.' Dad peeked at me as he drove. 'I'm sorry. I know this isn't fair to you. If you want to come to work with me, we can find another school for you.'

It was the last thing I expected to hear. 'Do you mean it?'

'Of course,' Dad said. 'It's completely your decision.'

He was tense, his whole body on edge as he waited for my answer. For the first time since we found out about the other daughter, I had his full attention and it was intoxicating. Maybe I shouldn't throw this gift away? Going to St Albans High might be my chance to bring back the Dad I knew, but who'd been missing in action for the past three months.

'What about Mum?' I asked.

'I didn't tell your mother because I didn't want any outside influences to affect your decision,' Dad said.

Anytime there was a reference to the other daughter, Mum stiffened and went on the defensive. She'd fought against the move and lost, and was furious that Sabiha refused to see Dad after our sacrifices.

'I'll tell your mother tonight.'

'But—' I was betraying Mum by even contemplating going behind her back.

'Sabiha is a part of my life now and your mother knows that. She'll see that this is the best decision for all of us.' Dad smiled.

I felt compelled to smile back, even though I didn't agree. There would be hell to pay when Mum found out. Dad stopped the car in front of the school and I looked with concern at the empty schoolyard.

'We're late,' Dad said as he got out of the car.

We were supposed to arrive at the office before the bell, see the coordinator, who would introduce me to Dina, whose job was to show me around the school and take me to class.

Dad reached into the backseat and got out a gift bag. 'I got this for your first day.'

I had a spring in my step as I peered into the bag. He'd bought me a purple organiser, matching pen and water bottle.

When we reached reception, Dad gave me a rushed hug and a peck on the cheek. I closed my eyes, inhaling Dad's cologne, and tried to remember the last time he'd held me. It was way back before we moved to Melbourne.

'Give your sister a chance,' he said before he left.

An admin worker walked me to class and introduced me to the teacher, while the students inside the classroom erupted into chatter.

'Everyone, settle,' Ms Partridge called out as I followed her back into class. 'This is our new student Alma Omerović.' Ms Partridge's forehead wrinkled for a moment and she looked at the back. 'Are you any relation to Sabiha?' she asked.

Time stopped as I followed Ms Partridge's gaze and met Sabiha's eyes. I felt *déjà vu*, as if I was looking at myself in a mirror. We both took after Dad and had his blonde hair, dimpled chin, and high cheekbones. But the longer I stared, the more the differences became apparent. We had different shaped eyes and mouth.

I'd wondered what Sabiha looked like, but at home she was a conversational black hole and I'd had to make do with my imagination. My fantasy revolved around Dad realising he'd made a mistake and casting off his fake daughter. Our lives would return to normal, and we'd go home to Hobart.

There were so many times I wanted to ask Dad if he got a DNA test, how could he be sure, but the questions burnt in my throat, never to pass my lips. Now I knew why he was so determined to establish a relationship with her. There was no mistaking that she was her father's daughter.

'No,' Sabiha spat out, breaking the spell. 'We're not related.'

I had to fight not to run for the door. She looked at me with such anger and disgust; I was scared she'd vaporise me with the scorn shooting from her eyeballs.

'You can sit next to Dina,' Ms Partridge continued, oblivious to the tension in the air.

Sabiha stood and collected her things, her resentment obvious as she slammed her notebook and slapped her pencil case together. She looked like a girl lumberjack; she had on a denim mini and pink leggings, and her feet encased in chunky worker boots. Her outfit should have looked all wrong, instead she looked cool and fierce. I was frumpy in my too-new jeans and bland top and couldn't wait to hide behind the desk.

'Sabiha, quiet.' The teacher shushed.

Sabiha moved to an empty desk in the last row. The two boys in front of her turned around and whispered to her, but she shook her head.

I slid into the seat next to Dina. 'Hi,' I whispered, trying to make eye contact, but Dina snubbed me.

I stared at the teacher stiffly, trying to focus on *To Kill a Mockingbird*, but it was no good. I felt Sabiha's stare like ants walking on my neck. Abruptly, I turned to look behind me, catching Sabiha off guard. I'd expected her to still be staring at me with rage. Instead she looked miserable. I remembered how Dad had implored me to give Sabiha a chance, as if I was his last hope.

Sabiha had determinedly rebuffed his every attempt to establish contact. In the end, their relationship was reduced to him paying weekly child support, a too generous amount that we could barely afford, according to Mum.

After English double period, the recess bell rang, and I turned to catch Sabiha madly packing her things to make a dash for the door.

'Can we talk?' I followed her.

'About what?' Sabiha whirled around. 'How your mother is a home wrecker?'

'No,' I stuttered to a stop, my train of thought evaporating. 'My Mum isn't—'

'Then how do you explain the fact that we're the same age?' Sabiha snapped, turning around again.

Sassy Saints Series

Sabiha's Dilemma was my debut novel that was traditionally published under the title *The Good Daughter*. This story was inspired by my own experiences of being from a Bosnian background, growing up in the Western suburbs of Melbourne (a low socio-economic suburb) and being brought up by a mother who suffers from Bipolar.

I loved the characters that I created and kept imagining their lives beyond the pages of the book I wrote. The year after publication I wrote a follow up novel about another character, Alma, who finds out she has a half sister she never knew, Sabiha, and through Alma's story I continued Sabiha, Jesse, Brian, Dina and Adnan's stories.

When I embarked on my indie publishing career and was preparing *Sabiha's Dilemma* for release I was hit by a wave of inspiration. What if I expanded this universe and created a series where each character had their own book? This would give me the opportunity to recreate so many of the experiences that happened off-page for each of my characters and to extend their storylines.

And so the *Sassy Saints Series* was born.

Sassy Saints Series

Follow the lives of six sassy teens coming of age in St Albans, as they navigate their sexual and cultural identity and search for belonging.

These books will be an inter-connected series that can be read out of order (I'll be keeping any spoilers off the page). If you want to follow the *Sassy Saints* journey join my mailing list and stay in the loop.

Sabiha's Dilemma

Sabiha's dilemma is being the good daughter so that her mentally ill mother is accepted back into the Bosnian community.

Alma's Loyalty

When Alma finds out that she has a half sister she never knew, she is faced with competing loyalties.

Jesse's Triumph

After Jesse's debut novel is published while he's a high school student, he contends with becoming popular.

Brian's Conflict

Brian's dreams of being a designer are in conflict with his father's hopes he'll join the family business as a bricklayer.

Dina's Burden

Dina carries the burden of living up to her parent's expectations to make up for her brother's errant ways.

Adnan's Secret

Adnan is the perfect son carrying the weight of his migrant parent's expectations, who lives a secret life.

About the Author

Amra Pajalić is an award-winning author, an editor and teacher who draws on her Bosnian cultural heritage to write own voices stories for young people, who like her, are searching to mediate their identity and take pride in their diverse culture. Her short story collection *The Cuckoo's Song* (Pishukin Press, 2022*)* features previously published and prize-winning stories. Her debut novel *The Good Daughter,* was published by Text Publishing in 2009 and won the 2009 Melbourne Prize for Literature's Civic Choice Award and is re-released as *Sabiha's Dilemma* (Pishukin Press, 2022).

Her memoir *Things Nobody Knows But Me* (Transit Lounge, 2019) was shortlisted for the 2020 National Biography Award. She is co-editor of the anthology *Growing up Muslim in Australia* (Allen and Unwin, 2014) which was shortlisted for the 2015 Children's Book Council of the year awards. She works as a high school teacher and is completing a PhD in Creative Writing at La Trobe University.

Amra Pajalić publishes her dark fiction using pen name A. P. Pajalic. She also publishes romance novels under pen name Mae Archer.

CONNECT WITH AMRA:

goodreads.com/author/show/3310015.Amra_Pajalic

facebook.com/AmraPajalicAuthor/

instagram.com/amrapajalicauthor/

https://twitter.com/AmraPajalic

bookbub.com/authors/amra-pajalic

tiktok.com/@amrapajalic

youtube.com/c/AmraPajalicAuthor

SIGN UP FOR AMRA'S AUTHOR NEWSLETTER

For news, giveaways, bonus material, and sneak peeks, please sign up to her newsletter below.

www.amrapajalic.com

PLEASE LEAVE A REVIEW

If you enjoyed this book and would like to show Amra your support, please consider leaving a star rating and/or review on the website you purchased the book from.

'If you struggle to read, then you haven't found the right book format.'

I'm Amra Pajalić, the owner and publisher of Pishukin Press, an independent press dedicated to the publication of own voices fiction and nonfiction, as well as genre fiction.

There is a quote that states 'If you don't like to read, then you haven't found the right book.' I would like to extend that further and state that 'If you struggle to read then you haven't found the right book format.' As a high school teacher I have taught students with various individual needs and recognise the need to make books accessible for all kinds of readers. To this end I am committed to publishing all Pishukin Press titles in as many formats as possible. This includes:

Dyslexic Format Edition—printed in Dyslexic Open font in 14 point
Large Print edition—printed in Large Print Open Sans No Italics font in 18 point font size
Audiobooks AI—narrated by artificial intelligence using Google technology.
Audiobooks—narrated by performance narrators.
All books are also available in paperback and hardcover editions.

To get 10% off use discount code 10OFF

https://www.pishukinpress.com/

A guide for international readers

This book is set in Australia and uses British English spelling. Some spellings may differ from those used in American English.

Australia's seasons are at opposite times to those in the northern hemisphere. Summer is December–February, autumn is March–May, winter is June–August, and spring is September–November. Christmas is in summer.

In the Australian school system, primary school is for grades Kindergarten to Grade 6, and high school is for grades Year 7–12. Secondary college is a name frequently used for high school. Tertiary education after high school is either at universities and TAFE (technical and further education) institutions.

In Australia, each school year starts in late January and finishes mid-December.

The legal drinking age in Australia is 18 years old.

AUSTUDY is financial help if you're 25 or older and studying or completing an Australian apprenticeship.

Also By

Memoir

Things Nobody Knows But Me

Growing up Muslim in Australia

Young Adult

The Cuckoo's Song

Sabiha's Dilemma

Alma's Loyalty

The Climb

Romance as Mae Archer

Return to Me

Hollywood Dreams

Dark Fiction/Horror as A.P. Pajalic

Woman on the Edge

www.ingramcontent.com/pod-product-compliance
Lightning Source LLC
Chambersburg PA
CBHW030608310726
48979CB00003B/619

* 9 7 8 1 9 2 2 8 7 1 0 0 8 *